THUNDER DREAMER

by
Ron Robinson

University of South Dakota Press
1996

Thunder Dreamer is a work of fiction. Any similarity between the characters of this novel and any persons living or dead is strictly coincidental.

Thunder Dreamer, by Ron Robinson
Published by University of South Dakota Press

Copyright © 1996 by Ronald Robinson

First printing, June, 1996

Library of Congress Cataloging in Publication Data

Robinson, Ronald, 1936-
    Thunder dreamer / by Ron Robinson
        p.   cm.
    ISBN 0-29925-33-5 (softcover)
    I. Title.
    PS3568.03147T48   1996
    813'.54--dc20

                                        96-21302
                                        CIP

ISBN : Softcover 0-929925-33-5

dedicated to the memory of

Lee Robinson

1.

Deposition, Rodney L. Deuce, made of his own free will, this 10th day of July, 1980.

Look, I know people are dead, you don't have to remind me. More maybe than you know. That woman, what did you say her name was? Anyway, I never heard the name. I just knew her by her looks, is all, if she is the one they found up in the valley. I never had anything to do with her, and if Mr. Quick was here, he could tell you.

As for that rancher out in the Badlands, nobody got killed in that. Besides, it wasn't my idea, and the only thing I did there was to drive the getaway vehicle, the way you call it. And that was just to save my hide.

The fact of it was, none of it was my idea. The mistake I made was only going along with it, because I couldn't see another way. But I tell you one thing, it wasn't all bad. There were times when it was nothing but pleasure, even on the res, at Deadwood, up in the Hills, down at Golden West. We got around all right. And it wasn't all murder and mayhem, like the newspaper says.

Maybe the easiest thing is just to tell you how it started. You know how it ended. I wish to God it hadn't ended like it did, but nothing can be done about that. It was in the cards, as old Mr. Quick would say. I heard him say that many times.

I want to make clear this is not a confession. The lawyer made that plain. She says I have done nothing that I have to be put in jail for. But now you want me to tell it start to finish. Just bear in mind I don't have to give this to you. And anybody that had anything to hide wouldn't give you anything at all. So that alone ought to to count for something.

If I hadn't been late that day in March, I might not've got to know the old guy like I did and maybe nothing would've happened. The night before I was out with my friends Harold Joli and Lymon Twobows, and we had a sip or two to drink. Lymon doesn't like to drink all that much, really, so mostly it was Harold and me. Lymon is Lakota. I've known him since I was a kid in grade school. We always got along pretty good, and we worked together, but he always drew the line at drinking with me. At first I thought, well, he's Indian and he's afraid of getting like those you always hear about. But he told me once he doesn't drink mostly because he doesn't want people to see him and get to thinking that he is an Indian and so he's a drunk. I didn't get it at the time, but I think I see now what he meant. It's a matter of pride, as far as I can see. He is what he is, and he can't do a thing about that, but what other people think he is, that he can do something about. Myself, I guess I never had the spine for that kind of thinking. When you are a poor bastard like me, I guess you just go along being what you are and let the people point and say, "Look at that poor bastard."

The funny thing is, I never even knew I was poor or a bastard until I was almost out of high school. My mother always managed to keep me fed, and she told me my father was a soldier and that he died in Viet Nam. She went by his last name of Deuce and that was the name that was on my birth certificate and later on my Social Security card. But I finally got out of her that they hadn't been legally married and that as a matter of fact he wasn't even dead, but had run off with another woman when I was five. He was a soldier, though, so that much was true. He'd been stationed at Ellsworth Air Force Base.

About the only thing I remember about him is him pushing me up in a tire swing. He pushed me higher and higher, until I almost got scared. I was thinking I would go flying off into the sky. It's funny what you remember and what you don't.

When you're a kid, I guess you don't think rich or poor, and only realize it when you think back later on and see how your mother had to scrape and how you had to mow lawns and have paper routes and bag groceries and everything else, just to get a little spending money. And then you get out of high school, and just about everybody else is talking about going to this college or that university, and you just don't have the money for it. And you see that you have been poor all the time and didn't know it. And you have been a bastard all your life and didn't know that either. And your almost best friend, who you used to play cowboys and Indians with in the trailer park where you lived, really is an Indian.

So there I was in Rapid City, at the Hillview Home for the Elderly, rolling old farts in wheelchairs around and emptying bedpans and stuff. Not to mention taking all kinds of crap from Ef-ef-Freddy Fitz. But it's a job anyway. It was hard enough to get, so I'm not going to badmouth it too much. In fact, it was Lymon who put in a good word and got me hired there. But when I woke up that morning after going out drinking and looked at the clock and it was already eight-thirty and I was already an hour late, I thought I was in big trouble. I felt sick. So I thought about it and I made up my mind that I was sick. How else do you know you're sick? So I called in sick.

The supervisor, Miss Frank, she's a tough old girl. "Rodney," she said, "get your butt over here."

"I'm sick," I told her again. And I coughed a little on the phone just to show how sick I was.

"Don't pull that stuff with me," she said. "Where are you calling from?"

"The booth on the corner by Domino's." It was the closest phone to where I lived, in this kind of rooming house. Lymon and Harold lived there too.

"If you were really sick, you would not be able to get to the phone," Miss Frank said.

I hadn't thought of that before, so I coughed again.

"Cut out that phony cough," she said.

"I'm late already," I said.

"Just get over here," she said. "They're getting out of hand here. Everyone is going crazy. We need help."

"I'll be right over." To tell the truth, I didn't feel sick any more.

When I got to the home, there was a pretty big uproar going on. Nurses were running up and down the hall. Ef-ef-Freddie was wrestling a guy down the corridor in an arm-lock, but he couldn't help stopping to take a pot-shot at me. He hauled up and rattled off something like, " I s-s-see you g-g-got h-here at l-l-long l-last." Too bad for Ef-ef-Freddy that the old guy he had hold of took advantage of the long pause caused by the delivery of the snappy line to break loose and take off in a kind of a limping run, like a chimpanzee. Ef-ef-Freddie threw me one of his Terrible Stares before jogging off to collar the old joker again. A Terrible Stare is what Freddie makes do for a nasty remark, because even "up yours" can turn into a long conversation where he is concerned. What this particular Terrible Stare meant is that he blamed me for letting the old guy get away and that he would get on my case good when he got the time. Somebody forgot to tell Ef-ef-Freddy that people who stutter are supposed to be shy and retiring and sensitive and not bullies. Maybe he just didn't watch enough television.

The residents, which is what they call the old farts who live there, were mostly standing or sitting in wheelchairs in the doorways to their rooms looking dumb with their mouths open or giggling or even clapping like they were at a show and getting a big kick out of what was going on. They sure knew more about it than I did.

I grabbed a nurse running by who turned out to be none other than Miss Goody Twoboobs herself, Karen Stephenson. To tell the truth, I'd been wanting to grab her for a long time. It was plain to see she did not believe in harnessing her team, even under that stiff white uniform. And when I saw who it was I had my arms around, I forgot why I stopped her. It was childish, I realize now. I guess I've been through some changes in the last few months. But back then the female body tended to turn me into a complete idiot. I was just standing there with her bustling around trying to get loose, and get to looking at her, I suppose, with some kind of silly-ass grin on my face such as I tended to get at such times, and I couldn't think of a thing to say.

"Damn it, Rod," she said, "let me go. All hell's breaking loose in the recreation room."

And it came back to me what I stopped her to ask about. "What's going on?"

"A fight," she said. "A free-for-all. It started over checkers or something. And pretty soon everybody was in there swinging." She pushed away from me. "We're trying to get everybody calmed down," she said, and she started off again. The team was pretty good, I was thinking, but the wagon is a bitch. That's the way I thought at the time.

"Rodney," somebody said behind me. It was Miss Frank. I turned around. She is a little bit of a lady but tough and sharp as a splinter of flint. "It's about time you showed up," she said. "We need you down on the south wing."

"But I'm on north," I said.

"We've got Lymon on north. And he's got his hands full. So get down to south, room 107." She talks real fast, Miss Frank. She's got this real gray hair on her that's cut real short and a skinny body and a face all grooved with grin and squint lines, and this funny knuckle of a nose. But she hired me for this job, and you always knew where you stood with her.

So I went down on south which was not familiar to me. And when I got close to 107, I heard a great commotion in there something smashing down on the floor and a string of language which I'd never heard before in real life, it was so raw. So I slowed down and kind of peeked around the door into the room and that was my first sight of Mr. Quick.

He was an old fart, but not so old as some of the others, as near as I could see. He had a full head of hair, for one thing, with still some dark in it, and he had some fullness in his face yet, not so bony and sunk in like others. But he had a short body on him and a stomach sticking out over his belt that looked like maybe was at one time cinched up a whole lot tighter.

There are some individuals you can see right away how they could've looked when they were younger. I was willing to bet that he'd been a scrappy character that could take care of himself pretty good. And he was right then not doing too bad in that respect. He was standing beside the bed and had got the bed tray between himself and the nurse who was standing there holding a hypo needle pointed up to the ceiling like a gun that she was afraid might go off. The nurse was none other that hers truly Karen Stephenson. She had her back to the door, but I had not long before given that particular view some study.

"Mr. Quick," Karen Stephenson said, "this will make you feel a whole lot better."

"Shit it will," said the old fart. And he pushed the tray cart toward her with both hands, the way a person would jab a stick toward the face of a dog that is growling at them.

Nurse Stephenson backed up a step. I slipped in behind her and moved over to the side where she could see me. The old fart, he saw me too, of course, and edged around behind the cart to show me he could just as well shove the tray at me.

"Reinforcements," he said. "It's Wild Bill and the McCanles gang all over again."

"You'll have to hold him for me." Karen Stephenson was talking to me in the the kind of voice a person uses to talk about a baby they think can't understand them.

But of course the old fart could understand. "Let him try it," he said, "and I'll take his head off for him."

I started to edge around the side of the room to get some space between Nurse Stephenson and me so that he would have to divide his attention between us.

"Get the wagons in a circle," the old fart yelled, and turned the cart around until he was behind it and between the window and the bed.

Under my feet I felt the crackle of a glass or something that had broken. Nurse Stephenson saw what I was trying to do, and she started moving to the other side of the room, still holding the hypo up like a six-shooter with the safety off.

"You can't give me medication against my will," the old fart said, and for the first time I saw something in those steel-blue eyes besides ornriness. What I saw was strange, kind of a sadness, but deeper than that. I have seen that look in the eyes of other gentlemen in the home, like they are going to yell or cry or something. It is my personal opinion that it is the way individuals get to looking when they see that they have not got charge of the situation any more like they used to.

"Give us your permission, then," Karen Stephenson said. "It will only take a second and you'll feel a lot better afterwards."

"I feel fine now," he said. "Stick it in your own ass, if it feels so good."

I was kind of embarrassed to hear the old fart talking to Nurse Stephenson in that fashion, so I said, "That's no way to talk to a lady."

And the old gentleman, he looked at me kind of surprised to hear me speak and said, "I know that line. You stole that line from the Duke. Which one was it? *Stagecoach*? *Rio Bravo*?"

"It's my own line," I said. I was trying not to look at Nurse Stephenson, who was coming up behind him now on the other side of the bed.

"It's not either your line," he said. "It's John Wayne's. I can hear him saying it plain as anything. Dammit, I can't think which picture. *True Grit* don't sound right either. I've seen so many of them I can't keep them straight any more." He started to shake his head, then he saw Karen Stephenson diving for him across the bed with that hypo aimed for his rear end. He shoved the tray at me and jumped out from behind it and headed for the door between us. I caught the corner of the tray under my ribs, but I managed to push it away and sidestep over to get ahold of him. To be truthful, what I got ahold of was a handful of his shirttail. But it jerked him around and kind of got him off balance.

"No holds barred," he yelled. "Fight like a man." And he spun and put up his fists like a prize fighter on television. He got into a kind of crouch and held his fists up to his face and his elbows down. It was a good imitation.

"If you want my opinion," I said, "you're putting up an awful big fuss over a little hypo shot." I didn't want to hit the old fart.

"Screw your opinion," he said, and he kicked me in the shin.

I've often thought that a person can be thinking something and something will happen that makes them do the exact opposite of what they were thinking. And that is what that kick did for me. I was thinking it was such a shame to punch an old gentleman like that, and then he kicked me and I just kind of reached over and swatted him on the jaw with my fist where I saw him drop his guard. And he went down like a tree cut down, if you've ever seen that, a little shiver first and then swaying so slow you can't hardly see at first, and then just picking up weight in the falling until it seems like it will just drive right into the ground.

I was afraid I had killed the old fart. I bent over and rolled him over to see if he was hurt bad, but he pulled his eyeballs back from somewhere up in his head, rolling them in my direction but with a far-off look to them so I didn't think he really saw me, and he said, "Shit," kind of weak. I was glad to see that he wasn't dead, anyway.

I got him under the arms and got him over to the bed and kind of draped him over the side and got his pants down. Surprise, he had on some of them old fashioned long underpants. I had to unbutton the flap and drop it before Karen Stephenson could get the needle in his behind. Then I buttoned him up and pulled up his pants and laid him out in the bed. All the time he was kind of moaning and talking weak, all kinds of raw words, starting with the ones everyone knows and going on to some he must've made up. But he was pretty tame outside of his language.

If you have ever hit someone in the jaw, you know that it can hurt as bad as anything. I was of the opinion that my hand was busted from where I hit the old fart, and after I got him taken care of, I started rubbing my knuckles and looking at them and I saw that I had actually banged them up pretty good.

Karen Stephenson saw that I was looking at my hand and she took it and looked at it herself. I suppose she couldn't help it, being a nurse. "It's not bad," she said. "I don't think you broke it."

While she was looking at my hand, I was naturally looking at her. All the diving across the bed and wrestling the old fart and everything had got her kind of mussed up. Her cute little cap had come off and her hair was spilling down over one eye. And I think she had popped at least two buttons on her uniform, and her team looked like they were going to bust out of the barn. She looked up and saw me looking at her and all the concern seemed to run right out of her.

Who can understand a woman, I sometimes had to wonder. A person would think that where she saw a person looking at her with the kind of admiration I was feeling that she would at least take it as a compliment the way it was intended and give the person at least a smile of thanks. But that person would not know hers truly Karen Stephenson.

She was just looking at me in the coldest kind of way, and she let my hand drop and said, "I've got to get back to the station. You'd better stay here a while to see he doesn't do any more damage before the hypo takes hold. And clean up some of this mess."

And she looked around and saw the glass broke over on the side of the room and went to pick it up. She bent over and put a great strain on the seams of that uniform, which had already seen a great deal of wear and tear. And it kind of rode up behind on her and presented a very scenic overlook all the way from the Badlands to the Black Hills almost. It was a special effort for me not to reach out and grab something like I did with the old guy—only not just a shirttail—so taken up with such things as I was then. She paid no more attention to me than a fly on the wall, but went about picking up the glass and the little pieces very careful and then went on out of the room with me looking after her.

It is hard to say what goes through a person's mind when such a thing as that happens. According to my way of thinking, it is not far away from the feeling a person gets when he is watching somebody do something like play basketball, where a person kind of leans and rolls with the motion that the other individual is making so that just by looking a person can kind of feel the motion themselves. Is this maybe what a person means to say when they said they are moved? Anyway, in the state of mind I was in then, I was sure moved watching the motion of Karen Stephenson receding out of the room.

"I would give a quarter for one of those," I heard the old gentleman say. I looked and saw him eyeing my crotch. "You ought to pull her into a closet and take some of the starch out of her spine."

"I'm not much of a one for pulling women into closets," I said. "That could get me fired, not to mention twenty years in the pen in Sioux Falls."

"Then you better brace for a long, lonely life. Because they ain't gonna be too much attracted to a skinny, ugly bastard like you." He started rubbing his jaw. "You got a great right cross, though. If you ever want to go into the fight game, I'll manage you."

"I'm sorry I give you such a hit," I said. "It was a reflex."

"Well, you got damn good reflexes, then."

"How's your jaw?"

"Not that bad. I've taken worse punches. But it shook me up some. How is your hand?"

"I believe it is almost broken."

"Good," he said. "I'm glad to see I did some damage to you anyway."

"You skinned up my leg too, with your boot," I said. "And my stomach is feeling none too good where you caught it with the tray."

He laughed at that, a flat, mean laugh. I could see I was wasting my time if I expected any sympathy from the old fart. I made up my mind to change the subject. "What happened in the rec room? The nurse said there was some kind of a ruckus."

And he laughed again, even meaner than before. "Teach them to cheat," he said.

"Teach who to cheat?"

"The bastards who do all the cheating. The senile sons-of-bitches must think I'm blind, moving pieces with their elbows, nudging my color right off the board. That's the only way they could beat me though. I was checker champ of West River before I was seventeen."

"Checkers?" I hadn't believed the nurse before when she mentioned it. "You started a ruckus over checkers?"

"It's not the money that was laid—"

"You were playing for money?" The old fart was full of surprises.

"Five dollars, two games out of three. But it wasn't the money, much as I could use it. It was principle, pure and simple." He was lying there knocked out and weak on the bed, but he got a stubborn look, holding his chin up so you can see he meant business.

"What's your name, kid?"

"Rodney Deuce."

"He put out his hand to shake. "Daniel O. Quick," he said. "I don't think I've seen you around here before."

"I'm usually up on north," I said, and grabbed his hand. "What does the O stand for, Mr. Quick?"

"Ought," he said. "Zero. Nothing. I gave it to myself when I saw my mother forgot to give me a middle initial and everybody else had one. If anyone complains, I am prepared to show I have added nothing to the name I was born with." He yawned. I figured the hypo was starting to work on him. "How old do you think I am, Rodney Deuce?"

"Old enough to be in here, I guess."

"Eighty," he said. "Just as old as this century. And that's not the reason I'm in here either. I got the body and the brains of a fifty-year-old. I'm here because I tried to lay the Meals-On-Wheels lady." He yawned again, and laughed at the same time, that evil cackle. "Meals-On-Wheels," he said, laughing. His steel-blue eyes were looking pretty sleepy.

"That sounds like quite a story," I said, meaning that it sounded like an out-and-out lie.

"I'll tell you all about it sometime," he said. And he closed his eyes.

I started to pick up the room and straighten it up. It was a pack-rat's nest, like a lot of these old farts' rooms, but it did have some interesting things. Like the window sill was loaded with books all the same colors, but different names on them, and all written by the same individual, one Zane Grey. I had heard of this writer before, and I picked up one of the books and looked at the first few pages and it looked not too bad. This individual who had a bone to pick with someone was setting off down a river, is the way I remember it. I was thinking that I might like to borrow it and read it all the way through sometime.

And another thing was his desk, which every room in the Hillview Home for the Elderly has got, was loaded down in this par-ticular case with the strangest bunch of stuff I'd ever seen in real life. There were plastic bags of feathers of every size and description and furs and hair and string of all colors and thread and silver tools that had jobs I would hate to guess at. I was beginning to think that he was some kind of medicine man of the kind Lymon talks about having on the reservation. And I was beginning to conclude that he was about the most peculiar old fart I had ever laid my eyes on and that I would like to find out what all that stuff is for and what he sees in all those books, not to mention the rest of the Meals-On-Wheels story in the first place.

If I'd known what a bunch of trouble this gentleman would get me into, I would've backed out of that room right then and not put a foot in it again ever. But live and learn.

I looked over to where Daniel O-for-nothing Quick was snoring like a chainsaw cutting through hardwood, mouth open, and I saw that I was going to have to wait a while for any explanation of the feathers or the books or the Meals-On-Wheels. In plain fact, I might have to wait forever if Ef-ef-Freddie came down too hard on me.

2.

When I first got the idea of getting transferred to the south wing, I went to Nurse Frank. It wasn't just because of Quick I did it. It so happened that Karen Stephenson herself was assigned to south, and all the wrestling around in Quick's room that day got me to thinking even more about her. I was a little worried about Ef-ef Freddy, who was the orderly in charge of the wing, so I thought I would go to Nurse Frank and tell her I wouldn't mind too much getting transferred to south.

She looked up from her desk with her fisty face even more knotted up than usual, like she already had enough crap to worry about without this. "Why?" she said.

"Everybody needs a change of scene once in a while," I said, which I figured was safe and true enough. But the look she got, like she had just taken a bite out of a dead mouse, got me to seeing how weak a reason it was. So I added on fast, "There's a guy down there, the one that started the ruckus in the rec room yesterday. I think I could help him out. I think he just wants company, someone to talk at. It could keep him more under control." From the way her face unclenched, I must've been hitting the right buttons.

But now she was looking at me in a different way, like a nurse looking at an interesting urine specimen. "You are a surprise, sometimes, Rodney. I've been looking at your high school transcript. You did quite well in most subjects. Why didn't you go on to college?"

"I'm not too much of a college type, I guess," I said.

"What type is that?" she asked me.

"You know. The type that wears sweaters tied around their necks by the sleeves. I don't even own a sweater."

"You don't want to go to college, then?"

By that time, I was entirely confused, wondering how we had travelled from getting on south to going to college. "I guess not," I said. "I would have to get a sweater and one of those packs for books, not to mention the books in the first place. And anyway, I would be two years behind everybody else. I would never get caught up."

Miss Frank gave me one of her tight little grins. "It's not like a race, Rodney. People who start later sometimes do that much better. They work harder because they know how things really are."

"I know about hard work, anyway," being the only thing I could think to say.

"The organization that runs this home sponsors a scholarship. They always ask me for nominees. This year I want to put you and Lymon on the list. Do you mind?"

I shook my head. As far as I could see, it was like buying a lottery ticket or sending back one of those sweepstakes letters. It can't hurt, even if you know chances are about one in a trillion. "What about transferring to south?" I said.

"Who will take your place on north?"

"I talked to Lymon already. He said he'd switch with me, if it was all right with you."

"That's Freddie's wing. Talk to him. If he goes along, it's all right." And she ducked down to the papers on her desk and that ended that. I was right back to what I was trying to get around in the first place.

I went from there to the locker room, where the orderlies hang out on their break. Ef-ef-Freddie's got it set up like a little gym in there, with a bunch of weights and an exercise bench and stuff. See, muscles were Freddie's hobby, sort of. He'd started in junior high, lifting weights and all that. I think the thing that clinched it, after he'd built his biceps up a little, was that he stopped getting kidded too much about his stutter. When he'd got to the point in high school where he could press more than anybody else, he'd figured he had as much school as he needed, and he was probably right. Between his Terrible Stare and cracking black walnuts in the crook of his arm, he'd got all the grammar he needed for this job, anyway. My hunch is that's why Nurse Frank hired him, knowing he could strong-arm the patients, mixed in with a little sympathy for his stutter.

So there was Freddie, sure enough, with his orderly jacket off, and just his tee shirt and white pants on, doing some presses on the exercise bench. He's got hair the same color as his teeth, somewhere between gray and yellow. And he is one of those people, no matter how hard they scrub, their faces always look a little dirty. And he's got gray eyes, too. Altogether, I never knew anybody else in real life who looked any more like a faded snapshot like my mother's got in her album.

I went to my locker and got out a Butterfinger bar and started to unwrap it, thinking just how I was going to go about this. Ef-ef-Freddie swung the weight over his head and set it in the notches on the bench and slid out from under and sat up on the edge of the bench and said, "Thanks a l-l-lot."

I didn't say anything, knowing he was just getting off one of his snappy insults. I took a bite of the candy bar.

"You g-g-got them l-l-laughing at me," he said, just about Terrible Staring me to death.

I swallowed and said, "The old farts, you talking about? They were in such a state they would've laughed at a weather report."

He wasn't sold yet. "I could l-l-lose your job f-for you."

That I knew well enough. I'd seen him do it before, with none other than Harold Joli, who had been hired about the same time as me. Harold is half-Indian, which means according to the manual followed by the television and movies that he should be a low-down snake, thrown out by pure-bloods on both sides. The fact was, though, that Harold was just about the nicest person around. He wouldn't hurt a fly if it was biting him. So, naturally, Ef-ef-Freddie took a dislike to him and went to Nurse Frank and told her Harold's been jerking off in the locker room when he was supposed to be on duty. For some reason, Nurse Frank paid special attention to what Ef-ef-Freddie said, maybe because she had to listen close anyway to make out what he was saying. Harold was out on his ass before he knew it.

So I said, "I'm real worried you think so, Freddie, because I know for a fact it was me they were getting a kick out of. You were probably too wrapped up right then to notice, but I dressed so fast yesterday, being late, I forgot to zip my fly."

Ef-ef-Freddie started to flash his yellow-gray teeth and I knew I had him. It is pretty hard to grin and stay mad at the same time. To put a seal on it, I offered him what was left of my Butterfinger, which was about four-fifths, and he took it and stuffed it in his mouth all at the same time and handed me back the wrapper. While he was occupied with chewing, I got in my idea for getting trans- ferred to south. I had to be real careful, because I could not get off my real reasons. Ef-ef-Freddie himself had a thing for Karen Stephenson. And he just wouldn't get why I'd like to know Daniel O. Quick better. If I let on I thought I could do more for one of the residents on his wing than he could, he'd be insulted. "It's the smells," I told him. "You probably noticed it on north when you worked it yesterday. For some reason, they all seem to congregate up there." The truth is, the whole place has a terrible foul odor, no matter how much antiseptic and stuff we spray around. It is enough to smoke out a civet cat. After a while, working there, you get used to it, but I noticed more than once, the smells will strike you in par- ticular as you move around as being of a slightly different quality or something. I wound up, "So how about it, Freddie? Lymon and me trade, okay?"

Now, Lymon didn't take anything from Ef-ef-Freddie, so I could see in those gray eyes that he was thinking this might not be such a terrible trade, someone he could push around for someone he couldn't. But of course, he couldn't just leave it at that. He poked his tongue into various corners of his mouth, digging out the stray chunks of my Butterfinger bar that'd got stuck, doing what might pass for thinking. "W-wh-what do I g-g-get to b-b-ah-boot?"

I'd seen that one coming, and I was all ready for him. "I'll throw in my kitchen clean-ups." See, the orderlies took turns cleaning up the kitchen, each one getting one or two nights a week. The reason nobody minded too much coming back after hours to scrub around and stuff is that whoever did got to help themselves to the leftovers. And there was nobody there to stop you from taking as much as you wanted. The food was fairly pathetic, for the most part, but the catch was that the best of it tended to get left over, anything that was too tough for the old farts to chew, such as beef roast, or too rich, like cherry pie. So you could put together a pretty good meal for yourself and make the mopping worth the trouble. I especially appreciated the two nights' duty I got, seeing it took some strain off my grocery money. But I figured a few more grabs at Karen Stephenson was more than worth it.

So Freddie grinned, thinking he'd got the best of the deal, and says, "D-done." But after I started out of the locker room to tell Nurse Frank, I heard him say to himself, "Poor d-d-dumb bastard."

He was probably not too far off at that, the way it turned out. Because all my effort trying to get hers truly Karen Stephenson interested in me came to nothing. To be painfully honest about the whole thing, I do not think she was at all interested in me or anyone else either, except maybe herself, which come to think is not so bad to be interested in.

The old gentleman was for a while something a little bit different to break up the daily routine. It wasn't until later he got really weird, but I don't want to get ahead of myself. I learned a whole lot more about the old fart than anyone in his right mind would care to know.

The feathers and furs and stuff it turned out were all for the tying of flies for fishing. I'd somewhere heard about that before, but I'd never before seen it in real life. He'd fasten a tiny little hook in a vise to hold it and wrap thread around it and catch the thread over tiny little pieces of feathers and scraps of fur and wrap string and Christmas tree tinsel on top of that, and to tell the truth it did come out looking like something a fish might eat. I watched him for many spare minutes, and he talked as he went, just carrying on like a regular one-man band. How he could twiddle around with those tiny little pieces of fluff and things at his advanced years is a whole lot more than I know. But his hands were actually not so shaky at all.

"After a while," he said, "it gets to be second nature, like throwing a sidearm curve or wrestling an eighteen-wheeler down the road or dealing seconds at blackjack."

"You did all those things?" I said, not meaning to throw any doubt on the truthfulness of the old fart, but owing to my naturally suspicious nature.

"I did do all that," he said. "And a whole lot more. And some of them I can do as well as the next man right now. I can rope and tie a steer, I can do a backhand palm and an absolutely invisible one-hand pass, I can juggle three oranges, cascade or shower, I can box, I can—" But he stopped there and looked over his shoulder at me. "In my own weight class and with someone who hasn't got the reach on me, I can still hold my own." His sore jaw and my sore knuckles did not seem to slow down his argument any more than a prairie dog would slow down one of those eighteen-wheelers he was talking about.

"What I don't understand," I said, "is what you are doing in the Hillview Home for the Elderly in the first place. To tell the truth, you are not so feeble and flat on your ass as the other old individuals here."

"Meals-On-Wheels," he said, and chuckled in the wicked way he's got. But then he got all interested in the fly he was tying, having come to a ticklish place. Then he got by that place and whipped the thread around the end of the hook to finish it and cut the thread with his scissors and dabbed on some stuff like airplane glue and leaned back in his chair. "There you are," he said, "about as perfect a nymph as you'd ever want."

"A nymph," I said, looking at the hook real close. It was a pretty good imitation of those little wormy things you see swimming in the creeks sometimes. "You believe I could make one of them?"

"Hell," he said, "anyone can make a nymph." And he gave out his wicked chuckle one additional time. "What you ought to try and make is a nurse." He was of course referring to hers truly, you know, who I have spoke about many times before. He had given me his personal opinion on any number of occasions as to how I ought to go about the process of getting Nurse Stephenson interested in me, which where I am concerned amounted to nothing more or less than rape and would without the slightest bit of doubt on my part get my ass fired as quick as she could yell it, particularly if Ef-ef-Freddie would happen to be the one to hear it. And to be very truthful, I was pretty tired of his instructions on the matter. I made up my mind to change the subject back to what it was.

"You were telling me about Meals-On-Wheels," I said.

"It goes back farther than that," he said. He took the nymph, as he called it, out of the vise and put it into a plastic box with about a hundred others just like it. Then he clapped in another hook and looked back over his shoulder at me. "You want to try it?"

I shook my head. "It is not second nature to me," I said. "I'd make a horrible mess of it, I think."

But he got up out of his chair and waved for me to sit down. "You don't get it to be second nature by watching," he said.

So I sat down and tried to do it in the fashion I had seen him do.

He went ahead and lighted up another one of those smelly cigars that he had me smuggle in to him.

"I wish you wouldn't do that," I said. "If Miss Frank was to catch you with that it would be both our asses."

"What the hell am I supposed to do with them?" he said in a kind of muffled up way of speaking, being as how his mouth was stuffed with cigar. "What am I supposed to do, use them for suppositories?"

So I just shook my head and kept on wrapping up that hook with thread, If there was only one thing I'd learned in my short acquaintance with the old fart, it was that you couldn't argue with him any more than with a tree stump.

Daniel O. Quick sat at the edge of the bed watching me and talking in his usual habit. "You know my daughter Loretta?"

"I have seen the lady," I said. In the fact of the matter, I had seen her exactly once, when she was called in by Miss Frank after the recreation room ruckus. I thought they might try to get rid of the old fart after that, but the daughter must've talked them out of that notion, or bought them out of it, or maybe even wrestled them out of it, seeing as how the daughter Loretta is a large individual of the type that looks like she could throw a steer and hold it down while it was branded.

"Loretta flew me back from Phoenix when I got sick," Mr. Quick said. "I was down there for my retirement, which isn't all it is cracked up to be if you don't play golf. I wasn't that sick, really, just a slight hesitation of the heart, but it left me weak. Loretta thought I ought to have some care. And I had no objections to getting out of Phoenix. Mr. Zane Grey wrote a lot of good stories about that part of the country, but it is a damn sight too hot and dry for a man born at six thousand feet of altitude. Besides which, it is a hell of a town. They talk about your heart of town, but I believe Phoenix has got no heart at all, not that I could find. It's nothing more or less than a conglomeration of little towns, spread out as thin as an overgrazed pasture. So I flew back here and goodbye to palm trees and orange trees and good riddance for all I care." He reached over and picked up a little piece of feather and handed it to me to tie onto the hook.

"I don't deny I was sick for a while," he went on. "Damn sick, in point of fact, But I believe Loretta was afraid I was gonna die, which I was not about to do. It just wasn't in the cards. I started to get better as soon as I got inside sniffing distance of those Black Hills Spruce, which smell just like an elixir to me. But I stayed weak for a long time. She decided she's got to go back to work. Her and her husband both work and still don't seem to make nothing that amounts to a hill of beans. She is an accountant and he is a mechanic." He tapped the ashes off his cigar into a glass which was sitting on the bedstand. The ashes sizzled in the water that was left in the bottom of the glass.

"I won't say Loretta was disappointed I didn't die, but she did act like I was a great inconvenience to her alive, something she hadn't counted on. What with her working, I was left to home all by myself most of the time. Once in a while, one of the kids would be sick and would stay home from school with me, but they never seemed to want to do a damn thing but watch the TV, so that's not much of an improvement. Pretty soon Loretta got tired of coming home at noon to fix my lunch, and if it was left to me it would be oatmeal and a hot dog every day, so she gets Meals-On-Wheels to come around." He gave his evilest chuckle of all.

"The Meals-On-Wheels lady is a looker, Rodney. She's got a set of knockers on her that would make your Miss Stephenson look like a cardboard cutout. Right away I got a whole lot more interested in them than the dried roast beef and watery mashed potatoes she brings me around to eat. And when I think of Meals-On-Wheels, it's them that looms up in my mind. Meals. On wheels." And he chuckled again to make sure I have got the joke which I'd got so long ago I'd got over it already.

"It was actually pretty good therapy, as they call it," Mr. Quick went on. "I began to lay plans to get Meals-On-Wheels in the hay with me. You'll find, Rodney, that every woman takes a different plan. They are each one as different as the four seasons. Some will go for the fast ball, like your Miss Stephenson, but I figure Meals On Wheels for a change-up combination — a fat one high and inside, a slider, and a sidearm curve to polish her off. So I start with flattery — her hair, a new dress she was wearing, that sort of thing. Then I get her to talking about different things. I've been around enough I can talk about almost anything. But the conversation always gets around to loneliness, meaning me, and consolation, meaning Meals-

On-Wheels. Then comes the sidearm. I tell her I am impotent, which considering my years is I guess pretty believable."

"You said what?" I'd never heard the word before.

"Im-PO-tent," he said. "Meaning I couldn't get it up. You must've heard of such a thing."

"I did, but I thought it was a lie."

Old Quick gave me a look at that which I can't explain, like he could hit me and cry doing it. "This story is wasted on you," he said.

"No, go ahead," I told him. "You told her you were im-PO-tent. Then what?"

"I tell her it's never happened to me before, but sometimes, when she's around, I get the feeling maybe, one chance in a million, she could cure me. In fact, I believe that there is proof positive. And by God, Rodney, it works. She crawls in under the sheets with me and says she's got something to help me, something that's always worked for her husband."

"Husband?" I was a little shocked at hearing that. Up to then it seemed fairly innocent.

"Keep tension on your thread," he yelled at me. "Keep tension on it or you'll lose the whole damn business."

I tightened up the thread on the hook.

"Of course she's got a husband," Mr. Quick said. "There would be something wrong if she didn't with her bricks stacked the way they were. But the point is, she crawls in with me, and she is a natural wonder of the world, just as I thought. And she has certainly learned some unusual things to get a man in condition to do his duty to God and country. I figure her husband must be a pretty desperate man himself, sometimes, the way she is showing such invention. She takes me for an ice cream parlor, a double dip and a raspberry popsicle. And when the drunken sailor tries to stand up and salute, she tucks him in and starts in to rocking until I think I am going to spend all my small change right then and there. And she is humming and singing 'Dick Me, Daddy' like it is the Star Spangled Banner."

And then he went quiet. I was kind of froze, holding on to the vise with one hand, still trying to keep the tension on the thread with the other. "What the hell happened?" I said.

"Nothing," he said. "I suppose it was the recent sickness that sapped the spunk out of me. I just wilted like a goddam violet pinched off at the stem. I'm im-PO-tent after all. The joke is on me."

I started in to chuckle, but the old fart snapped, "It's not that funny." And in a calmer, sadder voice he went on, "It certainly isn't like we didn't try. We lost track of the time. The dried roast beef and the watery mashed potatoes have been cooling on the sideboard for hours. We both don't want to give up. It's a matter of pride for both of us. But then the real catastrophe. Loretta comes home from work and catches us at it. And Meals-On-Wheels decides to save her face, if not her ass. She jumps out of bed horrified, like she'd just been molested, and screams that I am a dirty old man. I figure it was in the cards. You seduce a woman, it is just like any other deal. You've got to follow through on your promises. Anyway, Meals-On-Wheels grabs up her clothes and beats it out of there. And the next day Loretta has me in this joint. I had a slight relapse brought on by the heavy exertion of the day before, and I was in no condition to fight."

"You're in pretty good shape now," I said.

"Sure," Mr. Quick said, "but now they've got me by the balls. When I was sick, Loretta got power of attorney."

"What's that?"

"A license to steal, where I'm concerned. I had over thirty-thousand dollars in a CD. A lifetime of savings. Near as I can tell, she's got it all. She's got my bank account and my pension money and my social security. What happens when all the money is used up, I don't know. She'll probably yank me out of here and kick me into a ditch to die, like an old smelly dog." He blinked a time or two, looking off. "It's not the money, so much as the betrayal. I can't believe she's her mother's offspring."

It was kind of a shock to me. I didn't know anyone could do something like that, but it explained some things I'd been wondering about.

"How are you doing?" he said, looking at the fly I had tried to tie.

"About finished," I said. "How does she look?"

"Wonderful," he said. "Like something you picked out of the radiator on your car."

"I guess I need practice," I said.

"Christ," Mr. Quick said. "I've got enough flies now for twenty seasons. And who knows if I'll ever get to use them?"

I turned to look at him and saw he was looking out the window up to the hills which is where they get the Hillview in the name of the home.

"It's getting to be spring now," he said. "The snow's going out. I'd give my left eyeball to get up there one more time, catch me one more good trout, take one more woman to the hay——"

I thought he was going to add on something else, but he didn't. "My wife, she loved to go fishing, too," he said. "Only she used worms. She would never try a fly. She said worms were more natural. Sometimes she'd go with me, but sometimes she'd just go off by herself and come back at the end of a day with a pretty good string. It's a rare thing in a woman to like to fish like that. I haven't found one before or since." He was still looking out of his window.

"She was a big woman," he told me, "just like climbing into a feather tick mattress. Loretta takes after her in that, but not in the size of her heart. My wife was about the biggest hearted woman I ever knew. And always smiling and joking. I believe she could've joked a person out of his deathbed."

He got out his wallet then and opened it up to some old faded pictures and showed them to me, pointing to a picture of a large woman. I could see the resemblance to Loretta. There were pictures of Mr. Quick in there too, looking a whole lot younger and more wiry. One of them showed him with a beer bottle and making a face like he was drunk.

"She loved to take snapshots," Mr. Quick says. "She used an old box camera she bought and took snapshots of everything, like she was trying to get everything into that camera that meant something to her. Loretta has boxes of them in her attic. Hundred of pictures of Loretta, a little girl. Thousand of me. You can see me go from thirty to fifty almost day by day. Fifty is when the snapshots stopped. Brain tumor." He took back the wallet and put it back in the drawer of the stand and looked up to the hills again.

"I got the sweetest little travel rod," he says. "I've been carrying it everywhere I go the past ten years." He squashed out his cigar in the glass. "You know what these stogies need to go with them is a good shot of bourbon."

I'd heard that one before, so I was kind of braced for it. "There I draw the line," I said. "If Miss Frank was to find I got booze for you, she would fire my ass like that. Besides, they give you a quota of wine every couple weeks or so."

"May wine," he said, making a face. "That stuff's as bad as panther piss. When I was a harbor pilot down in Galveston——"

I'd believed what he'd told me about his wife was the truth, but I couldn't be half sure of the rest of it, for a sample that he was born in Deadwood and was the grandson of Charlie Utter, who was partners with Wild Bill Hickok. And it was hard to swallow that any one individual even twice as old could've held so many jobs as he claims——miner, truck driver, rodeo clown, lumberjack, blackjack dealer, smuggler, bank robber and fruit picker, just to name a few I recall. And I think he could've been pulling my leg in regard to the matter of his ventures with the women, for the fact that it is hard to buy that he could've been married twenty years and get in all that much snorting around the fair sex before or after. But I do believe that there was more than a tiny bit of truth in that tale he told Meals-On-Wheels, that he was lonely.

I looked at my watch and saw my spare minutes were long past, so I got up and started out. I left him looking out the window, and I knew what was on his mind, so I was not in the least surprised later on when I came to work one day to find out he had run off. But that wasn't until he came near to killing me with embarrassment.

3.

That gray Easter Sunday is what did it for both me and Mr. Quick. It kind of brought things to a head like a ripe pimple and popped, too.

That morning, I went to see my mother. She still lived in the same trailer where I was brought up, in a park on the outskirts of Rapid City, the prairie side. The sandbox where I had played as a little kid was still there beside the trailer, only she had tried to make it into a flower bed a long time ago. It never worked out, being so many thistles and dandelions and weeds she could never seem to get out, until it just got all overgrown, a weedpatch all boarded in, and now the boards rotting. And there in a cottonwood alongside the trailer was still the tire swing, but the rope all frayed until it looked like it was ready to break. She said some kids from the park still swung in it sometimes, so she didn't want to take it down.

I never knew what to expect, knocking on the ripped-up screen door. It was usually some man who for me was Uncle Blank. I called them all Uncle Blank, because when I was a kid she would say to me that this is my Uncle Jimmy or Jackie or Wayne or whatever, until I got the idea that I had such a bunch of uncles that I would just call them Uncle Blank, fill in the blank. Usually they would hang around for two to six months and then I would never see them again. I never blamed her. She was still young when Lonnie Deuce left her with me, not too much older than I am right now. It had to be hard for her, I expect. And she met a lot of men in her job waiting on tables. And every one of them she hoped would be the one who would stick, but they never did.

And sure enough, it was another Uncle Blank who came to the screen door and stood looking at me like I was some kind of nuisance that he would have to shoo away like a stray dog. He was wearing a tee-shirt and jeans, but his brown hair was all mussed up and his eyes watery and red like he just woke up. "Who you?" he said to me.

"Is Vicky here?" I said. Her old beat-up VW squareback was in the drive, so I figured she was there.

"I'm a relative," I said. At a certain point, my mother didn't want Uncle Blank to know that I was her son, and she would try to pass me off as a younger cousin. I went along. It was one of those harmless lies, it seemed like to me.

"She's sleeping," Uncle Blank said.

"Maybe you could wake her up," I said. "Tell her it's Rodney."

And then I heard my mother from inside. "Is that Rodney?"

"He says he is," Uncle Blank said, looking like he was not too trustful I was telling the truth. And then my mother squeezed in between him and the door, tying up her robe, squinting at me and smiling the way she always does when she first sees me.

"What you doing here? What holiday is it?"

"It's Easter. I brought you a flower." I showed her the potted plant I was carrying. It was one of those white lilies, wrapped in shiny green plastic, that I'd got on sale at K Mart. She opened up the screen door and took the pot out of my hands and looked at it. I could tell she was hung over. I'd seen her that way enough before.

"It's pretty, Rodney. Thank you, honey." She pulled me down by the neck to where she could give me a smack on the cheek. "Come on in."

Inside, it looked pretty much like usual, kind of a mess, and smelled a little sour. She would go on a rampage two or three times a year and get things all spruced up, but then it would all get ahead of her again. She tended to hang onto things like old mail and what not until it piled up in drifts. She had a hard time sorting. It all seemed important to her, I guess.

"This is Red," she said.

Uncle Blank nodded. I don't know why he was named Red. His hair was actually brown, with white sprinkled through it.

"You want some coffee?" my mother asked me.

"I can't stay long," I said. "There's a to-do at Hillview this afternoon I have to help with." But I sat down at the booth and she started in drawing some water and heating up the stove.

"We're all out of creamer," she said. "Red, get on your shoes and go out and get some creamer."

"I don't need creamer," I said.

"Well, I do," she said. "Red?"

Uncle Red hadn't moved, but now he grunted and got up from across from where he'd been sitting and shuffled into the living room area. My mother sat down in the place Uncle Red'd just left and looked at me. "You getting enough to eat? You look like you lost weight?"

"I'm about the same," I told her, which was a harmless lie in itself, since I'd dropped a little since I'd turned over my kitchen cleanups to Ef-ef-Freddie Fitz.

"Red," she called out to the livingroom, "get some rolls, too."

Red grunted something that sounded about halfway between "uh-huh" and "screw you." He finished pulling on his shoes and got out the door before anything more could get added to the grocery list.

"Red is all right," my mother said. "He works at the 7-Eleven."

"As long as he don't hit," I said. My mother had a way of picking out Uncles who would as soon give you a sock as say howdy.

"Red isn't like those others," she said. "He has an education. He was a college professor at one time."

I nodded. I'd never seen a college professor except on television, so I suppose it was possible.

"He had a little trouble getting his degree. It gave him a nervous condition."

It was the same as always. Uncle Blank was always a sweet man until he turned nasty. At least she didn't have any bruises that I could see.

I dug into my pants pocket and pulled out a twenty-dollar bill I'd saved from my salary. I put it on the sticky table in between us. "This'll go toward what I owe," I said.

"I think you're already ahead on your payments," she said.

I don't remember when it started, this idea that I owed her a big amount of money and was paying her back ten or twenty dollars at a time when I could afford it. It made it easier for her to take the money, which I knew she always needed. We never mentioned how much exactly I owed and how much I got paid off. It was just another harmless lie.

"You sure you don't need it?" she said, still looking at the bill.

"I got all I need," I said. In a way, it was true. I always got along all right on the bare necessities. You could always get by as long as you didn't run into any hitches like accidents or getting sick or losing your job. You just didn't have any fat to live on when the pickings were slim.

She picked up the twenty and stuck it into the pocket of her robe.

"Uncle Red doesn't have to know you got that," I said.

"Red's not like that," she said. "He's got his own source of income."

"Right," I said. "The 7-Eleven. I suppose he is rolling in clover."

"He's counting on an inheritance, too. His father was in business."

I don't suppose my mother would've lasted that long if she didn't think things might get better soon. I've never seen another woman collect so much evidence on how tough life can be and how unreliable men can be and still have a load of faith that things would turn out all right. A couple years ago, I might have gone along, but the Hillview Home opened my eyes about a lot of things.

"You got a girlfriend yet, Rodney?"

I had to give the question a little thought, being that I had Karen Stephenson so much on my mind, but I had to conclude that Hers Truly was not really too friendly. I gave my head a shake.

"There is too a girl," my mother said. "I can tell. You are sweet on someone."

I could feel my face getting hot.

"What's her name?" my mother asked me.

"There is a nurse," I said, "but she won't give me the time of day."

"Have you tried asking her out?"

"I don't even know how to go about it." I'd never gone out with a girl in high school, unless you count Mary Beth Tubbman, which is another story entirely and almost as embarrassing to me as this one. I never had much spare time, for one thing, with all the part-time jobs I was juggling in those days. And for another thing, I couldn't feature myself like someone in one of those black and white movies, going down to a soda fountain and buying a couple of Cherry Cokes. There weren't any soda fountains left that I knew of, or any girls who drank Cherry Cokes, either. "I guess I am not much of a one for dating," I said.

"There isn't anything to it," my mother said. "Just strike up a conversation."

"About what?"

"About anything. The weather. The news of the day. Then you work it around to some compliment on her appearance. If you get a smile out of her, you ask her out."

It sounded simple enough, like someone saying, well, if you want to go to the moon, you just hop in a rocket ship and take off. But you know there's more to it than that.

"What if she tells me to take a flying leap?"

"Then give her a great big grin and say goodbye. Let her know what she's missing out on. And try again later on. Your daddy was such a charmer, I know you could be, too."

I held back saying that my father must have been a real charmer to run out on her and me. Besides which, by her own account, he was a handsome man, not like me. It is probably a whole lot easier to sell yourself to a woman when you've got something worth buying. It seemed to me women were all at the advantage of me in that respect. The fact was, I figured women could just about rule the world, considering the edge they had in bargaining.

"Are you going to talk to her?"

"Sure." Meaning maybe I would and maybe I wouldn't, depending. The teapot whistled about then, and my mother went to fix instant coffee and Uncle Red came back from the store and we all sat down and had coffee and rolls. But I suppose it was that talk with my mother that did it for me as much as anything, because if it hadn't been on my mind, I might never have spoken up to Karen Stephenson and got into such a fix.

What they do at Hillview, on Easter they throw a shebang for all the old farts to make them feel a little better maybe. In the morning they had what they call an Easter Parade where the residents get on their best clothes and march up and down the halls showing off. I'd seen it last year, and it is just a little bit pathetic, and I was glad to miss it. Mr. Quick wouldn't have nothing at all to do with that kind of stuff, of course, and in point of plain fact said he'd keep the door to his room shut tight during that part of it so he wouldn't have to watch the other old farts make a fool of themselves.

In the afternoon they have a non-denominational service in the rec room followed by a non-denominational what they call brunch, with a considerable amount of eating and drinking of May wine which I guess the Hillview Home must've got a wholesale vat of at some point in the past. It is a place where everybody kind of mingles on a social level and enjoys themselves to the best of their limited ability.

A great many of the relatives of the old farts visited with them on this occasion, and a pretty good meal of ham and sweet potatoes was served, which was already a far sight better than the kind of thin stuff they usually give to the individuals here. If I hadn't've traded off my kitchen duties to Ef-ef-Freddie, I would've had a great feast of leftovers that night.

For entertainment they got together a band they called the Kitchen Klatters, which was a bunch of old individuals playing things like a bass made out of a wash tub and clothesline, a washboard raked over with thimbles, kazoos, and such, and their particular rendition of "In Your Easter Bonnet" was a great strain on the ears. The individuals in the band, to make things that much worse, were all dressed in the silliest kind of outfits such as hats with flowers, gaudy shirts, and outrageous big handpainted ties, so you'd think a person would have a little more sense than to conduct themselves so ridiculous as that. But the old farts and their families seemed to like it, and I could put up with it if it didn't go on too long.

Being the relatives were keeping company with the old farts and spooning food into their mouths and wiping their chins and things of the kind the nurses and the staff usually did, there was not a lot for the nurses and the staff to do except watch close to see that no one gargled on the ham or got too tight on the May wine. It was a great opportunity, I got thinking, to try out my sidearm curve.

Of course I was a little put off by Ef-ef-Freddie, who was keeping a couple of the other orderlies amused at one side of the room by the foosball table by tearing in two the Fall and Winter Sears catalogs, now out of date because the Spring and Summer ones'd just come out. The catalogs were standard reading fare for the residents. Nurse Frank was of the mind that it gave the old individuals more hope looking at the catalogs and filling out orders in their head than any number of religious tracts could do. Anyway, Freddie liked to do his strong-arm stuff on the old catalogs, ripping them right in two with an awful show of gritting his gray-yellow teeth and bulging out the muscles at the sides of his neck. I figured there was some trick to it, although it is not a bad show at that. But then I noticed that Freddie seemed to be keeping an eye on me, like he was the slightest bit suspicious about the way I was edging up to Karen Stephenson. And when I went so far as even to sit down next to her, he gave me another one of his Terrible Stares just as he grunts and pulls the halves of another catalog apart. It was a pretty clear warning, I guess, and if I'd had any sense at all, I'd've paid more attention to it. But just getting even that close to hers truly had got my nerve up way past the sensible point. And since Ef-ef-Freddie was out of hearing range anyway, I figured a little pitching wouldn't hurt too much, so little did I know.

"That is a cute little hat," I said for a start.

"It's the same hat I always wear," she said. She was not even looking at me, but sipping her May wine out of a little bit of paper cup they use at the home to hold pills the old farts were supposed to take, and she was looking out over the rec room from where we were sitting on stools in the corner by the window. I felt I was not off to such a great start, and I looked across the room to where Mr. Daniel O. Quick was standing, looking kind of grumpy because, so I believed, Loretta had not even shown up to wish him a happy Easter. He saw me looking at him and he threw me a kind of raw salute with his hand which I can roughly translate into "Haul her into the closet."

But I decide to give her another chance. "Those are real nice flowers you got pinned on you." They were little yellow flowers of some kind.

"They are the same that all the nurses have," she said. I was having quite a time getting a ball past her. She seemed to be hitting on me quite regular.

"Your hair looks real pretty," I said. I thought maybe I had a strike at last. She turned to me and gave a little flicker of a smile and said, "Why, thank you."

I looked over to where Mr. Quick was to show him I was getting somewhere at last, but he wasn't looking. He was talking to Miss Frank. And for someone that called it panther piss, he seemed to be swallowing an unusual amount of May wine out of a glass about as big as a vase. In fact, I saw that it was a vase which he had stolen off the stand in the hall for the purpose.

So I turned back to Karen Stephenson and tried another one.

"Have you ever read the books of Mr. Zane Grey?" Books are a good thing to talk about to women, Mr. Quick told me, and I had been going through his collection at a fairly rapid rate of about one per week.

"No," Karen Stephenson said. I was in trouble again.

"They're real good," I said, trying to save something. "There's something happening at all times and the scenery is something beautiful."

She didn't say anything. She was back to looking over the room again. I was slipping pretty bad. I was giving serious consideration to throwing her the curve right there, but it didn't seem just the right place, I wished I was like Mr. Quick, who was never at a loss for something to say.

Speaking of which, I couldn't help looking over at the old fart, and he was still talking to Miss Frank, only now he had kind of got her pinned against the door of the storage room, leaning with his arm braced up and talking to her earnest, and it was hard to believe, but I was of the realization that he was trying to put the make on her, and from the looks of it he was doing considerable better than me.

So I looked back to Miss Karen Stephenson. I had to resort to the last thing which I could think of to talk about, which was the weather. "It sure is coming down," I said, looking out the window.

And, some little success, she turned to look too and said, "It certainly is."

And I just rushed right ahead and tried to keep her going. "The rain," I said, "makes me feel — " But there I came up dry. I didn't know just what it was that rain made me feel. But then I remembered what it was I was supposed to be driving at and I finished, " — makes me feel lonely."

"Me too," she said, and gave me a kind of sad smile which would melt an icicle. "The sound of it," she said.

"The smell of it," I said.

But then something went wrong with her eyes and I thought maybe I was getting too strange for her, so I hurried up and tried to explain. "The rain's got a smell," I said. "Sometimes you can smell it before it gets here even."

But that was even worse because she was starting to look kind of bored. "Really?" she said, but with the kind of a sound in her voice which meant she could give a shit about the smell of the rain.

Sometimes no amount of planning is as good as a simple hunch, and that is what saved the day. I looked around and made sure that Ef-ef-Freddie is nowhere to be seen, then I got off my stool and slid the window open a ways and said, "Come on, I'll show you what the rain smells like."

And she said kind of casual, "Sure," and slid down and walked out onto the porch. There was a roof over the porch so we weren't getting wet, but it was a little cool out there. She had her arms folded up already to keep them warmer and stood looking out into the garden. It was a poor excuse for a garden, if you want my feelings. Even in the summer there was nothing there but flowers. And this time of year it was not too much better than a pig wallow, all the grass worn off by the old farts getting out as soon as the snow was gone to get some sun and then the rain stirring it up to mud. A few tulips were sticking their green spears up by the side of the porch, though, and the maple was starting to have its buds swell up. I came up and stood by the rail between the post of the porch and her. "Just smell," I said, and she took a deep breath.

It was a sight a whole lot more lovely than that garden in full flower to see hers truly Karen Stephenson take a deep breath. I think I took a gasp or two myself, I was so moved in the way I have explained earlier on.

"It doesn't smell like anything," she said, letting out her breath with a motion that was just beautiful.

"Smell again," I said. I wanted to watch her breathe deep again, and she did, but it was beginning to dawn on me that I couldn't just keep her breathing in and out for very long. I would have to do some fancy talking to keep her interested. So I started in talking, just trusting in blind luck to give me some words that made some sense. "It's not so much what you smell," I said. "It's what you don't smell."

Her eyes were looking at me suspicious again. I was beginning to see that she could think I was just a little bit crazy. I'd better start making some sense pretty soon, I thought, or I could forget my sidearm curve altogether. So I said, "You don't smell any dust nor pollen, no coal nor oil smoke nor car exhausts. You don't even smell those deodorant sprays and disinfectants like what we are all the time spraying around the home, and you don't smell that smell the rooms are full of that belong to the old — individuals." I was afraid I'd almost slipped and said old farts, which would've broken the tender feeling I was getting across, no doubt. "What you smell," I went on, "is just the sweet, pure air that you were meant to breathe, washed clean by the rain."

I was looking at her and kind of holding my breath after I got all that out, not knowing what the funny look in her eyes was telling me. Then she says, "You know something Rodney? You are heavy."

It was something I had in secret thought for a long time, so it was good to hear from someone else, especially from hers truly Miss Karen Stephenson. What I did then I have no sound explanation for, except it seemed the most natural thing to do, seeing she is shivering with the cold air. I reached over my arm and put it around her shoulders and she let me. I figured maybe she hadn't noticed yet and I'd better keep talking before she saw what I was doing. So I started out, "The water when you drink it out of a creek in the spring, what does it taste like? It is what you don't taste. The chemicals, the germs — " And so on and on. It was not so hard to talk once you got the idea of it, just like walking, one foot after another, one word after another. I was beginning to see how individuals like Mr. Zane Grey were able to put so many words in those books. Mama would've been proud.

So I talked and talked and got my arm more and more around her until my fingers were about an inch away from her right hand bosom, as they call them. It was amazing to me that I could've got that far already, and there didn't seem nothing more to do than to let fly with my curve. So I got ready in my mind and let her sail.

"Miss Stephenson," I said, "can I tell you something I wouldn't want the other nurses to know, nor Ef-ef-Freddie, as he calls himself?"

She looked at me with the concerned look that was what I am fairly convinced was what called her to be a nurse in the first place. "Sure, Rod," she said.

I wanted her to catch the full seriousness of what I was about to say, so I grabbed hold of her right-hand bosom. "It is something you can probably do me a very great favor on, as a matter of fact. It is something I have very often felt when you are in the presence of myself. It could just as well be that you could change my life for me, or even save it."

She was now maybe a little more concerned than what I wanted her to be. "Rodney," she said, "what's the matter?"

"Nothing, nothing," I said. "Nothing that anyone would notice. It's just — "

The thing is, the fact was finally coming to me that I was actually clamped onto her in a fashion that I'd very often done in dreams, and it threw off my pitch. I didn't believe it myself when I came out with it. "Miss Stephenson," I said, "I am afraid I am important."

She was looking at me again like maybe I was crazy, and I quick tried to cover my tracks. "Im-PO-tant," I said.

She shook her head. "IMP-otant, you mean?"

"Right," I said, trying to grin my way out of it.

"What is THAT then?" she said, pointing to the region of my crotch.

I looked down kind of filled with a horrible idea of what I knew I would see. Even then if I'd've been able to think faster, I could've said maybe it was a green banana or something I had stuffed in my pocket. But now, I took way too long. In point of plain fact, I could not say anything at all, I was so shocked.

And then she reached down and snapped with her fingers the way nurses are, I am told, taught to do about the first day of nursing school, the way you would thunk a watermelon to see if it was ripe, and that was all to that. It didn't hurt all that much, but it did the trick, and I hadn't got a thing to be shocked about any more.

Miss Karen Stephenson pulled away from me, which was not hard considering how suddenly weak I felt, and she went back inside kind of shaking her head and snuffling into her hand like she'd all of a sudden got a bad cold and was trying to keep from sneezing.

I stayed out there for a while trying to get real interested in the rain coming down in the garden and as accidentally as I could tending to my tenderness. Then I heard this voice behind me that made the limp and sore little traitor want to shrivel up entirely and beat a retreat into my stomach maybe. "D-d-d-Deuce?"

And as I swivelled around, Ef-ef-Freddie stepped out from behind a pillar and stood there with his feet spread apart and his hands on his hips, throwing me just about the most Terrible of all the Stares he had in him to throw. But the worst part is that I had no idea at all of how long he'd been there or how much he'd seen or heard. I tried grinning at him, but that didn't do a thing but make his Stare a little more Terrible. "Wh-wh-what the hell," he sputtered, "you th-think y-y-you're d-doing?"

"Me?" I said, looking around like maybe there was a crowd of us here and he'd got the wrong one. "Me? I'm just smelling the fresh air."

"Hah," said Ef-ef-Freddie. "You're sn-sniffing around that n-nurse's t-t-t-tail, is what."

In actual fact, when I heard him say that, I was a little bit relieved, because it told me he couldn't've seen or heard too much of what went on or he would know that I got a whole lot farther than just sniffing. "We were chatting," I said. "About the weather and stuff."

You've seen dogs give their head a tilt when they are puzzled or undecided whether to wag their tail or take a bite out of yours. Well, that's what Ef-ef-Freddie did then. And it did give me some small hope maybe he would decide not to rip me in two like a Sears and Roebuck catalog. "I s-s-seen you g-g-iving her the eye b-b-before," he said. "Th-that's why you w-w-wanted on s-south, ain't it?"

I just kind of shrugged, taking what I could get out of this mess.

"I sh-sh-should fire your b-b-butt." He tried that out just to see how much of a quiver he could get out of me.

I gave another shrug, trying not to show how that would just about pull the rug out from under me entirely. It is a pretty scary thing watching an individual trying to decide on the best way to make you suffer, like there is a pretty difference between using pliers to pull our your toenails or just roasting your balls with a match. "B-b-better yet," he said, getting a new idea, "I could j-just put you back on n-n-north." And he raised his pale eyebrows to see how I'd go for that.

Well, I figured that was better than being without any means of support at all, so I tried to dig a worried expression into my forehead, not too hard a thing to do, given the situation. "Please, Freddie," I said, "You wouldn't."

And at last he flashed his gray grin, and I could see it was settled. He turned around and went on back in through the glass doors. And I waited a couple of seconds and did the same.

I was probably only thinking it, but it did feel like everybody looked at me when I came back in and knew what a complete idiot I was. So I just climbed on my stool in the corner and picked up a cup of May wine and drank some of it and grinned a little to myself and listened to the horrible noise of the Kitchen Klatters which had started up their scraping and banging again, and waited until things went back to normal.

Actually, I was pretty mad at myself for letting Ef-ef-Freddie catch me out. And it began to settle on me how I was going to miss those long talks with Quick, not to mention the mere presence of Karen Stephenson. I guess I was feeling pretty sorry for myself at that.

But in a little while I got curious about Mr. Daniel O. Quick, who got me into this situation in the first place with his sidearm curve story and bad pronouncing of words. So I looked for him and he was not there. So I looked for Miss Frank and she was not there also. So that was all I needed. The old fart had without a doubt got Miss Frank into the hay with him, even though it was hard to see why he wanted to. I was getting embarrassed all over again to think that he could pull it off and I couldn't. But I could just as well've saved my feeling sorry for myself, because just when the Kitchen Klatters were striking up "April Showers" for about the fiftieth time, there was a yell and across the room the door to the storage room flew open like it was on a spring and out rolled none other than Daniel O. Quick in the flesh, ass over headbone, like he was thrown from off a Brahma bull, and unfolded on the floor right in the middle of all the other old farts and their families which were beginning to think that Mr. Quick was part of the entertainment, and some even started to clap. And out of the storage room after him stepped Miss Frank, looking just as tough and flinty as ever, jerking her skirt down like she is all business and stepped over Mr. Quick and marched on out into the hall.

4.

"It was a simple miscalculation," is what the old fart told me later. "She does not appear to be the type you can pull into a closet."

But I think it hurt the old guy a whole lot more than he let on. I didn't get to see so much of him any more, since I was kept pretty busy on the north wing and if I hung around south too much Ef-ef-Freddie hit me with a T.S. But when I did get a chance to see him, Quick was quieter and appeared to be thinking a good deal more than he was talking, which up to then was rare. And he spent not so much time tying flies and a whole lot more looking out of his window up to the hills.

To be perfectly honest, I was not feeling so wonderful myself. Even though my run-ins with Karen Stephenson were rare, the giggling of the nurses in my presence had seemed to've picked up since Easter. And maybe I was only thinking it, but it did seem that the word "important" was getting a tiny bit more of a workout than it did before. Like I would go to the station and tell the nurse on duty there that I needed her signature on a checklist or something, and the nurse would say as innocent as she could, "Is it important?" or "How important is it?" And then she would try to keep a grin from busting out on her face. And one day I came to work and find pasted on my locker a little sign done in real fancy letters: "Very Important Person."

I ripped the sign down off the locker, leaving ragged edges where the tape'd been, and looked around to see who could've done it, and just then Ef-ef-Freddie walks in. Ordinarily, I wouldn't be so bold as to suggest he was capable of any mischief, but by that time I'd had about as much of this important business as I could stand. I handed him the sign and said, "I suppose you think that is pretty funny."

He squinted at it and gave a pretty good imitation of somebody who didn't know what the score was. "Is it s-s-supposed to be?"

"No," I said.

"Th-then I'm n-n-not l-laughing." And he handed me back the sign and got down on his exercise bench to press a few weights. I saw right away it wasn't him. It wasn't his style to be so dainty about his torture.

"Maybe you saw who did it," I said.

Freddie got down a barbell off its holder and lifted it real careful into position. It must've been pretty near to the limit of his ability, because I saw his arms waver a little bit with the effort. "M-m-maybe it's from Qu-qu-Quick," he grunted out.

But that didn't make any sense to me at all. "What the hell are you talking about?"

"H-h-he didn't l-l-leave n-no other n-n-note." It was pretty obvious by then that Freddie was having a hell of a time working the muscles in his arms and the ones in his mouth at the same time. It looked like it was taking all his concentration. In the meantime, I was trying to add up what he's saying, and it's starting to scare me. The first thing I think about in connection with leaving a note is suicide. There are a few that will take that way, sometimes, which is one reason there isn't but one floor at the home, and the way old Quick was acting lately set me off in that direction right away. I got closer to the exercise bench and bent over it and yelled down at Freddie's face, "What're you talking about? What happened?"

It startled Freddie so much he almost let his elbows buckle. "G-g-god d-d-damn!" he sputtered. He was already as mad as he could possibly get. He would've slugged me with a Terrible Stare if the effort of it wouldn't've done him in altogether.

I guess seeing him at slight disadvantage, plus what kind of horrible things could've happened to Quick, made me braver than normal. I dropped the sign and put my hand on the barbell and leaned over to yell into Freddie's face. "What happened to him? What did he do to himself?"

But my weight plus whatever enormous amount was already on the barbell was altogether too much of a burden for Freddie. "Sh-sh-shit," he said as his brace crumbled slowly away and the barbell came to rest on his adam's apple. I saw right away I'd got myself in a fine fix already. If I was to let him up, he would've killed me outright.

Now, added to his usual problems of talking, Freddie was almost gagging, trying to lift the weight of the bar off his throat. "G-g-get orf m-me!" he croaked out.

I leaned down on the bar a hair more. "Tell me what happened," I yelled. Truth to tell, I didn't know what else to do.

"H-h-h-he r-ruh-er-ruh — " See, the R's were the hardest of all for Freddie. Once he got started on them he just kind of ground on and on like a motor with bad points you try to get started on a damp morning. I suppose it didn't help too much the barbell crunching down on his vocal cords. Ef-ef-Freddie wouldn't've stood any kind of a chance on one of those third degrees you see on the TV sometime. He would've got his ass beat off with those rubber hoses before he could confess. But he finally got it out. "He run off."

Like I said earlier on, it wasn't a great surprise to me. Quite a ways from it. As soon as I heard it, I knew I'd kind of been expecting it. And I could almost bet where he was to be found. So I pushed myself away from Freddie to head for the garage. For half a second, I was afraid Freddie was going to jump right up and come after me, but his biceps had caved in completely by now. He was getting a little more air, but the barbell had still got him pinned onto the bench. "G-g-get it orf!" he was sputtering. And as I took off, he left me with a parting shot, like I think they say, only it was more machinegun fire in this particular case. "Ef-ef-ef-ef-fuck you!"

Lymon was just pulling into the garage in the Hillview Home pickup when I got there. He'd been out picking up some supplies. "I've got to use the truck," I told him. And I explained about Mr. Quick running off.

"What makes you so sure you know where he is?" Lymon said. He was unloading the back of the truck.

"I've heard him talk about it hundreds of times."

"What do you care where he is, anyway?" Lymon said. "He would show up back here sooner or later."

"I don't care that much," I said. "But he was pretty good to me when I was on south."

"He just about broke your leg and he used you to get cigars," Lymon said. "He fed you a lot of hog slop which got you into trouble and made you into a bad joke. I don't see you owe him anything."

Of course, he had a point. I couldn't explain it. "I'd hate to see him get hurt." I said finally. It wasn't much of a reason, but it was all I could come up with.

"Take the truck, then," Lymon said. "But you'd better get back fast or you'll get my ass in a sling too." He tossed me the keys.

"Thanks," I said. "I'll buy you a pizza tonight."

"I'm not going to be here tonight. I'm catching a ride to the res. Aunt Celia is having a giveaway. Don't ride the clutch like you always do." He motioned for me to take the truck and go.

I set off up the Rapid Creek road west where it winds up into the hills. It was for sure spring now and kind of a nice warm day, and the willow brush and bushes along the creek were still low enough so it was not great difficulty to spot Quick finally. He was fishing in the creek a good long ways up, which again was not too surprising since he must've took off sometime before the sun came up. I stopped the pickup on a pullout and got out and watched him a while. The fishing he was doing was pretty to watch, seeing as he was whipping this rod and line so that it curved back and forth making lovely bends in the air. It made you wish you could do it.

He was moving along up the side of the creek kind of slow, stopping to throw the line into the pools and wide places where the creek turned. Once in a while he would jerk the rod back fast, but then he would look disappointed and say "Shit" real soft. He'd got a vest with all kind of pockets and some rubber knee boots and a kind of funny cloth hat that didn't seem to have any shape a person could see, and around his neck he had slung with a piece of string one of those plastic zipper bags with Western Airlines printed on the side. He was starting to edge away from where I was parked, so I said to him, "Get any fish yet?"

And he said, "Nothing," pretty calm, like he knew all along I was there. "My reflexes are off. I'm getting hits enough, but I can't seem to hook any. I'm getting closer, though."

"It's almost lunch time," I said. "You'll be getting hungry."

"I got my lunch," he said, patting the airline bag. "I got everything I need. The older you get, the lighter you travel. The last hike you take, you don't need a thing."

So I watched him a while longer. It was beginning to look like this was not going to be so easy after all. Besides, I would've kind of liked to see the old fart catch something. For one thing, I guessed he would come along with me easier once he got one. I walked along the side of the road to keep even with him. But it was no go. I could even see the fish suck in the fly sometimes, but the old guy was just a little slow in jerking the rod and the fly got spit out again. I saw that I was going to have to think of something else. "There is one thing I could get you haven't got in that bag," I said in between his throws once.

He didn't say anything, I just went on. "I bet you haven't got a bottle of bourbon in there."

He threw his line and looked back over his shoulder at me. "You making me an offer?"

"Go back with me quiet," I said, "and I'll get a bottle of bourbon for you."

"What makes you think I can't get my own bottle?"

"Because I seen you get cleaned out of your spending money at the checker table yesterday."

"The bastard cheated," Mr. Quick said. "I was trying to win a grub stake." And he turned around to me and I saw that kind of completely helpless look on him again and I knew I had him.

A little while later we were both in the pickup and heading back to the home.

"Don't forget the bourbon," Mr. Quick said.

"I'll get it," I said. "But you'd better not let anybody catch you drinking it at Hillview."

"I'll drink it before I get there," he said. "A deal's a deal."

So I pulled into the first liquor store I saw, which was a fairly ritzy looking affair by the name of Adolph's. I turned off the motor and was real careful to stick the key in my pocket, and I went on in.

One look and I could see that this place was a whole lot different than Domino's On/Off Sale Liquor where Harold and me buy our wine. It had a great deal bigger range of selection, for one thing. And thick carpet on the floor and stuff. It took me a long time to find the bourbon and a long time after I found it to make up my mind which kind to buy, there were so many kinds. I was kind of shocked that booze could cost so much for a small bottle like that. So finally I found the cheapest kind, which already was going to take my last penny almost, and I went up to the counter to pay.

I thought as soon as I saw the gentleman behind the counter I had some more trouble coming my way. He was a good deal redder in the complexion than any Indian that is called "red." It's like his blood just got all pumped up into his head like his body was being squeezed like a bottle of catsup.

I set the bottle down on the counter and got my billfold out. The gentleman behind the counter just stared at me so that I couldn't look at him any more, his look was so ugly. I looked down into my billfold and acted like I was hunting for my money, even though to tell the truth there wasn't but that one five-dollar bill which I knew all the time was there. It was supposed to go for my part of groceries for the week. I was hoping Harold and Lymon wouldn't get too mad about that.

The gentleman behind the counter so far was not making a move to wait on me, and in the meantime another individual had come in and grabbed a six-pack out of the cooler and slammed it down on the counter beside me. And the counter gentleman, he picked up the six pack and put it in a sack and took the money from the other individual and rang up the cash register and gave the other individual change and thanked him. And the other guy went out and I was still not waited on.

There's not a thing in the world that makes a person feel lower or more sick and nasty than to be ignored like you were a window to see through. Anyway, sick as I felt and kind of weak, I pulled out the five-dollar bill and placed it on the counter and pushed it toward the gentleman.

"You took a long time making up your mind," the counter guy said.

I nodded. I wasn't in the mood for conversation.

"What you got in your back pocket?" he said.

I suppose I must've let my jaw drop then and looked pretty stupid. "Huh?"

"I think you got another bottle in your back pocket," the guy said. "You want to pay for that one, too?"

"This is the only bottle I got," I said. I turned around and pulled up my jacket and showed him.

"Under your jacket then," he said. "I know you got one salted away somewhere."

I unzipped my jacket and held it open to show him. By then I was about ready to throw up.

"Why do you look so goddam guilty, then?" The counter individual said. "What are you up to? You got an I.D.?"

"I'm almost twenty-two," I said. By which I meant it was less than a year away.

"You don't look that old," he said.

So I got my driver's license out of my billfold and handed it to him. He held it about as close to his face as his big nose would let him. Then he looked up at me and down at the card and up at me again and said, "This ain't you."

See, he was looking at the dumb picture on the driver's license. All in a flash I remembered when that picture was taken right after I finished with that stupid eye test. The driver's license lady, she told me to look into the machine and asked me what the letters and number were and which number looked closest. Then she switched to three squares of color—red, green and blue—and said, "And the colors?" By which saying I thought she meant which color was closest. And it had me stumped. They didn't none of them look closer than the other. So I said after a while, guessing, "The red maybe." And she laughed at that and said no, what are the colors, and I felt foolish and told her and then she said to step back to the line painted on the floor and then to look up and then to smile and then she flashed the light at me and took the picture. And the picture got all the feeling of foolishness in it that I was feeling, and the silly, shit-eating grin, which was what the gentleman behind the counter was looking at.

So I said, "No, it's me. It's my picture, see." And I tried to grin like the picture in spite of the fact that I did not feel like grinning in the least bit.

"You little bastards," the gentleman said. "You think a man can't tell the difference between you. But I can see when one is uglier than the other, anyway." I wish I knew to this day which one he thought was uglier, me or my picture.

About then Mr. Quick came in carrying his airline bag with him. He looked at me and he looked at the counter gentleman and put his bag down on the counter.

"Yes, Sir," the gentleman said. "What can I do for you, Sir?" But he was still holding my license and staring at me like he was trying to burn me right down to the ground with his eyes.

"The kid is ahead of me," Mr. Quick said. He'd unzipped the bag, I saw out of the corner of my eye, and was scratching around inside like he was trying to find something.

"I think the little bastard is trying to pull something," the gentleman said. "They think they can come in here and just take whatever they want, like it is a welfare kitchen or something." And he looked over to Mr. Quick and smiled that kind of snarly smile that such individuals put on their faces when they're trying to sell you something. But something happened to that smile as I watched. It caved in like a gopher hole and he was looking at what Mr. Quick had pulled out of the bag, and I looked too. I'd never seen anything like it before, not in real life. It was one of those old-fashioned guns with the long barrels like a rifle set on a pistol-grip. And Mr. Quick had it pointed right at the counter individual, and he said, "Give the kid the bourbon."

So the gentleman handed me the bottle. And I said, "Keep the change." And to Mr. Quick I said, "All right, we can go now."

But Quick, he still had that gun pointed. And he said, "Maybe you better open up your cash drawer," to the counter gentleman.

"Mr. Quick," I said, "this is maybe not such a good idea. I got the bourbon."

But the other individual, he'd rung open the drawer already.

"In the bag," Mr. Quick said.

And the counter gentleman started to scoop the bills out of the drawer and stuff them into the flight bag.

"You try anything," Quick said, "and this cannon will blow a hole in you a horse could run through." This line sounded awful familiar to me. I was thinking he probably stole it from Mr. Zane Grey or Mr. John Wayne.

"Mr. Quick," I said, "this is in my personal opinion a not very good thing to do."

But the old fart was not paying any attention to me. The other gentleman was finished by that time with the bills. "You want the coins?" he said, looking at that long barrel like it was the one giving the orders.

Mr. Quick told the counter individual to do something with the coins that was a little raw, according to my way of thinking, and would be painful too, if the individual really was to do it, like it looked like he might, that gun barrel had him so interested.

"Take the bag, kid," Mr. Quick told me. "I got him covered."

I started to give him my personal opinion on the matter again, but he got mad. "Take the goddam bag and get out to the car." He waved the gun, and it did cross my mind that he just might shoot me.

So I did it. I freely admit that it happened just that way, and if there is a crime in that, then I am a criminal, even though I happen to believe that I didn't do a thing a cop or judge wouldn't do if it was him.

I threw the bottle and the bag in the seat and I got behind the wheel. I was a nervous wreck, and I had a good mind to drive off and leave the damn fool to get out of this himself. I got the motor started and got it in gear, but I waited like a damn fool myself until the old fart came out. He was carrying that big gun in one hand and another big bottle of whisky in the other. He shouldered out the door and shuffled his old bones over to the truck and got in, tucking the bottle under his arm so he could get the door handle. Then he climbed up in the cab and said, "Drive."

"Mr. Quick," I said, "maybe we should just take the money back and say it was a joke."

"Drive, dammit," he said. "I think the son of a bitch has a gun under the counter."

So I let out the clutch all at once and the wheels ground into the gravel for a second while the truck just sat there, and then the wheels caught and shot us off, laying us back in the seats. We were halfway down the block when I heard something hammering on the cab, like someone outside knocking to get in.

"What's that?" I said.

"Keep driving," he said.

But the hammer pounded twice more and I heard glass tinkling and when I looked around, the back window was shattered like a sheet of thin ice.

"I was right," Quick said. "And he is a rotten shot, too. He should aim for the tires. He could get someone killed."

I by that time was a complete crazy person. "Shoot back," I yelled. "Shoot back anyway."

"I can't," Quick said. "It's not loaded." And he dumped the gun in the seat beside us and started twisting the cap on the bottle to break the seal. "Take a right up here."

So I squealed around the corner so fast Quick almost fell over, but he was still working at the whisky bottle.

"You can slow down now," he said. "He can't shoot around corners."

I slowed down a little and tried to figure out what to do next. But I couldn't think about that because I'm thinking so hard about what happened already. Quick had the bottle opened now and was taking a big swig, and I kind of pointed all my feelings at that.

"Why in hell did you have to grab another bottle?" I said.

Quick finished his snort and pulled the bottle down and away from his mouth. It made a little pop as he pulled it away, he'd put so much suction on it. He made a hoarse, satisfied sound in his throat. "I saw that rot-gut you picked out for me," he said. "Might as well go first class if it don't cost extra."

And right there I almost gave him up for a complete idiot. But my thinking went back to the red-faced gentleman who got the whole thing started with his meanness. "Asshole," I said.

"Who, me?" Quick said.

"The counter guy," I said.

"It is a startling fact of nature," Quick said, "that there are more assholes in this world than there are people."

"What was he thinking?" I said.

"Assholes don't think," Quick said. "They know what they know. They take it on faith."

"He must've taken me for a juvenile delinquent or something," I said. I figured it was because I was still in my grubs, jeans and plaid shirt and ratty old sweater and nylon jacket. I hadn't had time to change into my orderly outfit back at Hillview.

"Did you see him look at the gun?" Quick said. "I thought he was going to offer to suck it off."

And we both laughed thinking of the red-faced gentleman looking crosseyed at that long barrel. But I sobered up real fast when I
thought more about it. "What are we gonna do?" I said. "He got a real
good look at us."

"Relax," Quick said. "Assholes like that, they got weak powers of
discrimination. He just saw an old guy and a punk kid."

But there was a groan that it took a while to understand was me,
my own voice groaning because I'd just remembered something. "My
driver's license," I said. "The asshole kept my driver's license."

5.

"They know who I am. The counter guy no doubt saw the sign on the truck, and even if he didn't it won't take them long to put it together. The pickup will give us away faster'n anything."

Quick pulled the whiskey bottle away from his mouth again. "We can't get to Deadwood on foot very easy," he said.

"Who says we're going to Deadwood?" He's got a lot of gall, where I am concerned. "Who says we are going anywhere?"

"A deal's a deal," he said.

"I don't know nothing about a deal." I guess I was downright mad now.

"You get the bottle, you said, and I was to come with you." He took another drink.

"Fine. You can come with me down to the police station. You can explain how this was your own dumb idea."

"Was it?" he said. "I forget."

I looked over at him and he grinned at me and toasted me with the bottle and took another slug.

"You wouldn't tell them I put you up to it?"

"Didn't you? I don't have such a good memory. I'm old."

"You bastard," I said, "you'd lie, wouldn't you?"

"Hold on," he said. "For one thing, my mother was at least engaged when I was born. And for another, I don't intend to go back to that goddam home. I already stole and I'd just as soon lie and cheat to that purpose. I have not got a damn thing to lose. They can't do a thing to me worse than putting me back there. So I am what they call in checkers a renegade piece. I am as good as gone anyway, so I can just as well do some damage with my last gasp. In short, I am dangerous. And lying and cheating are things that I'm even more practiced in than stealing. So you just try me, if you want to find out." All that talking must've got him thirsty. He took a long swallow from the bottle and hiccuped.

I was thinking which the Rapid City police would believe most, a poor bastard like me, who according to the liquor store guy has the stamp of a sneak thief all over him, or an old fart like Mr. Quick, especially if he plays innocent. In addition to which, I am wondering what would happen if I was to go back to the home, what with Ef-ef-Freddie bound to be a slight bit upset by my rash action of earlier, plus leaving him wriggling belly up back there like a tipped-over beetle, not to mention the explaining I would have to do about the way I handled the whole situation. There were bound to be limits even on what Nurse Frank would put up with to give a break to a person.

"You know how the three-foot midget got to be the best barroom brawler in town, don't you?" Quick asked me.

I shook my head.

"When any of the six-foot bullies tried to knock him off his bar stool, he would just grab hold of their balls and jump." He laughed, getting a big kick out of it.

"That still don't mean we've got to stick together," I said.

"You know, I am halfway beginning to believe that you've got no sense of humor."

"Maybe you better explain the joke," I said.

"The joke is, you can't do without me. If you dump me, there is no way of telling what I might say to the police. Lucky for you I am willing to tag along if you inshist—insist." He gargled out a little laugh. I think he was getting a little tight from the bourbon.

"Here comes the police now," he said. "I can flag them down if you want me to."

Sure enough, there was a cop car headed in our direction in the street ahead of us. All of a sudden I felt like I had a rock stuck in my throat. I checked the speedometer to see I was under the limit and held the wheel steady and didn't breathe until the car got by. Then I checked the rearview mirror to make sure it kept on going.

"I take that as an affirmative," Quick said. "That makes us partners, I guess. Like my grand-dad Charlie Utter and Wild Bill. You want to shake on it?" He held out his hand.

I just looked over at his hand and kept on driving. "I got to put up with you," I said, "but that don't mean I've got to be your sidekick. You just better be able to keep up with me."

"You better be able to keep ahead of me, then."

So if you want to know what kind of a partnership we had, that was it. From that time on, I was hurrying to keep ahead of him and he was hurrying to keep up. It was just impossible all around. The old fart was just about the most impossible individual there ever was.

Being we were on the prairie side of town, I drove on to the trailer park. The VW was in the drive. I parked and got out and tried the door. Nobody answered the knock.

Quick had tumbled out of the truck and was weaving up the gravel path, his rubber boots flopping, still lugging his bottle. "What are we doing here? This is no kind of a hideout."

I paid no mind, but just knocked again, rattling the screen door hard. "She must be off with Red somewhere," I said.

"Red who?" Quick says. "If you want a hideout, you should get out of town, anyway."

I wasn't talking to him. I got out my old key and opened the door to the trailer. It was just lucky she hadn't changed the lock again. She usually did after she was washed up with one of my Uncle Blanks.

"You live here?" Quick said.

"What if I do?"

"Nothing, except it looks kind of—" He was inside, alongside me, by that time, and goggling at the piled up mail and last night's dishes still in the sink and what was left of breakfast still on the table.

"Looks kind of what?" I said.

"Looks kind of—lived in," he said. "You got a girlfriend?" he was looking at my mother's shriveled up panty-hose hanging over the back of one of the kitchen chairs.

I found the spare set of car keys in a mug on the counter. I also scratched up a pencil and slid an unopened envelope off the pile and scribbled out a note saying I was borrowing the car and that I was in a little trouble but she wasn't to worry. I left the envelope on the table where she could find it and pinned it down with the truck keys.

"We're taking the VW," I said. I needed time to think what I was going to do about this mess. I figured I"d head east, toward Sioux Falls. My mother had a brother in Sioux Falls who worked as a mechanic. I thought I might hole up with him until things straightened out.

Quick slogged to the truck and got the flight bag and his rod case and the other bottle. "You could at least carry some of the baggage," he said. I was already in the VW.

"I don't want a thing to do with that money," I told him.

"That's just fine with me. Take one of the bottles, anyway."

"I don't want a thing to do with the bottles, either." It was my opinion that it might go a whole lot easier with us if we kept all that stolen stuff together so we could give it back if we were after all caught.

"Nobody touches my travel rod but me."

"Just get your ass in here."

"It's not my idea of a getaway car," Quick said, and I couldn't argue that. It was rusted out in the panels behind the front wheels and was kind of a popsicle orange in color. Plus it cranked kind of hard, starting. It was my guess it was overdue for a tuneup.

I pulled the VW out of the drive and headed her east.

"We're putting Deadwood behind us," Quick said after a while.

"I don't give too much of a crap to go to Deadwood."

"I suppose," Quick said, "that is the first place they'd look for me."

The first place they'd look for me was in that house I lived in with Harold and Lymon. And what would they find? My clothes, about three pairs of jeans, the white tee-shirts I had to wear to work, some old shirts I wore for not working, some gloves, a winter jacket and stocking cap, a bunch of socks and underwear and an extra pair of shoes. And my alarm clock which I bought after I got the job at the home. It was setting on a chair beside my cot. And my blankets and things for the cot I have in a little room off the front room with nothing but a thin curtain across the door for privacy. And my magazines under the cot. They would probably take one look at those magazines and think I am some kind of a sex fiend. And the little notebook which I sometimes write some of my ideas down in. They would read that and they would know I am a sex fiend. I believed I had got down in there all the feelings I felt about hers truly Karen Stephenson and was not meant for anyone else to see, but I guess it couldn't be helped. Outside of that, not much. They would not even find my share of the groceries for the week, for all I had not yet kicked in my five dollars worth.

And the second place they'd look would be the trailer park, and that's where they would find the pickup with the shattered back window. But they damn certain would not find me.

"We are going to Sioux Falls," I said. That was the last place they would look. And by that time I was counting on something to've happened to get me out of this. Up to then I was travelling lighter than Mr. Quick and watching what I touch so I don't rub off on nothing.

"You are looking pretty sorry for yourself," Quick said after a bit. "You are thinking of that coochy-coochy nurse of yours, that you won't see her anymore and what a blow that would be."

Let him think what he wants to, I said to myself.

"You would do just as good to forget her," Quick said. "You can bet she'll lose very little sleep thinking about you. And while you are pressing your flowers in a Bible, some jerk will climb on her and grab her reins and teach her to gee and haw."

"I don't even know what that means," I said.

"You are at a dangerous age, Rodney," he said. "It's easy at your years to get confused and think that you've found true love when all you've found is an easy lay."

"There is nothing easy about Karen Stephenson."

"But if she was to give in sometime? After you got over the shock, you would go out and spend your last dime on a ring and one of those silly outfits they wear to weddings. And it would take you the better part of a month to figure out that you are the one that got screwed all along. Tell me what color her eyes are."

I thought a little bit about it.

"Go ahead," he said. "What color are they? Hasn't anyone ever told you eyes are the windows of the soul?"

I wished he would've asked how many buttons on her uniform instead. "I think, blue. Blue."

"You think." He gave a laugh, one of his evil kind, and took another swig of whisky.

"I'm sure of it," I said. "Blue. Maybe a little bit of gray mixed in." He just laughed.

"But mostly green."

He laughed so hard he got the hiccups. "Your IKgirl has got more colors in her eyes than a mutt has UKcousins."

"Try holding your breath for a change," I said as a gentle hint.

"IKhere," he said, holding out the bottle. "Have a snort. It will help you to relax, get your mind off nUKookie.

"It's stolen merchandise," I said.

"Not this one," he said, holding up the bottle whose seal hadn't been broken. "This one you pAKaid for."

I almost forgot about that, it seemed like so much had happened since. "To tell the truth," I said, "I am not much for strong drink."

"Suit yoursEKelf," he said.

"Not while I'm driving."

"I'll drive."

"You are in not very good condition yourself."

"GoddAKammit, if I can wrestle an eighteen-wheeler on an over-doze of no-doze, I can damn well peddle this IKiddycar on a little booze."

Never mind that I doubted he even had a driver's license, because I am not so hot in that department myself. And to be entirely honest, I was pretty tired. I felt like my head had been put through about a dozen hoops and had been made to set up and beg. Besides, there appeared to be a lot in what he said earlier about not having a thing to lose. So I pulled over to the side of the road.

We were in the country now, and there was grass off in all directions, the real green grass you see only in the spring in this country, before it goes to brown the way it always seems to. I was surprised how good I felt to be out in the grassland and away from Rapid City. Most particular when I got out of the car to stretch and switched seats with the old fart, I was awful tired, but I felt strange and satisfied too, like this was something I had been waiting to happen even though I was afraid of it too, but now it had, it was really a considerable relief. It was like one of those high-wire individuals, when he starts to fall. He knows it's going to happen sooner or later, so now that it has, he can give in to it. At least I wouldn't have that shitheel Ef-ef-Freddie Fitz socking me with his Terrible Stare every time I stepped across the lines he had drawn all over the place. You got to take the good with the bad, like I think they say.

The old fart drove about the way I figured he would. I had to keep telling him to slow down to somewhere near the speed limit. All we needed was to have an accident or get picked up for speeding. And he was all over the road, too. But he was going in the right direction.

"That place back there," Quick said, "that was your folks' place, wasn't it?" He was over the hiccups by then.

"My mother's if you've got to know. Home sweet home. What about it?"

"Nothing. Curious, is all." He gave me a look. "I come from working people myself."

"Just keep your eyes on the road."

I took a couple nips from the bottle I bought and I remembered again how much I can't stand the taste and it just makes me sleepy. I kind of nodded off there, and it was the most peculiar feeling in the world, giving in to your tiredness that way with the wind wheezing by and the feeling that you are being thrown off into space.

It's funny, as I gave in to my sleepiness, it was like I was a small child again, and I was back in the tire swing and someone was pushing me higher and higher up, and he kept pushing, and the wind was blowing across my ears as the tire swung up to the point where it kind of hung there and I knew I would fall, and I was crying for him to stop.

I woke up falling forward and had to put out my hand on the dash to keep from just going right on through the windshield. Quick was braking the car hard and the tires were trying to grab the pavement like claws and making that fingernail-scraping sound, and the car was shimmying and threatening to skid or roll.

"What in hell?" They were my first words.

"Damsel in distress," Quick said. "Might get your mind off your troubles."

Which I very sincerely doubted.

6.

I still couldn't figure out what he stopped for. There wasn't anything in our path except just the highway reaching straight out and the grass hills rolling on each side. I was still trying to pull my brains back inside my head when I looked up beside me and there was a woman standing right by the car grinning and kind of dancing and waving. She was a pretty good looking woman.

I rolled down the window. "What?" I said. It was a pretty dumb thing to start with, but I was still just barely awake.

"You can do wheels?" the woman said. She was speaking some different kind of grammar.

"What you want done to them?" I said.

She pointed back behind us and I swung around to look. There was a green van there, an older model Chevy custom it looked like to me. "Change wheels? Do you say? Inflate my wheels if you please?"

"She's got a flat," Quick said.

I looked at the woman again. She did not look too flat herself, to be honest. She was not as blessed in that regard as hers truly Karen Stephenson, but the kind of woven shirt she was wearing did a good deal more for her than what a starchy uniform would do.

"You can do?" she said. "You can help me please?"

"I guess so." I started to get out.

"I am very glad?" she said. "I am afraid no one comes?" She had a funny way of making everything she said into a question.

"It is not a well-travelled road," I said. I had on purpose kept off the interstate as being too likely to have state police.

"No? Not travelled?" She had on a tan skirt and had kind of sandy hair cut short and a roundish kind of face with a small nose. I made a big point to check the color of her eyes. They were blue. She held out her hand to shake like a man would and straightened up to her full length, which I put at five-five, and she said her name. I didn't really catch much of it except the first part, which was Ingrid. The rest I let go as too much of a strain. Then she asked my name.

"Rodney," I said, and all of a sudden thought I shouldn't let her know my actual name, so I went on, "James Alexander Hamilton Jefferson Adams. The Third."

"It is so long?" she said.

"Well, I was born here."

"Native American?" Her eyes were getting wide and her grin just dazzling.

Then I saw what she was getting at. It wasn't the first time I"d been taken for an Indian. I don't know what it was about me. My complexion isn't that dark, but I do have prominent cheekbones like my mother. And who knows what else from my mother's family in Arkansas? And who knows what from my father? "No," I told her. "I am just a plain American, not a name brand."

"Name brand?"

"Nope. Generic," I said.

"Generic?"

"Right."

"Right?"

"Correct."

"Correct?"

I was afraid we would go on forever like that, but Quick jumped in about then. He'd got out and was slogging around the car in his rubber boots. "He means yes. Javold."

"Ah?" she said, her eyes and her grin both getting bigger yet. And then she laid down a string of some foreign grammar that would knock a horse over.

"No," Quick says when he can get in a word. "Nein. I don't speak German enough except to know it when I hear it. I picked some up when I was in the merchant marine. Javold and nein, that's about my limit."

"Javold und nein?" Ingrid said. "You are not Cherman?"

"What I am, I guess, is the same as him, only elderly. And Alexander Hamilton here is my faithful sidekick." He ignored the mean look I threw him.

Ingrid looked at me again, the grin fading on her face. "You are not Native American?"

"Not to my knowledge," I said. "I know some, though."

"We go to reserve, yes? We are very much interested in the plight of Native American?"

"Who is this we?" I was beginning to suspect she had some guy in a black leather overcoat with her like the movies and TV.

"I think she means her girlfriend." Quick said. He nodded in the direction of the green van. There was another woman climbing out of it.

If you have ever noticed, women who go in pairs, one of the two will be not so bad looking as the other. I have often suspected so much as a general rule, and these German women clinched it. It is the same with almost any kind. One is fat, the other is thin, one is pretty and the other is an orangutan. But the tricky thing is, it is the plain one that has got all the personality. She is the wisecracker and the good sport and the other one is all the time looking in the mirror and fixing her hair or her makeup. If you end up with the good-looker, she gives you heartaches, and if it's the pleasant one you finish with, somewhere along the line you get to looking at her and just wondering if you would be able to eat breakfast across from her.

Hannelore is the name I got from what the pretty one called the not-so-pretty one. "You can call me Lorrie, yes?" She had a kind of dished-out face and yellower hair and wore slacks and the kind of heavy wool sweater that looked like it maybe served some time as a turnip sack. It was of course the pleasant one that saw no particular profit in dresses or show-through shirts.

Ingrid talked a lot of foreign grammar to Lorrie. Meantime Quick and me got started on the flat. They had the tools all laid out there. I guess they just weren't sure how to use them.

"Maybe we can travel along with them," Quick said while I was cranking off the nuts. "If the cops are looking for us yet, they are looking for just the two of us. Four might throw them off the track."

"Sure," I said. "Us two Mormon missionaries, a foreign-grammar baby-doll and another one which looks like she could use her face to shovel gravel. We will blend right in."

"Too bad you aren't Indian," Quick said. "That would seem to raise your value in the eyes of the looker."

"I guess we haven't got a plight big enough for her. She is looking for a world-class plight." Lymon has told me about the individuals who hang around the reservation when the weather's good studying the plight of the Indian, like it is some kind of dull book to get through. God knows the Indians got enough trouble to talk about, but some of them add on quite a bit of fancy quillwork, just for decoration. And it all goes down in the notebook or the tape recorder and when the weather changes for the worst, the individuals doing the studying go back to their colleges and write another book with all the plights in it, fancy quillwork and all. It was without a doubt a book of this general nature which these German women had read to get them so interested in the plight of the Indian. I guess it is all right, but you would think that the Indians would get a better cut off whatever the book sold for. It would make their plight some easier to swallow, I would think.

We finished with the tire and were just standing up and brushing off when an old rattle-trap Ford pickup chugged by, and I heard someone give a yell. The pickup ground to a stop and I was surprised as hell to see Lymon Twobows jump out of the back of it where he had been riding.

"Damn, Rod, what're you doing here?" Lymon was looking around at the van and the women and Quick, like he was looking at a picture upside down.

"I would give a nickel to know, myself," I told him.

"You are in deep shit, you know that? The police were at the home, asking a lot of questions. They put me through a real grilling, on account I was the one that had the truck last and this guy at the liquor store said it was an Indian and an old guy."

"He thought I was Indian?" I ought to've known. That explained a lot. "What did you tell them?"

"Just what happened. What did you do with the truck?"

"Ditched it at my mother's. I took her VW."

"Jesus, Rod, why did you do it?"

"I didn't. It was the old fart. He had a gun, which I didn't know about. And he says if I try to turn him in, he will say I put him up to it."

"Jesus," Lymon said again, and looked at Quick, kind of surly. "And now he will most likely say I was in on it, too. The cops didn't want to let me leave town. I told them I had to because of the give-away. Nurse Frank vouched for me, or they never would've let me go."

By this time, Ingrid and Lorrie were by the pickup, talking to the guys inside, who were genuine Indians like Lymon, trying no doubt to get at the root of their plight.

"Who are the women?" Lymon asked me.

"German tourists, the way I get it. They are going to the reservation."

"Is that where you were headed?"

"Through it, only. On the way to Sioux Falls. What do you think?"

Lymon shook his head. I could see what he was going through, trying to figure it out. "I don't need this," he said. "I got troubles of my own."

"Forget it," I said. "Just go on with what you were doing. We'll get along. It's not your problem."

He looked at Quick again, who was half-sitting on the back bumper of the van, fanning his face with the floppy fishing hat. "He was always a mean son-a-bitch," Lymon said. "But I halfway liked him."

"He has a good side," I said, "but he keeps it hid good. The thing is, I feel kind of responsible for him, too. I'm supposed to be taking care of him."

"Shit," Lymon said. "Damn it to hell, I got my own problems." Then he looked at me and looked away again. "I don't know why I give a shit. Couple of fool wasicus." I knew he was really upset then, because he never called me a wasicu before, which in Lakota grammar means something like "white asshole."

Then he stomped back to the pickup and said something to the guys inside and the truck took off and left him. Ingrid and Lorrie were waving after the truck like they were saying goodbye to old friends. Lymon stomped back to me.

"You can stay at Aunt Celia's for a while. Until we can work out how to handle it."

I felt a big relief, even though I was sorry to get Lymon mixed up in this at the same time. "What about the women?"

"Are they part of the deal?"

"I don't know. I guess not."

"Jesus," Lymon said one more time.

So we ended up with Lymon and me in the van with Ingrid, and Quick driving the VW with Lorrie. Ingrid was nothing but questions. Lymon was glum, like he wished he was somewhere else. I wasn't feeling too peppy myself.

"Your socio-economic status," Ingrid said, as an example. "it is not good?"

"What is she talking about?" Lymon said.

"Wages, I think," I told him. Then I said to Ingrid, "Do you mean wages?"

"Yes? Wages?" She nodded.

"Low," I said.

"But you have a chob? she asked.

"I doubt it," Lymon said. "Not after this."

"You are between unemployed?"

"Between unemployed and out of work entirely," I said.

"Your comrades, they had no viable alternatives?"

"What?" Lymon said.

"In the geo-political construct?" Ingrid said.

"I don't get her even when she talks English," Lymon said.

I myself figured she got it out of a book, the one about plights, probably. But she was giving Lymon a come-on look if I ever saw one. Here was a real live Indian, and she looked like she was ready to wring him for all he was worth.

"The Lakota," I told her, "are a nation, the way I get it. They made treaties with the U.S., just like any other country, the only difference being they are inside instead of outside. I guess it is a big difference, because Uncle Sam treats the treaties with them like crap."

"Crap?"

"Doo-doo," I said. "Ca-ca. Shit."

"Shit?"

"Horse shit."

"Ah," she said. "Horse shit." Like that explained everything. Maybe it did, at that.

"The comrades can do nothing?"

"What's all this about comrades?" Lymon said. "Is she a Communist or something?"

"Communist? Yes?" Ingrid said, nodding again.

"I think she is one," I said. It was a first for me. I'd never seen a Communist before, and it took me by complete surprise, since I'd always got the impression that to be a Communist you had to be built like a tank and have a moustache. It was my understanding that even Communist women followed those specs. But here was one that looked about as much like a Communist as a fire hydrant. It was hard to believe.

"They are letting Communists run around this country doing whatever they want?" Lymon said.

"Well," I told him, "it is a free country, I guess."

"So I been told," he said. I suppose he was thinking it cost more for some than others.

It threw a peculiar light on the matter to realize that Ingrid was a Communist from stem to blossom end. She didn't appear different from the women that were one-hundred percent American. It was hard to believe that she's a threat to the free world. But I did give her advice not to mention her politics too much on the reservation for the fact, number one, that a lot of the Indians are actually fairly patriotic and, number two, the place is usually swarming with F.B.I. individuals.

She went into a long explanation about exactly what kind of a Communist she was and what kind she wasn't. To be honest, I didn't know there were so many brands of them. I guess it must be hard to decide what kind you want to be. And they all look to be at each other's throat, too, from the sound of it.

She got back on the plight of the Indian before long, and it seemed like she was out to make up for every bad thing the Europeans did to the Indians. Since Lymon wasn't talking much, I explained what I could about the settlement the Indians were hoping would turn the Black Hills back to them or at least pay a fair price for it, which would be considerable, when you thought what the Homestake gold mine alone took out of there. But Ingrid said that wasn't enough. She said the Indians should get the whole state or maybe two or three of them, along with a trillion dollars and a tearful apology.

Lymon grumbled at that. "I would settle for less," he said. "Like maybe decent jobs for people, and a roof over their heads. Maybe just a little justice thrown in."

He was talking about his uncle Zachary, I knew, but I didn't want to get into that too much with Ingrid, it was so complicated. Zachary was the type of person who was too proud to accept charity. He worked all his life at whatever he could do, starting back in the '40s digging sugar beets, later picking potatoes, later working on ranches. For a long while he worked on this ranch just outside the reservation for a man named Colton. He worked just the warmer part of the year, so he wasn't counted a regular full-time worker. I guess Colton got around some taxes or something that way. Anyway, about a year ago, Zachary went to Colton to get some money he was owed, and Colton came up short. Zachary figured he was rooked, so he complained, but Colton just stonewalled. He tried to make up for it by going to his freezer and getting out a package of frozen steaks, worth maybe a tenth of what he owed, and sticking it into Zachary's hands, like he was paid up full.

Lymon told me later that Zachary took the meat home, but the whole thing gnawed at him so he couldn't sleep. Finally Zachary went back to Colton's ranch, taking the steaks along with him. He took Colton by surprise, just outside the house, as Colton was headed for his truck. Zachary held out the package, and was going to tell Colton what he could do with them when Colton pulled out a pistol and shot Zachary dead.

The coroner's inquest said it was a justifiable homicide, on account of the witnesses, a couple of Colton's men, who said that Zachary approached in "a threatening manner." It was in the paper, and there were a lot of people mad about it, especially on the reservation, where Zachary was liked real well. The COUP bunch, Congress of United Peoples, got mixed up in it, of course, and tried to bring lawsuits and everything, but it all came to nothing. There were letters to the editor and such, but pretty soon it all fizzled out. Except maybe for Celia, who was Zachary's wife, and Lymon. I don't know about Celia, who I hadn't seen in five years, but I knew Lymon carried it around like a sliver under his skin and that it stuck there festering and swelling up with poison.

We were getting close to the reservation by that time. I'd been there two or three times before with Lymon, when we were younger. It's not at all the way you might think. I mean, it's not like there is a big fence or something, and you go through a gate and you are on the reservation. But you start noticing trash piling up in the ditches, and the skeletons of cars and trucks once in a while setting out in the middle of nowhere, going nowhere, stripped of everything that can come off. You see some cattle, sometimes, but the ranch houses and outbuildings you see other places have dwindled down to wooden shacks, unpainted houses without trees around them, wrecks of cars in the yards. The feeling you get is that there's been a war there, and there's nothing left but the people who lost it. And that's not too far from the truth, I guess.

Other places, especially in the towns, you can see some pretty nice houses and stores and things, and some government buildings that are fairly sturdy, but you also see a lot of people sitting around like they've got a load of time on their hands. But you see some bustling around busy, too, and the best part is the children, now that school is out, playing outside, shooting baskets and yelling and laughing just like kids everywhere. You can't call it a hopeless place. But you've got to wonder what kinds of spring traps and pits there are for people to step into and get dragged down to where they don't give a damn.

I suppose somebody could doze off, driving through, and miss the whole thing. And there are some, no doubt, who would as soon put on blinders. But the worst thing is, if you look as hard as you can, you can't see an easy way out. It's like a sink hole that you slide into fast and pay time and hell pulling free, and lose your shoes, besides.

Lymon directed the way off the main road to Aunt Celia's place. You think at first it is just a lane and the place has got to be right over the next hill, but the road goes on and on. I looked back to make sure Quick was still tailing us.

"It's about here I start to be Indian again," Lymon said. The last time we were down this road, Lymon told me how when he got close to his aunt's place, his head would kind of flip over into Lakota. Things actually started to looking different to him and snuggling in around him and making him feel like he was in the middle of it. And then, when he'd go back to Rapid City, his head would do another flip and the world would start to looking wide open and empty and like it didn't give a damn about him. So that is part of it, too, along with the other. The res is a dead end in one way, but it's where a person can feel to home.

Finally we got to Celia's place. It was nestled down between two hills. There were just a few cars around the weatherworn house, along with one or two that looked to be parked there permanent.

"I thought you said she was having a giveaway," I said. "There's hardly anyone here."

"It's tomorrow," Lymon said. "I wanted to get here to help her get ready."

Quick pulled into the driveway after us, and struggled out of the VW door while Lymon was hopping out and heading toward the house. The old fart was looking pissed as he flopped up to me in his rubber boots. "You aren't too concerned about an old man's bladder, are you? Where's the men's room?"

I pointed to the shed behind the house. "Help yourself."

Ingrid and Lorrie were on me with about a thousand questions as Quick cantered off to the outhouse. The women were just about ate up with the excitement of being there, and they wanted to know everything at once. I was a poor one to ask, being I got all my facts secondhand, but I tried to explain the situation as best I could.

The giveaway was in honor of Zachary. Celia had been getting ready all year long, and friends and relatives chipped in what they could until they were ready to throw a big picnic with about a ton of food for everyone concerned, along with heaps of presents. When she was done, there wouldn't be hardly anything left for her own self, but she would feel all right about it, because she'd done the right thing, according to the custom, and Zachary's ghost, which had been lingering around all that time, and which she had been tending to as best she could, would be free to take off to where ghosts are supposed to go.

Everything I told them, they had a dozen questions more that I couldn't answer, but I was saved by Lymon who showed up about then with his arm around his Aunt Celia. "You remember Rodney," Lymon said, and then he said the same thing over in Lakota. Celia understood English well enough, I think, if it was spoken slow, but she was more at home with the Lakota grammar.

Celia gave me a kind of sideways look and nodded and then she grabbed hold of my arm and gave it a squeeze. She remembered, all right, even if it had been five years ago. I was Lymon's friend, so I was all right in her book.

Then Lymon introduced the German women, who were for once struck dumb. There was something about Celia, sure enough, that just made you want to pay attention to her. I don't know if it was the network of wrinkles on her face, which had got deeper since I saw her last, or the way she held her frail body in a way that made you think she was strong as a horse. Maybe it was just the feeling you get around some people that they know things you haven't even guessed at.

Finally, old Quick slogged up, back from the outhouse, and Celia gave him a look like she was halfway afraid of him. Lymon and her talked in Lakota for a while, and when Quick held out his hand to shake, she gave it a weak little rattle. I think she might have been a little overpowered to see so many wasicus all together in a bunch, that she had to take care of some way.

"She can put you up tonight," Lymon said, "but maybe you better count on being away most of tomorrow. She's got to concentrate on the memorial, and it might make some upset to have you around."

I was the least bit disappointed to see he was talking about me, along with the rest of them. I felt a little bit like family. At the same time, for all that some took me for an Indian, there was never an Indian that did.

7.

Lymon tried to explain once how it was that Celia was his aunt but Zachary wasn't exactly his uncle. I had a hard time with that. It seems like his mother's brothers are his real uncles. His father's old sister was Celia, which made her a real auntie. And of course, he'd honored and respected Zachary, even if he wasn't a real uncle. Don't ask me.

We had caught Celia at a bad time, when she couldn't refuse anything to anybody, even if it is a strange bunch of wasicus. We all packed inside the house, which was warm and smelled something like a bakery from all the food that was being got ready. It got my mouth watering and my stomach to rumbling, being that I hadn't had nothing but a couple sips of bourbon since breakfast.

Aunt Celia said something in Lakota, and Lymon said, "She wants to know if you'd like to eat."

"What does she say?" Ingrid said.

"Are you hungry?" I said. "Eat?"

"Ah? Essen? To eat?" She nodded. "She is starving? In the van we have the fruit cocktail?"

Me: "No, do you want to eat?"

Quick: "Don't mind if I do."

Ingrid: "It is true she is forced to eat the dogfood?"

Me: "You mean dog. Dogfood is horsemeat." This was my small effort to make sense out of this turkey-gobble.

Lorrie explained to Ingrid: "It is the dog she is forced to eat."

Ingrid: "Ah? The hoont, yes?"

Me: "Actually, that about Indians eating dog don't hold too true in the modern day and age."

Quick: "Horsemeat is really not too bad of a dish. I don't know about dog."

Lorrie explained: "They eat dog and horsemeat."

Celia now had made out a little of what was being said, and she got a puzzled look on her face and said something. "Jesus," Lymon said, "she thinks the guests want dog meat."

I said I didn't think they had decided yet. It was a tossup between dog and horse.

Celia said something else and Lymon translated: "She says she is sorry she only has beef."

"I guess we will have to be satisfied with that," I said.

Quick, for his part, had already started to dig into the bowl-full that Celia had set in front of him. "Tastes a lot like rabbit," he said.

Ingrid and Lorrie went at the stew pretty slow, but they wolfed down the fry bread. Ingrid came out with a load of German grammar and Lorrie explained in American: "Ingrid wonders if collective action cannot be taken to get plumbing for this home."

Quick coughed, choking on his stew. "Plumbing, that's the ticket all right. Running water and a white porcelain shitter. And next television. The throne first, then the altar. Cornerstones of civilization. Lucy and Gilligan reruns, TV dinners, Salisbury saw-dust in gravy, a hot crap and a cold shower."

"You could do with the shower, anyway," I told him.

Celia said something and Lymon put it into American: "She wonders if something is wrong with the stew." Beside Quick's sputtering, she was probably worried that the girls weren't eating.

"Tell her they had their hearts set on dog meat," I said.

Celia shrugged and mumbled something.

"What did she say?" I asked Lymon

"Nothing. She just said they are German, Iashica. That's the word for German. What it actually means is someone who can't be understood in Lakota, French, or English." And that just about sums up the whole conversation.

Besides Celia, there were two or three women inside, fixing things at the cookstove, and a couple men outside. They were kin, the way I understood it, helping Celia get ready for the big day. Lymon talked to them a little bit, and I saw them looking at Quick and me and the Germans. I think he was trying to downplay us as much as he could.

The sun was pretty low in the sky by that time, and we figured out that Ingrid and Lorrie would just sleep in the van, which was one of those conversion kinds that could be used as a camper. Celia would find room for the rest of us inside. There were a couple small bedrooms off the main room. Celia wanted me and Quick to take one of them. She took the other, and Lymon was to sleep in a folding army cot out in the main room, which was a combination of livingroom, diningroom, and kitchen. Before we went to bed, she gave Quick an old pair of shoes to put on in the morning. She was worried about his feet getting too hot and sweaty inside the rubber boots. I suppose they were Zachary's shoes at one time.

After the other relatives left, we went to bed. There were a few pictures on the walls of the room me and Quick were in. The light hanging from the ceiling was dim, no better than 40 watts, it looked to me, but you could make out the photos well enough. There was Lymon's graduation picture, which I recognized, and another one which was I think his cousin Darrel. There was a picture of Zachary, too, when he was young, in an army uniform. I can't remember if it was World War Two or Korea he was in. And there was a picture of Lymon's father, before he went off to San Francisco.

I told Quick about Zachary and Colton, all of that. He was getting ready for bed and took off those rubber boots at long last. The aroma made me wish I was outside where I could get upwind of him. He tried on the shoes Celia had given him and allowed they were a fair fit. "He'll get what's coming to him," he said.

"Who will?"

"That rancher, Colton."

"What makes you think so?"

"He will," Quick said, getting out of the shoes again. He sounded just as sure as anything. "He'll pay. A man always pays, one way or another, sooner or later." It's hard to tell what he had on that crazy mind of his. Before I could ask him, he flopped down and was honking through a cord of hardwood with his patented chain saw.

I laid down and thought about the long day. It seemed like too much happened for just one day, like a week would hardly be enough to hold it. There were thoughts sticking to me like burrs and making me uncomfortable. If getting messed up with Quick and the liquor-store holdup wasn't enough, there was the business about Zachary. And Lymon had gone so far out of his way, I was afraid he might just end up hating me for causing all this trouble in the first place. I was thinking I could just about write a book of plights all by myself.

Between Quick's snoring and me mulling over the happenings of the day, I didn't get too much sleep. As soon as there was any light showing through the net plastic storm windows, I got dressed and went outside. It was kind of chilly in just my flannel shirt and jeans, and the whole world was colored that kind of gray-blue that comes over in between night and day. After I drained my bladder, I got it into my head to climb up that big hill that stuck up to the south of the place. So I started in climbing. I could still see the biggest of the stars sticking out, and before long I could make out the line between the sky and the land pretty clear.

When I got to the top, I stood there hugging my arms from the cold and watching the sky get lighter and turn the color of wild roses around the edges, and then the first bow of the sun bulging up. When the light hit me, I felt the heat of it right away. I think for a minute or two I forgot everything I every learned in science about the earth revolving around the sun and such. Because that's not what it feels like. What it feels like is a kind of gift. You feel like you just want to say thank you. I reached down and run my hand over a stem of grass and stripped the new pollen and held it to my mouth and blew the pollen off in the direction of the sun. It just came to me to do that, sort of like reaching out and shaking hands and saying much obliged.

Then I turned around and let the light flow over me. The morning is one time you know exactly where you are. The sun is east, and you turn toward the right and that's south, where you can make out dark shapes of scrub cedar on some of the hills, and right again, west, toward the Paha Sapa or Black Hills, and another right turn is north where the ragged Badlands are.

Looking north, I saw something that took me back. On a hill over there on the other side of Celia's place there was another person standing just like me. At that distance I couldn't make out much, but it looked like a man stripped down to the waist, leaning back and holding his arms out, facing the sun.

But then wham, and the hill shook under my feet and made me freeze. I didn't know where the sound came from right away, but then it hit me what it must be and I looked up in the sky and saw the jet trail cutting across the sky, orange in the morning light like a piece of yarn being pulled along by a needlenose and unraveling at the other end. The plane was most likely from Ellsworth. The explosion was its sonic boom. They wouldn't go booming like that over the city, but over the res it's all right because there's nothing but Indians. They even used part of the land to practice bombing.

When I looked back east, it was nothing but the sun coming up. And I looked back north, and the man was gone. I'd got snapped back to reality.

8.

By the time I'd climbed down off the hill, Lymon was up and doing. He was piling up wood that looked like it'd been ripped out of a old barn or something.

"It's for a cook fire," he told me. "Celia wants to do the main cooking outside." For the giveaway, he meant.

"Were you up on that other hill a bit ago?"

"What're you talking about?"

"I saw someone up there. No shirt on. It was strange."

"I've been right here. You're seeing things." He stopped tossing wood and looked at me. "You done any more thinking about what you're gonna do?"

"That's all I've been doing. I couldn't sleep because of it."

"If you stay here very long, you'll get Celia mixed up in it. I don't mind much for myself, but she's had enough trouble."

"We'll just move along, then."

"You can stay the weekend. I have to get back to the home, Monday. Miss Frank gave me to Monday noon off. I'm not gonna lose the job."

"I wouldn't want you to," I said. "I don't think there's much hope for me, though."

"Maybe you should just go back and give up. Explain how it was. It's not like anyone got killed."

"You think they'd believe me?"

Lymon looked at me for a second. "Maybe you're right. Only you can't just keep on running."

About then Quick clomped out of the house in the shoes Celia had given to him. He was carrying his flight bag and his rod case. "You better get inside if you want breakfast. Aunt Celia is fixing pancakes for the German women."

"Did you have something." I asked him. He was looking a little more sickly than usual.

"I had a pancake," he said. "My appetite is off."

Then I thought of something. "Your pills," I said. "How many were you taking a day, anyway."

"About a dozen, it seemed like. Good riddance to them. Except the pain ones. My arthritis is bad this morning."

I myself remembered giving him the pills and capsules in those little paper cups three or four times a day. The nurses doled them out into the cups, but the orderlies got to know what they were for, most of them.

"Maybe we can get to a drugstore," Quick said. He sat down on a wooden crate that was in the yard.

"You'd need a prescription," I said.

"Not for the pain pills. You can get them right off the shelves. I think I need a physic, too."

"What about blood pressure medicine? You had two kinds."

"And that little red one. What was that?"

"A stool softener. You could live without that."

"Easy for you to say. Wait a minute." He set the flight bag in his lap and leaned the rod case against the crate and zipped open a little side pocket on the bag. "Ha. They missed it." He pulled out a little brown pill bottle. "That's something." He squinted at the label, then handed it to me. "What does it say?"

I read the label. "This prescription is four years old," I said. "Dyazide. It's to take your pressure down." I shook the bottle. There were about a dozen capsules inside. The label said there was one refill left, but the date would make a drug store suspicious, it seemed to me.

"Anything else we need, we can get off the shelf," Quick said. "I want some vitamins, too. And garlic pills. They wouldn't let me have them in there."

I looked at Lymon, who just shook his head. Who knew what would happen if the old fart didn't get his right medicine? Just to add to all my woes.

"You better go up to Weed," Lymon said. "They got a drugstore. Wherever else you want to go. Pine Ridge, I suppose. You can come back here after dark."

"The women will be pretty disappointed."

"There's a wacipi tomorrow. They can go to that."

I went in and had breakfast and tried to explain to Ingrid and Lorrie what we were up to. They were pretty let down about not staying for the giveaway, but the news about the pow-wow cheered them up some. And of course, they wanted to see Wounded Knee, which they must've read all about in the German papers.

I drove the van up to Weed, about twenty miles off the res. On the way, we passed by the Colton ranch. It was a good-sized spread, with the house set off the road a ways, but right next to the road was a pen fenced in with white wood rails. And inside the pen was a big Black Angus bull. "Champion Noah's Forte," a sign on the pen said. I slowed down for a good look.

"A bison, is it?" Ingrid said.

"A tame kind," I said. I guess I was feeling smartass. It was hard not to kid the women, they had such funny ideas.

"For meat?" Ingrid said. She wrinkled up her nose. I had figured out that she was pretty much a vegetarian.

"You could say," I told her. "He helps keep the cows happy."

"He has no hump," Lorrie said. Not much got past her.

"He is not that kind of a buffalo," I explained. "There is the kind that has humps and there is the kind that gets humps."

"He will get humps?"

"If he gets lucky," Quick put in.

"Ah?" Lorrie said. I think she was suspicious of being put on, but she didn't want to miss anything either.

Quick was pretty quiet after that, riding along, staring out the side window.

"Are you all right?" I asked him. I was worried about him not getting his medicine.

"Thinking about Colton, is all," Quick said. "Every person's got a place they can be hurt in. For a lot it's the billfold."

"I don't think it's the billfold for Colton. He's got all the money in the world."

"Right," Quick said. "And he don't appear much to care what people think of him, either. A lot of people would rather pay ransom than get their name drug in the mud. Colton, he don't seem to give much of a shit. He's got all the guts in the world."

"There's not much left, then," I said.

"You could kill the son-bitch," Quick said. "That'd show him."

"Right," I said. "He'd never screw anyone again, that's for sure." I was trying not to let on how nervous he was making me.

"Eye for an eye," Quick said. "Damn right."

"What do you care, anyway? It's none of your affair."

"I was just thinking what the Duke would do."

"I wish you wouldn't think. It's your thinking got us into trouble in the first place, it seems to me."

"There is trouble?" Ingrid said.

"It's all right," I said. "We were just talking."

When we got to Weed, I found the drug store and pulled the van up in front of it. "We are going to need some money," I said.

Quick got his flight bag in his lap and unzipped it and pawed around a little and pulled out a bunch of bills and handed them to me. "That should cover it."

I straightened out the bills and stacked them in my hand. There was over a hundred dollars there. "I feel funny spending it."

"What else you gonna do with it? Put it into stocks and bonds?"

"You know what I mean. Dirty money."

"Spends just the same as the clean kind." Quick zipped up the bag.

"You gonna come in with me?"

"You think that's a good idea?"

"Maybe not." That's just what the cops would be looking for, I guessed.

Ingrid and Lorrie had already piled out of the van by the side door and were jogging their way down the street to a place that sold tee-shirts.

I left Quick in the car and scooted into the drugstore and plunked the Dyazide bottle down on the prescription counter. The woman in the white coat there read the label and looked at me quizzical. "It's an old prescription," she said.

I tried to make my eyes wide and dumb. "It's for my uncle."

She looked at me over the top of her glasses and blinked. There's some people, when they get a dumb answer like that, it throws them. Like she supposed it was for me? What would I do with Dyazide, pop some and pee a lot? So she just shrugged and gave up. "It'll be a few minutes."

I shuffled around the shelves and got together all the stuff Quick'd told me he wanted, the garlic pills and the laxative and the pain killer and the rest, and threw in some foot deodorant for my own sake. I wished I knew a little more about what really ailed him. I think it was mostly his heart, but I didn't know any over-the-counter cure for that. I heaped all the stuff on the counter and paid for it and got my change. When I strolled back outside, the van was empty.

I climbed back in the driver's side and sat and waited, hoping that Quick didn't get into any more situations on his own. He'd left the flight bag sitting in the passenger seat, and as long as he was gone, I didn't think it would do any harm to peek inside. I unzipped it and looked in, and the first thing I saw, of course, was the gun. It was a Buntline Special, according to Quick. I couldn't help but admire it, in spite of the fact that I wasn't too much of a

one for guns. You can see the loveliness in something without nec-
essarily hugging it to your chest. I remember when I was a kid,
kicking around in the brushland next to the trailer park with
Lymon, I climbed up on a big rock and there was a rattler there sun-
ning itself. I didn't move, but just looked at it. And it was a beautiful thing with its pattern like fancy beadwork and its grin. I could-
n't take my eyes off of it. And it moved lovely, too, looping and
stretching and pulling its length. But I didn't pick it up and pet it,
I can tell you for damn sure. And when Lymon came along and
took a stick and bashed it bloody, I didn't cry too much over it
either. My guess is loveliness is something that don't have a thing
to do with whether a thing is good or bad or tame or dangerous. So
I intend to avoid rattlers, however pretty they might be, and I feel
just the same about guns.

Under the revolver there was the money, all wadded and loose,
just the way it came out of the till. A good deal over a thousand dollars, I figured, seeing there were so many tens and twenties. I
reached down and felt around the bottom of the bag. There was roll
candy and loose change and a reel case and a holder for glasses and
a pack of cards and lint and all kinds of junk and garbage, but no
pistol shells that I could find. If there had been, I would've hooked
them and thrown them away the first chance I got. It was bad
enough when Quick was waving around that iron empty. I didn't
want him to get it loaded, not with the weird ideas he got into him.

Just about that time, there was a tapping on the glass behind
me and I jumped, feeling guilty and nervous like I was. I turned
around kind of stiff and awkward, half expecting to see a cop of
some kind, but it was only a guy with a face on him that looked like
it had got bombarded with meteors or something, like the moon,
all craters. He was grinning, showing a mouth of ragged teeth. He
moved his hand in little circles to tell me to roll down the window.
I was so relieved to see he wasn't a cop that I didn't stop to think
what else he could be. Public Enemy Number One, for all I knew. I

went ahead and rolled down the window and the guy leaned in and grinned and said, "Hau, kola. You want me to wacher for you?"

Whew. His breath was the most peculiar I ever smelled and for some reason reminded me of the Hillview Home. "What?" I said.

"Yer car," the guy said. "You want me to wacher?"

"It's not mine. I'm just driving it. For some friends. And it don't need washing, I don't think."

"Haw," he said, spraying me again with his breath, which all of a sudden I recognized for what it was: Lysol. No wonder it reminded me of the home. "Watch, I meant, not wash. I ain't a carwash. Haw." His eyes were all watery and red.

"You think it needs watching?" I said.

"New car like this, kids might pry off the hubcaps or something. You can't tell. I would be happy to keep an eye on her if you want to go shopping or something."

His disinfectant breath was making me sick to my stomach. "Maybe," I told him, "you could watch her from a distance."

He looked surprised, blinked a couple times, but bounced right back like a boxer too beat to know when to lie down. "How far away?"

I reached into the flight bag and pulled out a fistful of bills and poked them at him. "How far will this take you?"

He started to look serious, then, and plucked the bills out of my hand one at a time like someone pulling petals off a daisy. He dropped one and bent down to get it and popped back up again. Then he looked at what he had like he was trying to figure how many cans of Lysol it would buy. "It will go a long way," he said. Then he gave me a doubtful look with those rheumy eyes, not too sure if I really meant him to have the money.

"It's yours," I said. "Get yourself some wine for a change. If I was you, I'd lay off that spray-can crap. It will kill you."

"I ain't particular," he said. "Everyone dies somehow. Much obliged, friend." And he quick whipped around and started off at a fast clip down the street and disappeared around the corner. I guess he was afraid I'd change my mind.

Right away, I felt bad. Because of me, he'd go on another toot and get stinking and who knows how he would end up. And the white people in these little towns outside the res, they would say that's the way Indians are, dirty, drunk all the time, no self-respect, begging off the government and everyone else.

After I zipped the bag back up, I sat back and thought a while. Then I got back out of the van and stomped back into the drugstore and unhooked the pay phone they had in the entrance and put in a collect call to my mother's number.

It was Red who answered of course.

"Will you accept a collect call from Zane Grey?" The operator asked him. It was the name I'd given to her.

"Jane?" Red said.

"Red, it's me," I put in.

"Will you accept the call?"

There was a little wait. "Okay."

"Is Vicky there?" I asked him once the operator got off the line.

"What makes you think she wants to talk to you?"

"Is she there or not?"

"The cops were here asking questions, did you know that? She's all upset."

"Just let me talk to her."

"You've got a lot of nerve," Red said.

Then I heard my mother's voice: "Is that Rod?" And then she must've grabbed the phone away from him. "Is that you, honey?"

"It's me."

"Baby, you're in bad trouble," my mother said. "Where are you? No, don't tell me where you are. Oh, Rod, honey, how did it happen?"

"It just happened. I didn't do anything. It was this other guy."

"I told you about that crowd," she said.

"No, the old guy. A guy from the home."

"That's what the TV said. But in the movies, it's you."

"What movies?"

"There was a camera behind the counter. They've got your picture standing there while the clerk is putting money into the bag. They've got you carrying it out the door."

I couldn't help but groan. "I suppose it looks bad."

"And now he's in the hospital," she said.

"Who is?"

"The clerk. He had a stroke or something. He's in intensive care."

"The liquor store guy had a stroke?"

"Or something. Later in the day. It was from the stress, the TV said."

I couldn't believe my bad luck. If the red-faced guy died, they'd try to pin that on us, too, I supposed.

"Rodney?"

"I'm here."

"The police said if you give yourself up, they'd go easy."

"Go easy? What does that mean? I'd get out before I got senile?"

"I don't know. I'm just telling you."

"Thanks," I said. "Now I know. I had to take the VW."

"I know. The police came and got the pickup. It's all right. Red has a car."

"Mama, can I ask a question?"

"Of course, honey. What is it?"

"Is there any Indian blood in our family?"

"What a question. Because that clerk took you for Indian? Of course not."

"What about Lonnie Deuce? What nationality was he?"

"I don't know. He was from Ohio."

"What kind of a name is Deuce, anyway? It doesn't sound American."

"I think he told me once, French."

"He was French?"

"The name was French. I don't know how French he was. Not much, I think. What in the world are you asking about Lonnie for? You hardly ever talk about him."

"I just got to wondering."

"All you all right, Rodney? You're not hurt or anything?"

"I'm fine, mama. I'll be just fine. Do you think I ought to come back and turn myself in?"

"All I know is what the police said, honey. That they'd go easy if you did. I can't tell you what to do."

"Ask the college professor. Maybe he knows."

"Don't be mean, Rodney."

"I'll call you again later."

"You can call me at work, if you want to. You have the number?. Jake won't mind. I can pay him back for the call."

"All right. Goodbye, mama."

"Wait a minute. Wait a minute."

"What?"

"I don't know. There was something I wanted to tell you. I can't think what it was."

"I'm sorry I got you upset. It just happened. I'll call again."

"Rodney, be careful."

I thought I would feel better, but I didn't. It seemed like things were getting worse instead of better.

When I came back out, Ingrid and Lorrie were leaning on the front of the van. They both had on new tee-shirts. Ingrid had a Red Power one and Lorrie had that C.O.U.P. one you see so much, with the feather and the arrow. It was a change from the boycott- lettuce and save-the-whales shirts they had on before. They had bags full of fruit and stuff, too. "We have picnic, yes? Later?" Ingrid said.

"Sure," I said. "You seen Mr. Quick?"

Lorrie pointed up the street. There was nobody up there, but soon as I started off in that direction, I saw him coming out of the farm supply store. He was carrying a paper sack.

"We better get going," I said to him. "What's in the sack?"

"Supplies," he said. "You get the medicine?"

"In the car. You didn't happen to get shells for the gun, did you?"

Old Quick stopped dead in his tracks. "By God, I forgot. I better go back."

"Don't bother. I'd just as soon you left it empty. You could have an accident. Damn thing makes me nervous."

I had to do some more talking, but finally I got him to get into the van and we went on our way again.

On the way out of town I almost ran into a guy carrying a brown grocery bag across the road. He was so in a hurry, he didn't see me coming, and I had to slam on the brakes. When he heard the brakes yelp, he jumped and the bag got away from him and dropped on the pavement and split open and blue spray cans went rolling in all directions. It was the guy I'd given the money to. He scrambled after the Lysol cans and gathered them up in his arms, and then stood aside for me to pass. When he saw it was me, he spread his ragged grin at me and nodded. I drove on by.

"He must be planning to do a lot of cleaning," Quick said. He said it innocent, but he knew.

The Germans had a big discussion about what to see first and ended up deciding on the Badlands, then later Wounded Knee and Pine Ridge. So we circled around north and got into the Badlands that way.

I don't know what a person is supposed to feel about the Badlands. I'd been there once before and didn't much care for it. In fact, it kind of scared me, that time. All I could think was how desolate it looked, and dangerous, with all those spiky peaks that looked like they were warning you to keep out. A person could get lost in there and never get out again, I thought back then, but I was nothing more than a kid. This time I saw it different. It was still scary enough, but it was lovely, too. It wasn't all dead, the way I remembered. You had to look for it, but there was plenty of life around in the cracks and crevices. And there was something beautiful about the way the rock had got carved by the rain and wind. I supposed farmers coming in from the east would look at it and get kind of sick, thinking of their green corn and wondering how you could ever grow a crop in land like this. And I guess city people would look at those peaks and be reminded of their tall buildings, and the whole place would look to them like some place after the bomb dropped. For me, though, all I could think of was the time it took to get like this. It was all at the bottom of a big ocean once, the way the signs said, and it took all that time to build up and all that time to melt down again. And I got to thinking what we were looking at was like the stumps of candles that had been burning millions of years. It made me feel puny in comparison, and all my troubles nothing but fly-specks.

The women had to take a lot of pictures, of course, and Quick had to stop at the visitor's center to relieve his bladder. It all took time, and we ended up spending most of the morning. By that time, Ingrid was just demanding to have a picnic, so I pulled over in one of those little scenic view places and we got out and Lorrie spread out a blanket on the rocks and we squatted down and had a little meal consisting mostly of bread and cheese and apples and things like that, but no meat. It was all right, but a strange place for a picnic, it seemed like to me. When we were almost done eating, Lorrie opened the back end of the van and pulled out a bat and ball and a couple fielder's gloves. "Come on," she said. "We play the bazebull."

She and Ingrid put on the gloves and started to throw the ball back and forth something pitiful. Me and Quick looked at each other and shook our heads. It is a sorrowful sight to see the great American pastime made such a mockery of. We volunteered to show them how to play the game right.

Quick, naturally, started himself out as pitcher and gave the women pointers on winding up with all the proper flourishes, keeping your eye on the runner on first, tugging on your cap, squinting at the catcher's signals, shifting your cud, and spitting. I think Ingrid and Lorrie were amazed to find out there was so much to just throwing a ball.

I took the bat and showed them the rules about hefting the wood, choking up, lining up the trademark, dusting your hands with dirt, wiping them on your shirt, digging into the box, wiggling your rump, going into your crouch, and knocking the mud out of your cleats.

They caught on pretty fast. Lorrie made a whiz-bang catcher, seeing as how she had the natural build for it. We taught her how to hunch down and give signals between her legs, peel off her mask, and call for the catch of a high foul. And Ingrid was laying down bunts just perfect, and it was a lovely thing to see her look mean and dangerous at the pitcher or stagger away from an inside pitch. It was easy to forget she was a communist menace, and I was beginning to think that with a little more coaching she might get weaned off that stuff altogether.

We had to give it up, of course, when Quick lined a foul right over a cliff with about a 400-foot drop off. We all ran to the edge and looked down and knew at the same time our fun was over. "I'll tell you this, though," Quick said, "it is the longest ball I ever hit."

After that, we headed back to the res. Unless you've been there, you can't have much of an idea of how out-and-out big the place is. It just spreads out everywhere until you get to feeling lonely in it. You get to thinking what you would do if the car broke down or something, or if someone came down sick, where you would go for help. It gets you wondering, too, how the people who actually live there deal with all that space. Like someone who has to go to the hospital and it's 100 miles away. Or just going shopping. It must make people anxious, especially if their cars are none too good to start with. You can't catch a taxi or a train, that's for sure. And I didn't see too many buses, either. You can drive long stretches and not see phone lines or electric lines. The towns themselves look halfway decent, but in between it looks like a risky place to live.

At Wounded Knee, there wasn't that much to actually see, but it certainly gave a person a lot to think about. The women, of course, were about beside themselves with how terrible it was so many old men, women, and children were killed there. For me, it was more complicated. If you think about how such a thing could happen, you realize that it took a lot of people to pull it off, and not all of them could've been that bad at heart. You've got to figure there was some young soldiers there who just didn't have enough sense to know what a bad thing they were doing. Or else they had somehow got it into their heads that they were doing something that was all right. It doesn't get them off the hook, I don't suppose, but it is more sensible than thinking they were all some kind of demons. I can't accept that people are all that bad or all that good, either. And if I was German, I would be careful about drawing lines all that solid. It does seem to me that, get right down to it, it is more what people believe that's to blame for them doing bad things than what they are. In this place there was an awful risk of judging people by the worst they could be. It all makes you wonder how we could have come to this, people lined up on one side or the other with enough hate on either side, but only one side actually doing the killing. I have heard people say it balances out, what happened to Custer and then what happened here, but that doesn't help anything. Something that terrible, even if it happened 90 years ago, there is no forgiving and there is no forgetting. It is like a sore that won't heal, but just keeps on running and hurting until it kills you or drives you crazy.

We were all pretty quiet after that and drove on like we were in a funeral procession. Even Quick had enough sense to keep his flapper sealed up. In Pine Ridge we stopped at a gas station to get some gas and Ingrid and Quick both went to the bathroom. While they were gone, Lorrie said, "You have a problem with women, I think?"

Coming out of the blue like that, it hit me hard. Was it written on me that bold? "What makes you think?"

"I see how you look at Ingrid," Lorrie said. "Always here." She put her hands on her tee-shirt right over the feather and the arrow. "And also the legs."

"Not always," I said. "I have looked at her face, too. She's got blue eyes."

"She is very beautiful," Lorrie said. "She can not do anything about that."

I didn't see what she was driving at. "Why should she?"

"She also has a brain."

"Sure," I said. "Naturally." But I still didn't get it.

"She is not just a collection of parts," Lorrie said. "She is not a sack of candy in different shapes and flavors and colors. She is a person. She is something that has nothing to do with how she looks."

"All right." I was starting to feel uncomfortable. "She is not a bag of candy. I can see that."

"And I also," Lorrie said.

I looked at her. Her brown eyes were shining like colored glass in her long face. Her chin was kind of stuck out, maybe, which gave her a man-in-the-moon look, but her smile was pretty. Without Ingrid there for comparison, she was handsome enough. But there was something else there, too, which is hard to explain. It was like she knew things she could teach me. For a second it was like she was offering me something rare and valuable for nothing down and no payment for six months. Then her gaze shifted away and down and it was over. "Never mind," she said.

I didn't know what to say. "I'm sorry," I told her. I didn't even know where the words came from. I had no idea what I was sorry about. I guess I felt she was testing me, and somehow I hadn't come through.

Then Ingrid came back.

"How was it?" Lorrie asked her.

Ingrid made a face.

Then Quick climbed back in and we went on our way again.

One more time, I got to thinking about what I was doing there, only now I was beginning to see that there were complications I hadn't even dreamed about before. When you take up with people, there's more to it than asking them to dance and taking a couple whirls around a dance floor. Even if you never see them again, they might waltz around in your head forever.

9.

Another thing I never expected is what kind of a time of it we would have the next day. I thought I was pretty much braced for all that could happen, but I kept getting surprised. They say live and learn, only I seemed to get older but never smarter.

At first it looked like it would be a pretty nice day. It was warmer, and everybody was all primed up for the wacipi. For the Germans, it started to dawn on them that this was something that they would be talking about to all their friends back home. They hadn't counted on anything this good. So they were pretty much in tourist heaven all day long. I wasn't much better. I had been to a couple of wacipis with Lymon before, so I knew a little better what to expect, but all the same I was looking forward to it. That is just like me, I suppose. I didn't really understand what was going on, completely, but I always hoped that this time I would finally get it.

The way I understood, the wacipi had been planned for a long time and Celia just held the giveaway the day before to take advantage. From what I could tell, the giveaway had been a big success. There were still some people there when we got back at night. All the things that Celia and her relatives had been piling up for a year were all pretty much gone, the fire wood was down to a few sticks, and the food kettles were scraped clean. Celia seemed satisfied that Zachary had been sent off to the spirit world with the right spin.

Lymon was talking to an older man when we got there, and he didn't seem too much in a hurry to break off the conversation. The older guy was dressed in an old-fashioned way, with a polka-dot shirt and his hair in braids, and lots of beads and necklaces draped around his neck. He seemed to be doing most of the talking, with Lymon just nodding and sometimes sticking in a word or two while he picked up around the yard, gathering up the chairs that had been set up in a circle.

Celia had saved a couple things to give to the German girls and me. I guess she counted us as guests and thought it wouldn't be polite to leave us out of the giveaway altogether. Ingrid got a shawl and Lorrie a nice beaded belt. They didn't want to take the stuff at first but finally got the idea that it would be an insult to turn it down. I got a medicine wheel woven out of willow branches that looked pretty old, and I realized that it was something special. I suppose it was because she knew me from before. She said we should take the things to the wacipi the next day. Quick she had already given the shoes, so he didn't get anything else.

The day had been pretty hard on Mr. Quick. Even with his medicine, he was plain tired out, and he went to bed almost as soon as we got back.

I stayed up long enough to talk to Lymon, once the guy left.

"You were having quite a conversation," I said to Lymon.

"That was Leonard Fourwinds. He is kind of a holy man. He has this funny idea about me, that I am special in some way. He doesn't say anything outright, but I think he wants me to tell him that I agree with him and will do something about it."

"Do what?"

"I'm not sure. There are lots of things. Go after a vision, for one thing. I don't know. I keep trying to tell him that I am not that kind, but he won't give in."

"So what are you gonna do?"

"I haven't decided. How was your day?"

"All right. Long. A lot of driving around."

"Where are the women?"

"In the van. They're trying on what Celia gave them, trying to figure out what to wear to the wacipi, I think."

"That one, she keeps looking at me," Lymon said.

"The pretty one, you mean? Yeah, I've seen her. Me, she's just polite with. You, I think she's got different plans for."

"Makes me uncomfortable." He shrugged, a little embarrassed.

"She's a communist," I said. It just came out.

"So what?" Lymon looked at me.

"I'm not sure. She just has a different way of looking at things. Maybe she would like to do something about your plight. Take the edge off it, or something."

Lymon nodded, then laughed. "I never thought of myself much as a mercy case."

Which I guess was the big difference between him and me.

The wacipi got started the next day in the afternoon and ran right into the night. It was held down the road about ten miles at a place where they also had rodeos sometimes and even ball games. There was already a crowd when we got there, and lots of people already in their dancing outfits. Lymon and Celia rode down in the van with the Germans, and me and Quick took the VW. Ingrid and Lorrie were already having fits of tourist delight over seeing so many Indians in one place and dressed like Indians, too.

The day was warmer than any we'd had so far, and everybody seemed to be in the mood for a wacipi. First there was a grand procession where the flag was brought in and all the dancers following it. Then there was a flag song which for the Oglala I think is a beautiful one, kind of a remembrance of all the Indian soldiers who had ever fought for the flag.

The rounds of dancing began then, starting with open dances where everybody can dance, and then dances for young boys, young girls, fancy war dances, shawl dances for the women, traditional, and so on like that. Somewhere in there the judges picked out a wacipi queen, and this time they picked a girl the p.a. guy said was one Verine Manyponies. She was what Quick would call a looker, but in the Indian way, with those beautiful cheeks and long braided black hair, and a way of looking down with her eyes as she danced, modest.

I suppose the music takes some getting used to. The singers sit around a big drum, each with a drum stick, beating out the rhythm, sometimes a steady beat and sometimes alternating, BOOM-boom, BOOM-boom. The songs were strange, sometimes with words and sometimes not, but always repeated over and over. Lymon told me once that there was kind of a rule about that, they had to repeat everything at least four times, smaller parts and bigger parts too. You could say it was monotonous, I suppose, but not much moreso than a lot of rock songs I have heard that go on and on with "I love you love you Molly," about a thousand times in a row. And you surely can't say that it doesn't have a beat to dance to.

Lymon did a great job with the fancy war dance. That is the dance that takes the most energy of any. The songs they use for it are real tricky and mostly fast, and the dancers step high, and there is a lot of jumping and turning. Lymon has a way of doing cross steps in that dance that is real flashy and catches the judges' eyes often enough that he has many times come back with prize money. He wears these fancy bustles, one on his rear and one tied just behind his neck, plus the usual porcupine quill roach and head feathers and a shield and coup stick. He had bells strapped on his ankles and clouts in front and back decorated with Aunt Celia's best beadwork.

I watched the fancy war dances with Ingrid and Lorrie. They were both wearing what Celia gave them over their own clothes, longer skirts and peasant blouses that they hoped gave them a kind of Indian look. They did make awful blonde-looking Indians, though.

The way Ingrid watched Lymon was fierce, like some kind of meat-eater that had spotted a juicy field mouse. Or maybe, in her case, a vegetarian eyeing a crisp carrot. I glanced at Lorrie, and she was watching me watching Ingrid watching Lymon. I felt like I was part of a food chain or something. Lorrie just gave me a knowing nod, her eyes half-lidded, like she was saying, "What did I tell you." The only problem is, I had no idea what she did tell me. That Ingrid was not a sack of candy? All right. What was she, then? I guess it was all right that she was looking at Lymon like he was a whole candy store. Excuse me for being confused.

Lorrie hooked her arm inside mine and pulled me a ways away. "You are looking at Ingrid again?"

"And she is looking at Lymon."

"She can look if she wants. A woman can look, as can a man?"

"Fine. Then I will look if I want to."

"It is not that you look, but what you see."

"All right, then. You look at me, what do you see?"

She blinked a few times before she answered. "A lost boy."

"I know where I am. And I'm not a boy."

"A man if you wish. But lost."

"I have no idea what you are talking about."

"It is not where you are, but what you are. You have lost yourself."

What could I say to that? She was so serious, I didn't want to laugh, no matter how much like happy horse shit it sounded. And if it was true, I was in a sad state. "What am I supposed to do about that?" I finally said, playing along.

"It is possible I could help?"

"To find myself?"

"Yes. If you wish." She was looking at me with those solemn brown eyes and holding on to my arm like she was afraid I might make a run for it. Then she brushed me with her free hand, just lightly, like she was knocking some crumbs off my shirt, and just let her hand trail down and flicked at my crotch. She was now looking intent at the dancing, all of a sudden real fascinated. You might think the flick was accidental, but that's not the way it was taken by the part that got flicked. Benedict Arnold, of course, stood at attention, ready to do battle right then.

I looked at Lorrie again, and she pulled her hand away and started in applauding. I thought it was for Benedict Arnold, at first, until I realized that the fancy dance had ended. I gave a weak clap myself.

"When?" I said, when I could make myself heard again.

"When?" she said back to me, blinking like she didn't know what I was talking about.

"When do you want to help me, you know, to find myself?"

"Oh, I think later, yes? When it is dark? In the van?" And she let go my arm and went back to Ingrid, leaving me and Benedict both standing there feeling kind of woozy. The sun was setting. Somebody had started up a bonfire. When it is dark, I'm thinking.

Lucky for me the judges asked for another round to judge the fancy dancing. It gave me a chance to get a little settled down. Not so lucky for Lymon, though, because his neck bustle, which had got loosened up during the first round, started slipping bad and he had to walk off, disqualifying himself. He got some kind of consolation prize, though.

The next thing was a round of open dancing, which anybody could do, even us tourists. I wasn't going to, but Ingrid and Lorrie pulled me out into the circle, and I went along. I had the medicine wheel that Celia had given me, and I held it the way I'd seen the other men hold such things when they were dancing. The drummers started in with a real soft beat, then one of the singers began with that high, clear cry like the sound of a nighthawk, and brought it down, and the other singers joined in and the dancers started shuffling around the circle. The singers started pouring the sounds out now like a waterfall.

It took me a while to stop thinking how ridiculous I must look, out there in my jeans, but then I noticed that there were others dressed kind of ordinary, even many of them Indians. So then I started concentrating on the dancing and forgot everything else. I imitated the way I saw other people doing, and it wasn't so hard. Pretty soon it was like I didn't have to think at all, and the drums and the singing just got into me and was moving me around. The strangest thing was that I started to thinking what the Oglala men would've thought, back a hundred years ago or more. Maybe they were thinking about hunting, getting themselves fit to do brave things. I started moving my head around, the way I'd seen some of the dancers do before, like I was looking for something in tall grass. In my mind I was seeing ponies and buffalo and deer and antelope.

If I hadn't been so deep into the dance, I might have noticed that Quick was among the missing. The drumming stopped without any warning, and I kept stepping heel-toe a few more beats, which of course no Indian would do. I looked around, and I realized it was dark. And the next thing I knew, my name was being called over the p.a. to come to the judges' table. I didn't see how I deserved a prize, but I went to the table anyway.

"You Rodney Deuce?" the guy at the desk said.

"That's me."

"These gentlemen want to talk to you."

The gentlemen he was talking about had come in on either side of me and one was clapping me on the shoulder like an old friend and the other was grabbing my wrist. They were dressed in ranch clothes and didn't have any badges on, but they acted enough like police, that's what I took them for. I think my heart stopped for about a minute.

"Don't embarrass yourself by making a fuss," one says that has his hand around my wrist. They start marching me away from the table, in the direction of the cars. We probably looked like three old buddies, talking over past times. The night air was starting to turn cool.

"You know an individual by the name of Daniel Quick?" one of them said, the taller one.

"Who?" I was trying to play dumb.

The tall guy squeezed my wrist harder. I was beginning to lose feeling in my fingers. "You heard me the first time."

"Oh," I said. "Mr. Quick. Maybe I have heard the name."

"He's the one," the other guy said. "Let's go."

And they shoved me into a late model Ford pickup and started off with me.

The old fart has done it now, I was thinking. It was sure to be both our asses. I knew these guys weren't police, by that time, but that might be all the worse. The letters on the side of the pickup spelled out "C.T. Colton, Black Angus." The police at least have a little respect for the law.

Sure enough it was the Colton ranch that the pickup pulled into, finally. The orange VW was sitting in the yard. The two guys dragged me out and took me into the house. It was one of those one-level affairs made all out of stone. And inside it had carpet all over, even in the kitchen where we were. At first everything seemed real quiet and muffled, but then you heard this kind of hum that was made by the deepfreeze and the refrigerator and I don't know what all electrical stuff. The two guys made me sit down at the table and wait. In the bluish light I noticed the shorter guy had bad teeth. I had already smelled his breath in the car.

The bad teeth guy went into another room and in a half a minute he came back, bringing Daniel O. Quick, in the flesh, who grinned at me.

"Rodney, I'm sorry you got mixed up in this," Quick said.

"Shut up," the rotten-tooth guy said. I figured he didn't know Quick very well yet.

Quick's clothes were torn all over. He looked like some big cat had taken him for a ball of yarn. "You don't have to tell them anything," he said.

"Shut up," the guy said.

"It's all a misunderstanding," Quick said.

"Shut up." The guy leaned over the table and yelled in Quick's face. And finally Quick shut up. It could be the guy's breath that stopped him. It smelled like the guy had been chewing on dead mice.

Anyway, I had just about put the whole story together now. Quick had killed C.T. Colton and had got me messed up in it too. And it was just like him to call something like that a misunderstanding.

But then a man walked in who had to be none other than C.T. Colton. He didn't have a sign on him, or anything, just the way he carried himself, and that little smirk. Lymon had described him to me—six four or five, dark hair, moustache, cocky kind of walk. It was him all right. I'm afraid my mouth must've dropped open like a suitcase.

"You look surprised to see me," Colton said to me.

"No, Sir."

"What did you expect to see? A corpse?"

"No, Sir."

"What is this old billy goat doing with your wallet, anyway?"

"I didn't know he had it."

"We found it in the VW," Colton said.

"Must've fell out of my pocket. We were at the wacipi. I don't know what he's doing here."

"Dammit," Quick said, "I told these people a hundred times. I was heading to Weed to get a drink. I got tired of the barndance."

"Shut up," the bad breath guy said, but he was starting to sound discouraged.

"Colton was standing at the table looking from me to Quick and back to me. If you remember that guy in those cigarette ads a time back, that looked like his face was made out of rawhide and with that 4X beaver Stetson and that thick brush of hair under his nose, that was C.T. Colton. He must've modeled himself after those ads.

"What were you doing on my property?" Colton asked Quick.

"I told you that already."

"Tell me a second time."

So what Quick says is that the sun got in his eyes so bad he couldn't see the road, and he pulled the car off to keep from wrecking it. And then when the sun went down, he realized he still couldn't see very well, and he remembered he had night blindness. He tried to walk back to the house to make a call. He climbed the fence, he said, because he thought it would be shorter.

"How did you end up in the feed pens?" Colton said.

"I couldn't see where I was going. Night blindness, like I said."

"There must be something to that," the tall guy said. "I never seen anybody more tangled up in bob wire."

"What about the gun?" Colton pulled Quick's long-barrel pistol out of his belt and laid it down on the table.

"I didn't have it with me," Quick says. "It was in the car. And it's not loaded anyways."

Colton looked at me, then. "Where have I seen you before?"

"Don't know. I'm not from here. Just going through."

"You friends of the Twobows, any chance?"

"Which?"

"How much Indian are you, anyways?"

"None. I'm French, my papa's side. Arkansas on the other."

"You look part blood, to me."

I shrugged. "I been told that."

Colton shook his head. "I don't see how it could be a coincidence. But I don't see this senile old futz as a hired killer either."

"You still got a trespassing charge," Bad-breath said.

"No," Colton said. "It wouldn't be worth it. Might as well let them go. See they get well off the place." And he turned and started back into the other room.

The two guys started to take us out and I started to breathe normal again. But Colton swung around just then and said, "Hold it. Did you check out Forte's pen?"

"No," the tall guy said.

"Why don't you do that right now?" Colton said. "We'll wait here."

So Quick and me sat down again and Colton and Bad-breath stood watching us as the tall guy went on out.

I looked over to Quick, and I thought I saw a little bit of worry in his face. "What is a Forte?" he said.

"Shut up," Bad-breath said. But his heart wasn't in it any more.

So we all sat there looking at each other and listening to the house hum. It came to me that this is what being rich and being able to buy everything in the world that runs by electricity can do for you, make your house sound all the time like it is trying to clear its throat.

Finally the tall guy came back in. And when the door opened, I saw Quick stiffen up. He was worried, all right, and trying not to show it.

"The animal's all right," the tall guy said, "what I can see. He was pretty frisky, kicking up his heels. The old fart must've give him a scare."

"You give my prize bull a scare, old man?" Colton said. "You're damn lucky you didn't get in with him. He might've run right over you like a truck."

"Sheer luck is what it was, all right," Quick said. "Blind luck, you might say."

Colton looked about halfway amused himself, thinking what the bull could've done to Quick. People with money like that, they get amused easy, I think. They got money and all it can buy and are amused by all the little people scraping around trying to make a go. Put a big shot together with two other people who haven't got money, and you can pick out the rich one by the funny half-smile he's got on his face. See, the struggles of the world don't mean shit to the man with money. I saw men like that the year or two I caddied, and they were alike that way, different as they might be other ways. They might be tightass one minute and generous the next, whatever amused them.

Colton looked at me, looked at Quick. "I'm letting you drive away from here," he said. "And you better drive fast. But I'm going to tell you something before you go. If there is anything goes wrong around here in the future, you are going to be the first we come looking for. So you'd better keep close track of your whereabouts at all times, and see you have somebody can swear you were there. If not, we are going to have to assume it was you who did it. And you are going to be screwed." Then he looked at Quick, looked at me, shook his head again, and said, "Get them the hell out of here."

So before long we were in the VW heading back down the long lane toward the road. The pickup was following along behind us.

"Just move it along steady until they stop following," Quick said.

"What do I do after that? Get out and push?"

When we got to the end of the lane, Quick said, "Take a right."

"The res is the other way," I said. So was the wacipi. So was Lorrie and the van. It had been dark a long time.

"Take a right," Quick said again. "We don't want to lead them back there. Not when they find out."

"Find out what?"

Quick didn't say anything, and right away something sank down inside me like the feeling you get in an elevator sometimes when it jerks. I cranked the wheel right and slid out the lane onto the main road.

"You did something, didn't you?" I said. "I knew it. What did you do."

I looked over at him and in the faint light he was grinning one of his evil grins. "Did I ever mention to you I was a vet's assistant once? I would hold the shoats to get vaccinated and like that. As usual, I got to know a good deal about that particular profession."

"Oh, no," I said, because now I knew it had something to do with the bull after all.

Quick was half turned around, looking at the rear window and talking at his usual rate. "I bought the knockout stuff in Weed. Tied the needle to the end of a long stick, like a spear. I got him in the rump. He went down like he was hit by one of your right crosses." He turned back to face to the front. "They've given up on us. They're turning around."

I was beginning to feel that old sickness coming over me again. "What did you do to the poor beast?"

"Give him a little rest," Quick said. "Time for meditation, counting his blessings."

"You better not've."

Quick just chuckled, and I could feel that elevator cable snap. "No wonder he was frisking around the pen. He is feeling a good deal lighter on his feet, I suspect. He will be doing a toe dance before long."

"Jesus," I said.

"Don't take it so personal," Quick said. "Old Noah had his fun. Only he'll have to find another forte. Maybe take up needlework of some kind."

I was wondering what C.T. Colton would do when he found out he is the owner of a real expensive steer. He is going to take it personal as hell, I was thinking. And he is going to know exactly who did it. It was about at that point in my thinking that I started to groan.

"It's not like I killed him," Quick said. "I just castrated him a little. Probably do him good. Get his mind out of the gutter."

"If Colton catches us," I said, "he will do to us what you did to his bull."

"I wouldn't put it past him" Quick said. "I think you are beginning to see the need for haste."

I already had the pedal to the floor, but of course the car was going at its usual rate of speed. Quick was watching in the rear view for car lights.

"Is that true about the night blindness?" I asked. To be honest, I'd been halfway taken in by that story myself.

"Partly," Quick said. "It hit me after I done the deed. I couldn't find my way out of the damn place. Then I stumbled into the roll of wire. It give me a whole new perspective on fishing. What it is like to get hooked."

I couldn't help smiling just a little thinking about Quick tangled up in that wire. I got to wishing he was still there. But then it came to me how all-out satisfying it was C.T. Colton was finally getting back some of what he dished out. Killing him wouldn't have been near so fitting. I just wished I could be there to see his face when he found out. Or on the other side of the planet, maybe, watching it on TV, that cigarette ad face just going all to pieces. There is nothing near as sweet as seeing justice done. Nor as rare, neither.

Not that there weren't some regrets laced in with it. We would never see Lorrie and Ingrid again, for one thing. And who else would there be to take me on, even as a mercy case? And it would go hard on Lymon and Celia too, for a while, because Colton would try to pin this on them, of course, even if he knew better. Then I thought of something else. "What about the money?"

"It's in the bag, in the trunk. I guess they didn't think to look there. Maybe they couldn't figure out where the trunk was."

So it was pretty much the same as it was before, except for Uncle Zachary's shoes on Quick and the willow wheel Aunt Celia'd given me, which I'd tucked into my shirt. And in my head, Lorrie's face looking at me the way she had. I was feeling pretty let down about that, I guess. I had my hopes worked up without even thinking about it.

We went on through Weed and finally came to the interstate, and Quick pointed me on through, off on another side road. That would've been the place to head east, but I was in the wrong state of mind to think about any of that, with all those feelings churning through me. So I just kept on following the directions Quick gave me. I guess I figured his way was as good as any other, even when I saw how we were headed.

To hell with it. The elevator was surely falling, and I was thinking it was just a matter of time before it hit bottom.

10.

We got to Deadwood about the time it was starting to get light. We could've done it faster, but we had to circle way out around north to avoid Rapid City, and then Quick directed me in by some gravel roads to keep away from the highways where there could be patrols. He seemed to know the back roads around there pretty good. And when we rolled into town at last, I said, "Where now?"

"I don't know," Quick said. "We'll find some place."

There was hardly anything open at that hour, so I just kept driving, taking the turns that Quick gave to me. Finally he said, "Stop here."

So I stopped. We were on one of those steep streets with what looked like about two hundred steps going up from the sidewalk to a little house high up. See, all of Deadwood is just about built on the side of one mountain or the other.

"Where are we?" I said.

"Nowhere," he said. "I used to live here."

"I know," I said, thinking he meant Deadwood.

"No," he said. "Here. That house. It's pretty much the same, it looks like. New paint."

"The stairs must of been hellish," I said.

"Not so bad when you were young and you knew when you got to the top you were home."

"Who lives there now?"

"I don't know," he said. "Might as well go on."

So I did, but pretty soon he told me to stop again. It was a different house. He got out and looked at the mailbox and then got in again.

"Did you live here, too?"

"No," he said. "A friend of mine did. But there's a different name there now."

"Maybe we should get a motel," I said. I was pretty tired from driving and all we been through. "There were some vacancy signs up back there."

"Drive a while first," he said.

So we went on, winding around them empty streets. It was kind of weird, to tell the truth. It was so quiet. It seemed like everybody in town could be dead. He told me to stop a couple times more and looked at more mailboxes, then he told me to pull up into a kind of a parking lot and he told me to shut off the car and he got out and said he'll be a while. So I turned off the car and folded my arms across the wheel and rested my head on them and I fell asleep like that.

I woke up kind of in a state, and hit the brake. It took me a while to realize the car was standing still all the time. It was pretty bright by then, and I looked around. I saw we were parked by a cemetery. The sign at the gate said "Mt. Moriah." On the other side the land sloped off fast and you could see houses and tree tops down below and over across the valley was mountains with morning fog stuck in their creases. We had worked our way pretty high up. Quick was nowhere to be seen.

I got out of the car and trudged on up through the gate and into the cemetery. It was a lovely place, actually, with lots of ponderosa pine and spruce around over the gravestones. The grass and the tree needles were covered with dew, and the little drops were kind of winking in the gray light. I didn't have to walk very far before I saw Quick standing by a fence and looking through it at a stone.

When he heard me coming, he said, "How'd you sleep?"

"I would've rather had a down mattress," I said. "Who's this here?"

"Wild Bill himself," Quick said. He pointed to the marker and I read it.

"It doesn't seem real," I said. "You hear so much about a person like that, it seems like a made up story. You don't think about them having a grave. Is your grandaddy here, too?"

"No," Quick said. "He ended up in Panama. He was always quite a one to get around. Calamity Jane is though." He pointed out her marker. "She wasn't all that much. She made a name for herself as some kind of wild woman, but I just think she was kind of cracked. There were lots of lies told, too, about all of them. The truth is always more pathetic, it seems like."

"Is this what we came to Deadwood for?" I said.

He shook his head. "Lulu Bea is buried over there a ways." He pointed.

"Lulu Bea?"

"My wife. There's lots of friends there, too. More than I knew about."

I began to get an uneasy feeling. "You trying to tell me we came all this way and we got nowhere to go but a cemetery?"

"No," he said. "There is one other place, I guess."

"Whereabouts?"

He turned around, then pointed down into the valley. "You can see it from here, down there on main street."

"Who lives there?"

He grinned and said, "Pleasure." And I could see he was not about to explain himself. It was something I would have to figure out by myself.

About the liveliest place on main street when we got there was the Number Ten Saloon, which from the looks of the motorcycles lined up in front of the place had already pulled quite a crowd. It reminded me for all the world of one of those western movies, except motorcycles instead of horses.

As we got parked, a couple more cycles rolled in. A pair of fairly ugly individuals were driving the machines, kind of scraggy looking except for their leather jackets, no helmets or nothing. One had a red bandanna wrapped around his head I guess to keep his hair out of his eyes. The other one had this woman clamped on to his back like she's a pack of some kind. She was too skinny to be pretty to my way of thinking, but she's got one of those long, sunk-in faces with fierce eyes blazing out of her skull of the kind that can haunt a person.

They weren't too jovial a bunch, but got off and went on into the saloon like it was something they had to do, like a job or church, and the jeans the woman was wearing made me wonder if she had much trouble getting them zipped up.

"Seems early in the day for a pick-me-up," I said.

"That's not the point," Quick said. He was getting out of the VW with his flight bag. "The point is, it's kind of a shrine. That's where Wild Bill was killed. Some make a case that's where the wild west ended."

So I got out and started for the saloon. I never before had a drink for breakfast, but those jeans got me hoping for another look.

But Quick yelled at me. "Hold on. That's for pilgrims and tourists." And when I turned around to look he was heading off in the other direction entirely.

I caught up with him just as he was tapping at a door. The door was kind of stuck in between buildings on the street across from the saloon. And the main thing about it was, it was yellow. Over the top there was a little sign that a person could hardly see from the street that said, "Hotel." "You said we weren't going to a hotel," I said.

Quick gave me a kind of pitiful look and shook his head. "This stands up against a hotel the way a cathedral stands up against a wayside chapel." He knocked again.

"Looks like no one's to home."

"There's always someone home here," he said. Then he found an old push button beside the door of the kind you can't tell if they are connected up to anything or not, and he pushed it. I listened, but I didn't hear anything ringing inside. "It's broke," I said.

"They tend to sleep late," Quick said, and leaned on the button again.

"We could wait at the saloon until they get up."

"I know what you got on your mind," Quick said. "Don't take more than a set of tight levis to get you to forget your recent sorrows, does it? Well, there's something here will make you forget your own name. This is where they sell amnesia by the hour." But it was still no go on the button. He started to knock again.

"Maybe they all got amnesia and forgot how to answer the door."

"Shit," Quick said and stopped knocking to rub his knuckles, he's been whacking them so hard. It looked like he was just about to give up. But just then the door jerked open and a face looked out at us. It was a face that looked like it came out of one of those horror movies. The nose was flattened down, the lips were puffy and the teeth that showed through them were either set particular wide or were missing every other one. The eyes were wet looking and orange where the white should be and hung with pouches underneath you could keep your socks in. The one ear that could be seen looked like some kind of a pink flower that had been kept too long in the vase. I believed we must've stumbled on the original model for the jack-o-lantern. He was hairy as a bear from his neck down his chest and arms and had those big knotty muscles that made you wonder how he could even move. He only had on trousers. This didn't look much like pleasure to me, somehow. I was convinced we got the wrong door.

But Quick just barged right ahead in his usual way like it was not in the least strange to see a Halloween pumpkin setting on a gorilla's shoulders. "Is Mrs. Ball in?" he said.

The jack-o-lantern blinked at him two slow blinks. "It's too early. Fart off." And he started to close the door.

"I'm an old friend," Quick said. "I'm sure she'd like to see me."

"Mrs. Ball doesn't like to see anybody before noon." He just kept on swinging the door closed. But it got stuck with about half a foot to go and the pumpkin guy looked down surprised and saw that Quick had got his knee stuck in there.

"Get your leg out of here before I break it off for you," he said.

"Just tell her I'm at the door," Quick went on. You could not get on him for being a quitter. Stupid, yes.

"Take out your leg."

"Call Mrs. Ball."

The two of them had reached what I think is called a standoff. It looked like that, anyway, until the guy with the face reached down and started to squeeze Quick's knee between his thumb and fingers. Quick stopped talking for a change and started looking real thoughtful, like there was an idea that had him all wrapped up. His eye started to water.

Then I heard this woman's voice: "Ray, what's going on?"

"Guy won't get his leg out of the door," the pumpkin face said.

The woman must've gotten around to where she could see better who it was, then, because she said, "Good god, it's—Dan Quick, what the hell do you think you're doing?"

"Right now," Quick said, kind of between his teeth, "I'm kneeing the hell out of this gentleman's fist."

And the woman laughed and told the guy she called Ray to let Quick's knee go. So the old fart got his leg free and hobbled around on the sidewalk for a while getting his knee back in operation. Meantime the door swung open and the woman stood there watching Quick and laughing like a bartender. "You silly shit," she said. "I thought you would be planted by this time."

"I was planted," Quick says. "I dug myself up."

The woman was standing with her hands on her hips in the doorway. She was a big woman, but her proportions were pretty good. She was wearing one of those flimsy kind of robes made out of silk or something that just kind of floated around her like pink smoke. Underneath that you couldn't help notice she had on a red nighty, likewise quite thin. After that the view got a little more dim. In the morning light, without any makeup on, her face came in at what it must be for a fact, maybe forty some. It didn't exactly match the red hair, which I was pretty sure was dyed. She was displaying a good amount of white teeth, which I would guess were all her own.

"Dan Ought-for-Nothing," she said. "What brings you to the whorehouse door in the wee hours?"

"I'll be honest with you, Regina," Quick said, rubbing his knee. "I'm here because I got nowhere else to go."

"That sounds honest," she said.

"We could use a place to stay."

She laughed. It was plain already that she enjoyed laughing. "You want a place to stay? That's something new. Who's the child? Is he old enough to cross this stoop?" It was me she was looking over.

"He is old enough," Quick said. "And he is in great need. I believe his horniness is becoming a burden to him. Rodney Deuce, say hello to Regina Ball, the proprietress of this establishment."

I nodded to her. I guess I was a little embarrassed. She grinned back, then she herded us inside. There was a little entranceway, then stairs going up steep. It was dark and cool in there and smelled like stale cigarette smoke and whisky mixed with sweet perfume. When your eyes got used to it you can see that it was something like a big diningroom, with lots of little tables and chairs. A bar was set up in one corner. There were paintings on the wall with frames of gold leaves and flowers, and they were mostly of fairly heavyweight girls with not too much on and a few men with horns and beards and goat from the waist down. In the middle of the room was a big light-fixture hanging that was made out of about a thousand pieces of glass cut and shined up like big diamonds or something, and dangling there like something complicated that was caught in an ice storm.

"Reggie," Quick said, "seeing this place again is like stepping back about thirty years."

"Don't you wish," Mrs. Ball said.

We sat down at a table. It had a marble top. The whole thing was quite a change from the reservation.

"Lord, I need some coffee," the woman said. "Ray—"

The pumpkin head was standing in the doorway, his arms folded.

"Do you want some?" Mrs. Ball asked Quick.

"Some eggs would be nice," Quick said.

She looked at me and I nodded.

"Fry some bacon and eggs, too, Ray. But get the coffee ready first."

The pumpkin head twirled around and took off.

"He's new," Quick said.

"Ray?" Mrs. Ball said. "He was here twenty years ago. Don't you recognize him?"

"He looks familiar in a way, but I don't think I ever seen him here."

"Not here, on the television. He was Death's Angel, the wrestler."

"My God," Quick said, "I knew I seen that mug somewhere. He was one of the great villains of all time."

"He's a pussy cat," she said. "A bookworm. You ought to hear him get going on books."

"I'll have to strike up a conversation with him some time," Quick said. He was still rubbing his knee. "What's he doing here?"

"He came in on a tour, visited our facilities. I'd just lost my bouncer, so I offered him the job. Fifty dollars a day and all the tail he could use. He jumped at it. Said it leaves him more time for his books and is not as hard on his body. Usually all he has to do with a trouble-maker is grin at him."

She laughed. "What're you doing here yourself? What you been up to?"

"Water over the dam," Quick says.

And they got talking about stuff that didn't mean too much to me. I just looked around at the wallpaper, which was that fuzzy kind, and the fancy velvet curtains and everything. And I got to thinking what kind of a place this was, and I half-way wondered if it was a whorehouse, which I didn't really believe her when she said the word before. I wouldn't recognize one myself, never being in one before. If this was what they were like, they were pretty nice houses.

Before long Death's Angel came back with breakfast on a tray and set it on the marble-top and we tore into it. He cooked really good eggs for someone whose looks tend to spoil a person's appetite.

"Well now," Mrs. Ball said as we were mopping up the last of the egg yolk with the toast. "What are your plans?"

Quick wiped his mouth with the back of his hand. "I'm not much for plans, I guess. I just wanted to get up here and get a lungful of pine-scented air and clear my head."

"Dan," she said. "You and me, we're survivors, but we've got different ways of surviving. For you it's all fancy footwork. You make up the dance as you go along. Me, I've got it all mapped out. In a few years

I'm going to sell this place and move to California and sit on the beach in the sun and go to all those television game shows and nobody will be able to tell me from that widow from Iowa who is living off her husband's will and the sale of the farm. You will never see anyone so respectable as me. And I am going to just bask in the joke of it and it's going to keep me warm and cheerful till the day I die. And here you don't even know what you are going to do tomorrow. What kind of trouble are you in, anyway?" She looked from Quick to me and back again.

"It is a slight mistake," Quick said. "The cops are after us."

A change came over Mrs. Ball's face. She was looking a deal more serious. She stood up and walked over to the bar. "I thought so," she said. "That's all I need. Trouble with the fuzz. I've got an arrangement."

"We'll pay," Quick said. "We've got money." He was looking at the flight bag.

"You've had breakfast. No charge. Why don't you just go to a motel?"

"If we wanted a motel, we'd've got a motel," Quick said. "I thought I was a friend of yours."

"You're an old customer," she said. "And a regular customer. But that doesn't give you visiting privileges."

Quick didn't say a thing, but looked down at his hands like he was wondering what they were for.

"Shit," Mrs. Ball said. "One night. One night and then out."

"I appreciate it," Quick said. "We'll pay for it."

"Damned right. And booze and tail extra."

"Sure," Quick said. "Maybe we could go to our rooms now. Rodney's been driving all night."

So Mrs. Ball led us down the hall toward the back to a little room that had a double bed. "Lucky thing we're a girl short now," she said. "Seventy-five dollars."

I think she was halfway hoping we'd back out and go to a motel, but Quick got the money out of the flight bag and counted it out in her hand. Then he counted out another twenty-five. "That's for meals," he said.

She folded the bills together. I noticed she was pretty cool taking in the stack of bills Quick had been peeling. "Checkout time is noon tomorrow. I'll tell Ray to make arrangements for you." She started to go on out. Just then there was a burst of noise that sounded like it was coming from the door across the hall. You could hear men's voices exchange in words and laughing.

"What's going on over there?" Quick asked. "More roomers?"

"A friendly game of hold-me-darling," Mrs. Ball said.

"Poker?" Quick said. I think I saw a light come on in his eyes.

"A few johns like to get together here once in a while," Mrs. Ball said. "I give them a safe, quiet place, and they pay good. This one's going on to two days."

"This is a new sideline, ain't it?" Quick asked.

"Diversification, that's what my broker calls it. Besides, one of them is my dentist. He gives me a break on the girls' teeth and does mine for nothing."

"This hold'em game," Quick said. "Is it closed or open?"

"Open," she said. "But they've got to like your looks and see the color of your money."

"Maybe you could introduce me."

"Sure," she says. "I'll tell them here is a man in trouble with the law who wants to spread a little of his probably stolen money around. That will go over big with the one who is a big shot in state government. He is nervous enough as it is."

I looked at Quick, thinking maybe he'd change his mind about this game, and it did look like he was having something of a struggle in his head, but then he kind of lit up and said, "Colton. That's what you can call me. C. T. Colton."

11.

I am not too much of a card player, but I watched the game a while to make sure Quick didn't get into too much trouble right off. I was a little scared about this big shot business, but nobody paid too much attention to me after Quick told them he was a rancher out by the Badlands and I was one of his hands. There were four of them at the table when Quick sat down. The Big Shot was fairly easy to spot because like Mrs. Ball said he was pretty nervous, always played with his chips and stacked them and counted them. And when he bet, he slammed the chips down ferocious like he was daring anybody to say he didn't have the cards to back it. And he folded the same way, squinting around at the others like he was suspicious someone on purpose saw to it he got rotten cards. He was wearing one of those suits with vests and a skinny tie which he hadn't even loosened up yet. He had this kind of wavy hair like you see on statues sometimes that looked like it would break if you hit it with a hammer. And he watched deals real close like he knew there was something funny going on, maybe because he didn't appear to be winning much. In my opinion, it is people like that you got to watch out for special, because they are likely to be judging everybody else according to their own crooked instincts.

The dentist I figured to be the one with the biggest pile of chips in front of him and the big grin on his face every time he raked more in. I'd like to know who else would get more of a kick out of inflicting pain like that.

The other two, one was a store-owner or something, quiet and all business, who seemed to be playing pretty conservative, folding his low hands early and not pushing his good hands too far. Every time he came on strong, everybody else folded because they knew he must have them. He was more than breaking even, which seemed to satisfy him. The last one was a phony cowboy with levis and a denim jacket. The reason you knew he was phony is he had thrown his hat over on a side table which a real cowboy wouldn't take off except to go to sleep. He was a wild better that liked to bluff and was talking all the time and trying to fake everybody out.

It was past me to see how this bunch, which looked pretty smart on the whole, could buy the idea that Quick was a well-to-do rancher. His clothes were now all tattered by his tangle with the barbed wire. His hands and face were scratched up some too. And Zachary's shoes, which he'd got on, don't exactly look like what C. T. Colton would wear. But I believe it must've been greed that wore down any suspicions any of them might of had. When Quick plunked down that wad of bills, he made believers out of them. And when any one of them made any mention of the tears on his clothes or the scratches on his skin, he just said, "Teach me to wrestle with a lynx." And somehow they seemed to accept that, whatever it was supposed to mean.

Two things took me by surprise right away. One was that Quick had dug out of his flight bag a pair of wire-rim-spectacles and had put them on when he started in to play. He let them settle down on his nose and kind of peeked over them at the other players. They made him look all of his age and then some. And before long the other players were calling him Gramps and treating him like some kind of a harmless mascot or something. The other thing is he fumbled the cards so, come his turn to deal. It is hard to believe that he was the same individual that was tying flies so handy such a short time back. It was my belief that he was sinking into senility pretty rapid.

At first it looked like Quick was going to lose all the money off the bat, but he got a little back, then he got a little more, and he was ahead by maybe fifty dollars when I figured it was safe to leave him.

I went back to the room across the hall and lay down on the bed for a time, but I found out I couldn't sleep again. It seemed like to me that there was just one problem after another which had come up to cause us trouble, and it didn't seem like any of them was any closer to being solved. So far we'd made it so we couldn't go back to Rapid or to the reservation. The cops had reason to be after us for robbery, car-theft, and castration of a prize bull. There is that saying about burning bridges that seemed to fit our case pretty snug. And who knew what kind of sparks Quick could be setting off in the other room right now?

As long as I couldn't sleep, I got up and wandered down the hall to where there was a door standing half-open. I peeked in and it was a kitchen, and Death's Angel was sitting at the table reading a book. He looked up at me with those orange-colored eyes.

"I wonder if I could get some more coffee," I said.

"Help yourself." He jerked his big head toward where there was a coffee urn on a counter.

I found a cup and drew some coffee and turned around to look at Death's Angel. He'd got on a white shirt now and wasn't looking so much like a gorilla as before. He looked up at me again and I tried a grin on him, but he didn't smile. So I said, to make conversation, "Have you ever read the books of Mr. Zane Grey?"

"No," he said.

"They're real good," I said. "The characters and the scenery most of all."

"I'll have to read them some time."

The conversation was going pretty good, so I pushed on. "What's that you're reading?"

"Dante," he said. "The Divine Comedy."

"Pretty funny is it?" I said.

"No."

"Oh," I said. "Then it's not much of a comedy, is it?"

"It's a love story," Death's Angel said.

"I'm not much for them. They tend to turn out sad."

"Not this one," he said.

"How do you know?" I said. "It looks like to me you are only halfway through with it."

"I've read it before."

"Don't that spoil it for you the second time?"

"It's the third time," he said. "And it's not spoiled yet."

"I've done that," I said. "I forget exactly how it ends. I mean I know generally, but I forget the details."

"That's what I am looking for. The details."

It seemed to me he talked awful good grammar for a wrestler. "Is it true you were on television at one time?"

"It's true." He took a drink of his coffee.

"What was it like?"

"It was a living. That's all."

"Mr. Quick says you were one of the great villains of all time."

"Maybe," he said. "There were others just as good. But there wasn't anyone as dirty. They loved me. People are in love with outlaws."

It seemed like it was getting to be kind of dangerous ground, so I cleared my throat and stepped light. "Why, do you suppose?"

"They're tired of hypocrisy. They know better. There's no justice in this world."

I just nodded. I was afraid I was in way over my head already.

"Except here." He patted his book. "Nobody gets away with anything here."

Lucky for me someone else came in just then to get me out of this swamp I seemed to've got mired down in. Two others, in fact, both of them females. One was what the Lakota call wasicu sapa, or "black white person," and the other was Japanese or something oriental. They had about every color there is in that kitchen it looked like. It was a regular United Nations.

The Japanese one was wearing one of those fancy robes with pictures in red and yellow I think they call kimonos. She was pretty classy looking for a hooker, it seemed to me. I didn't figure her for more than thirty years of age, with one of those long necks and smallish heads, her black hair done up behind, and her face tipped up so that she either seemed to be looking over everyone's head or when she looked at you it was like she was looking down, in spite of the fact that she was pretty short and on the frail side. The brown one, the first thing I noticed on her was this white hair, which I guessed was some kind of wig, silver colored, really. And she had on a smoky white robe that looked like one of those thin curtains, and her body underneath was all motion. When she walked it seemed like she was doing some kind of dance, going every which way.

The Japanese one, she gave me a look and then to Death's Angel, and Angel said, "He's a guest."

"Since when do we take in guests?" she said.

"Yeah," the brown one said. "You think this a hotel or something?"

"We'll be serving Sunday brunch next," the Japanese one said.

"What your name, Sugar?" the brown one asked me. She was pouring some coffee.

I told her.

"I'm Delly," she said. "And that's the Doll."

I nodded to them.

The Doll was already setting at the table with the Angel. "What we take in last night?" she asked him.

"About normal," he said.

"How much for drinks?" she said.

"Two-twenty."

"We should be getting twice that," the Doll said.

Delly took two coffees over to the table and gave one to the Doll and sat herself down. "They don't nobody come here to drink," she said.

"That's the point," the Doll said.

"When you are running the place," Death's Angel said, "you can charge all you want for the drinks."

"If I was running the place I would for sure get rid of the dead-beats," the Doll said. "The customers that come in for conversation, the girls that don't pull their weight."

The Angel shrugged. He was looking maybe more grim even than usual.

"Business is business," the Doll said.

"Old time's sake," Death's Angel said.

"Screw old time's sake," the Doll said. She gave me a sideways look and took a sip of her coffee.

Delly turned half around and said to me, "Come on and join us, Sugar."

So I took my cup and went and sat down, feeling kind of uncomfortable.

"You ain't no deadbeat, are you Sugar?" Delly asked me.

"No," I said.

"You pay your way, don't you?"

"Yes."

The Doll sniffed a little and took some more coffee. Somehow that struck me the wrong way. "We got plenty," I said.

"You and who else?" Delly said.

"Friend of mine. Partner. He's in the poker game right now."

"That's another thing," the Doll said.

Death's Angel shrugged.

Delly reached over to a white bakery sack on the table and opened it and pulled out a roll and started in to eating it. She passed the sack to me.

"I ate already," I said.

"Everybody's ate, Sugar," Delly said. She licked the crumbs out of the corner of her lips. "Everybody going to eat again. Just like humping, don't last for all time." She took another bite and chewed and grinned at me. "I bet you never get your fill, do you, Sugar?"

Her eyes were so full on me, I couldn't look at her any longer. I took out a roll and bit into it. She had brought home to me what a terrible thing appetite is, the way it never lets up for long. Sometimes it seems like a person is nothing but thirst and hunger. It just eats into you so you can't think about anything else. And the same with sex, like she said. It was enough to make you disgusted with humans altogether. With animals, like for example dogs, it is at least a passing thing and you can lock them up until it is over.

"Mail come yet?" the Doll said.

"No," the Angel said.

"You sure? It's usually here by now."

"I just checked. It's not here."

"You expecting something?" Delly said.

"I'm always expecting something," the Doll said.

"Bet I know what." Delly had her elbows propped up on the table and was picking her roll apart and looking at it close and smiling.

"So what?" the Doll says.

"That sweepstakes thing you sent in. This week they say they gonna tell who won."

"So what?"

"So you been real curious about the mail all week. You really think you gonna win?"

"Just as well me as anybody," the Doll says.

"They ain't gonna give it to no prostitute," Delly said. "They couldn't put it on TV."

"They got to give it to somebody," the Doll said. "It's the law."

"What the law got to do with anything?" Delly said.

The Doll took a long drink of coffee and crossed her legs and looked up to the ceiling. "I'll get it," she said. "Sooner or later."

"You got to have luck," Delly said. "I myself never had none."

"You make your own luck," the Doll said. "I got twenty-six entries in the sweep. Twenty some I talked my regulars into getting for me and the rest I bought at a buck apiece from the other girls."

"I bet you lucky, ain't you, Sugar?"

I couldn't believe Delly was talking to me. "I never won nothing in my whole entire life."

"Either you win it or you earn it," the Doll said.

I started to get a little nervous the way the conversation was going. I finished off my coffee.

"Or you steal it," the Doll said, and she brought her eyes down on me in a way that almost made me wince.

"Me and my partner," I said, "we're in business."

"What kind of business, Sugar?" Delly asked me.

"Liquor store," I said. It's the first thing that came into my head, and right away I regretted it.

"They make money," the Doll said, "but they're risky. They're all the time getting robbed." She still had her eyes on me.

"Could you tell me," I said, "whereabouts is the bathroom?" All of a sudden I felt like I had to go pretty bad.

"There was one ripped off in Rapid less than a week ago," Doll said, real cool and casual, hooding over her eyes with blue-painted lids and sipping at her coffee.

"Bathroom?" I said.

"Down the end of the hall to the left," the Angel said.

I got up from the table. "All this coffee," I said.

"You coming back, Sugar?" Delly said. "They're lots more rolls." She gave me a kind of sly grin like we already got some kind of secret between us.

"I'm kind of tired," I said. I yawned to make my point. "I guess I'll try to get some shuteye." And I beat it on out of there. Behind me I could hear the girls laughing.

I went to the bathroom and then back to the room and lay back down on the bed. Old Quick was right about one thing. This is a great place for forgetting. Between Delly and the Doll I had pretty much put my other troubles out of my head. I had got a whole new set to bother with, like how much the Doll knew and how much I would like to get to know Delly. One was the whip and one was the sugar and they had my head going through hoops. I don't know when I fell asleep, but when I woke up I had a taste like something dead in my mouth and I was hungry again.

12.

It was dark again. From the sound of voices and music coming down the hall, I guessed it was the rush hour. I checked out the card room first to see how Quick was doing. He appeared to be losing ground again. At least there weren't as many chips in front of him. The dentist, the cowboy and the Big Shot were still all in the game, but the other one was nowhere to be seen. The dentist looked to be the big winner yet and just as smug about it as usual. The Big Shot was still looking nervous, but now he had at least loosened up his tie and unbuttoned his shirt collar and taken off his coat, though his vest was still on. He was holding his own, maybe picked up a little more. The cowboy had done pretty good and had his mouth running as usual.

"I keep winning like this," the cowboy said, "I may consider taking it up for a living." He had lit up a big cigar and took a puff on her.

"What is it you're in?" Quick said. He was eyeing the cigar like he wouldn't mind one himself.

"Oil," said the cowboy out of the free side of his mouth.

"For hair or for cooking?" Quick said.

The cowboy looked at him like he was undecided to grin or not. "For cars."

"You drain it or put it in?" asked the dentist.

The cowboy gritted it out. "Drill for it. We both make a living drilling, Doc."

"You drill it," the dentist said, "our political friend runs his campaigns on it—What do you have to do with oil, Gramps?"

"Take it for constipation," Quick said.

The Big Shot was looking more interested in the oil cowboy now. "You from this state?"

"Wyoming," the cowboy said. "Gillette."

"What are you looking for," the dentist said to the Big Shot, "a campaign contribution?"

"Just might shake his hand if he was a voter," said the Big Shot, and went back to hide behind his cards sulking like a kicked dog.

The dentist leaned over to the cowboy: "Shake his hand anyway. Keeps it out of your pocket."

"The pot is light," Quick said, a little grumpy.

The cowboy tossed in a chip. "You ought to come over to Gillette some time," he said. "It's growing like the creamery cat. Lots of oil money floating around. You can always find a game there."

"I'd like to find a game here," Quick said.

They bet a round.

"I was in Gillette last week," the dentist said. "I couldn't find the town. I kept coming out on the other side."

The cowboy said, "You should've parked and let the town find you. I know a guy bought ten acres of land outside the city limits, a year later it was downtown. Sold it for a shopping center and moved to Florida."

The Big Shot threw in his hand. The dentist raised. Quick stayed. The cowboy bumped. The dentist saw it. Quick stayed again. The cowboy showed his straight and Quick took it out on me. "Dammit, Rodney, get out of here before you bust me entirely. You carried bad luck in with you." He poked a five-dollar bill at me. "Go get a drink or something." He glared at me over his wire rims.

"Five bucks won't buy much of something," the dentist said. "Girls won't look at less than thirty. Buck a minute."

"And they lay down on the job," the cowboy said, pulling in his chips. "We're all in the wrong trade."

So Quick skinned three more tens off his roll and held them out to me. "Do me a favor, Rodney. Shop around a little. Thirty dollars could buy you a weekend in my day."

"In your day," the dentist said, "thirty dollars could buy you a slave for life."

"Did they have dollars in your day?" the cowboy said. "I thought they were still using beads."

"Get your beads in the pot," Quick said, snarly, "it's light."

So I took the bills and went on out and down the hall to the main room. There was quite a party going on there, it looked like. Death's Angel was behind the bar stirring drinks. Mrs. Ball was gliding around from one table to another, tossing a few words to the men she knew, with this filmy thing she's wearing billowing out behind her as she went, and letting her laugh boom out every other minute. There was country-western music yowling out of a phonograph by the bar, lots of sliding guitar sobbing in that mournful way that everybody seems to get such a kick out of. Some of the girls pulled their customers out into the open space near the phonograph to dance. They were whirling around in various kinds of dresses, all of which you could see through enough to get your imagination worked up. About the only thing in the room that didn't seem to be in motion was the Doll, who was setting under the ice-storm light in the middle of the room with her legs crossed and sticking out of the slits in this shiny dress, and her head tilted back as usual, holding a cigarette holder aimed over the head of the guy talking to her. She looked like a picture out of a magazine, just as slick as that, and just as still. If she was agreeing or disagreeing with whatever the guy was saying, she wasn't showing it.

I went to the bar and asked the Angel if he'd got any wine. He said only champagne, which costs fifteen dollars a bottle. He showed me the bottle, which was the size of a bottle of seven-up. I told him I would pass on that. He poured me a rum and coke, which he said was as close to wine as he could get, and took my money and gave me change. I took my drink over to the corner and sat at the table and tried to watch the girls dancing. But I couldn't keep my eyes off the Doll's table. The guy she was with was a fairly slick looking number himself, with dark curly hair and a sports jacket and open-collar shirt that showed off a few curls on his chest, too. He had a matchstick stuck in one corner of his mouth and rolled it around with his teeth as he talked. Whatever it was he was talking about, he was looking serious enough about it. Maybe he was arguing price or something.

Mrs. Ball came swooping over to me. "I see you woke up finally. You want to talk to a girl?"

"I don't know," I said.

"See any you like?"

"I don't know." I was watching the Doll blow smoke up over the slicker's head into the ice storm. Mrs. Ball saw where I was looking and laughed. "You've got high hopes, kid. I'll give you that. But you better learn to swim before you try for the English Channel."

"Guess I'll wait a while," I said.

She gave me a wink. "Don't wait too long." And swooped away.

In a little, Delly came in from the front hallway steering the guy who was missing from the card game, the conservative-playing one. He looked like he had a few too many a couple hours back. Delly was grinning and the guy had a kind of grim smile of the kind an individual gets when he's trying to show he don't care his dog just got hit by a truck. "You the greatest, Honey," Delly was saying. "You the absolute greatest, no jive."

The guy tried to pull himself up straighter, but he was collapsing at the same time, like a stump that's just been dynamited. Delly braced herself and got under his weight. "Hold on, Honey," she said. "You danced me ragged already. Wait for a waltz." She maneuvered him over to the top of the steps and launched him down them. She watched him go, wincing and shaking her head. There was a clatter like somebody running a stick along a picket fence, and Delly covered up her mouth with her hand. But the guy must've survived and picked himself up, because she threw him a wave and turned away from the stairs. When she saw me, she came over to sit down with me.

"Do me a favor, Sugar," she said. "Finish zipping me. Dude couldn't get it."

So I zipped her up the back while she held her white hair up out of the way. She had on a fake leopardskin dress that hugged her like a sock.

"Why I always get dudes like that?" Delly said. "First gets too stoned to make it, then pays me extra to let on he the great lover. Buy me a drink, Sugar. What that you got?"

I told her. She made a face. "Just tell Ray the usual," she said.

So I got her a drink from the bar and paid for it and brought it over. She took a long swig from it. "What you grinning at, Sugar?"

"Bet I know what that is," I said. "It's tea. I heard about that."

She shook her head. "You heard dead wrong, Sugar. Taste."

She held the glass up for me and I took a sip. I was a little surprised. "Whisky?"

"Scotch and water," she said. "Heavy on water. Get me through the night." She was spreading her teeth out for me to see. "You cute, Sugar. You want to dance?"

"I don't know," I said.

"Me neither," she said. "Can't dance to this cowpie jazz. What do you want to do then?"

"I don't know," I told her. I was looking over to where the Doll was again. She was talking to the curly guy now, or over him anyway, like she's trying to pretend he's not there at all.

"Hey," Delly said, seeing me look. "Lay with the China Doll and you horny again in an hour."

"I wasn't thinking that," I said.

"What then?"

"She really Chinese? She almost looks Indian some time."

"Korean," Delly said. "But who gonna know different? They's always been a Doll here, I guess. Johns expects it."

"The funny thing," I said, "I keep thinking I smell Chinese food."

"That not too surprising, Sugar. They's a Chink eating place down below. Half the time Reggie feeds us the stuff."

"They got one in Rapid, too," I said. "I like their egg foo young."

"Egg roll's my favorite," Delly said.

"I would settle for an egg sandwich," I said.

"We got eggs in the kitchen," she said. "Come on." And she took ahold of my hand and pulled me up and led me to the kitchen.

"Quieter in here anyway," she said. She went to the frigerator and opened it. "I like just about all kind of music, but some I can't take much of."

"Honky tonk," I said.

"Honky is right, Sugar," she said. "I'd like to pull the plug on all their steel guitars some time."

Sticking her head into the frigerator like that she was putting a mighty strain on the fake leopard skin. "How many you think you can eat, Sugar?"

"How many is there?"

"Even dozen," she said. She handed the carton out of the frigerator and closed the door.

"I don't think I can stand more than half," I said.

She looked at me kind of suspicious. I think she had caught sight of the way I had been eyeing her leopardskin. "Some egg sandwich."

"Me and Albert, we'd fix them sometimes back in Rapid. They got radishes in the frigerator? They're good sliced up with mayonnaise on the eggs."

"You go on and fix the eggs, Sugar. I be getting the radishes."

So I found a frying pan and turned on the stove and put in a stick of butter and waited till it's bubbling and smoking and then start breaking the eggs into it and swizzling them around with a fork to mix them up good. For sandwiches like that you don't want too much of the whites showing. Then I slid the eggs on the bread, and then mayonnaise and radishes, then bread again, with the eggs leaking out all around the edge, there's so many of them. I fixed one sandwich for me and one for Delly and sat down at the table to try them. They were so tasty that we didn't say nothing, but just sat there chomping and humming to show how good it was.

"You a real chef of fried eggs," she told me after she gets her wind back.

And I have to admit I am pretty fair at that. But now the edge was off of my hunger, I started to feel those other appetites more sharp. Watching Delly polish off the last of her sandwich and licking off her lips, seemed to get all kinds of other juices to going. She got up and put the plates in the sink and I stood and got up behind her and wound my arms around her. She kind of snuggled her rear end into me like she was trying not too hard to get away. "Them eggs put lead in your pencil, Sugar?" She turned on the water and rinsed off the plates.

I can't explain the feeling that came over me then. The only thing I got to compare it to is the way sometimes you start to get drunk and you just start to pour down the liquor like you can't get enough. Anyway, I was over her like a rash, and she was braced against the sink, squealing when I grabbed her sometimes a little hard.

"Sorry," I said. But I didn't let up on her much.

"You cherry, Sugar?" she said, stealing my line.

But I was way past the pitch stage anyway. I was trying to peel that leopardskin off her, but all I succeeded in doing was to set loose her bosoms, as they are called, and of course I can't keep my hands off them, neither.

"Hey," she said. "They's a zipper. Ain't no call to rip the dress."

"Sorry," I said again. But as soon as I got a hand free to go for the zipper, it's like I came out of a trance or something. I started to see what a dumb thing I was doing and I backed off of her, kind of sitting down on the table.

Delly turned around and looked at me, pulling the dress up to cover her bosom again.

"I'm real sorry," I said. "I wasn't thinking."

"You in no state to do no thinking," she said. "Unless you planning to run a flag up that." She was looking in the direction of my crotch area, which caused me to turn away a little embarrassed.

"We didn't settle," I said.

"We didn't what?"

"Settle," I said. "On a price."

"Oh," she said. "What it worth to you right now?"

It smelled to me like there was a little frost in the wind, so I turned back to see her. She was smiling one of those hard smiles.

"I got thirty some on me," I said.

"You got thirty worth already, Sugar. You need thirty more to finish the job."

"I can get it," I said.

"You better, then," she said. She's tugging and patting herself back together. "I be up front waiting. Name's on the door." And she went to the door, almost running into the Angel. "You can pay Ray the sixty," she said to me, and went on out.

I'm trying to figure out what hit me. Seems like the cold wave came on fast.

The Angel came in and got hamburger out of the frigerator and made patties and started to fry them just going on with his business like I wasn't there.

"Somebody always wants a hamburger this time of night," he said.

"I fried up some eggs," I said.

"I see that," he said.

"Me and Delly," I said, "we were having a sandwich."

But he looked at me with those pumpkin eyes. "I think you just blew a freebie," he said.

"Free," I said. "I didn't know they did that."

"Delilah has been known to have that weakness," he said. "For someone she likes."

"I'm sorry," I said, telling the plain truth. There couldn't be a sorrier person in the world, especially for himself.

"The Doll," Death's Angel was saying, "she doesn't give away anything. She'll own the place someday."

I got my money and counted it. Thirty-one dollars and some change. "I guess I need again as much," I said. It was beginning to come to me what a stupid thing I did. It shows you what happens when a person stops to think.

13.

So back I went to the card room. Quick was shuffling the cards when I came in and he gave a little groan when he saw me. "That was fast," he said.

"I need another thirty," I said. I noticed that Quick's pile was pretty big now.

"The boy has found himself some high-priced something," the dentist said.

"Seismo charts must show a dome," the cowboy said. "Nothing left but to drill."

The Big Shot just gave me a look out of the side of his eyes in his usual suspicious way. He was low on cash, it looked like.

"Just when I'm on a lucky streak," Quick said. He counted out thirty dollars and handed it to me. "Don't come back for more," he said. "Inflation can't be that bad, even on cattail."

"Hope she comes in for you," the cowboy said as I took the money and turned around to go.

Last thing I heard before I went out was Quick ruffling the deck. "How's about some draw," he was saying.

I went back to the kitchen and gave Ray sixty dollars and he told me to go on up front. I went through the big room and I noticed the Doll looking at me go like she was trying not to be too interested. The curly-headed guy was still talking to her.

I found the door with "Delilah" printed on it real neat at the very end of the front hallway. I knocked and heard Delly's voice say it was open and I went in. I don't know what I was expecting, but it was just a bedroom. It had that same kind of creaky cane furniture as what the one me and Quick had. There were some colored posters on the wall, was all that was very different, and lots of stuff on the dresser, and a stereo outfit on one wall. Delly was lying kind of diagonal across the bed with nothing on but her pink panties and her white hair. "You pay the man?" she said.

"Sixty, just like you said," I nodded.

"Then you bought thirty more minutes worth," she said. And she swung her top leg and propped it with her knee sticking up.

"You be wanting to get down to business." She bit her lower lip with her upper teeth in a nasty kind of smile and jutted out her hips all of a sudden in a way that almost made me pass out. I stumbled toward her in a kind of fog.

"You want to close the door first," she said. She brought her legs together again, kind of coy.

So I backed up to the door and caught hold of the knob and closed it, still watching her.

"And take off some clothes," she said. So I went over by the dresser and pulled my shirt over my head and took off my jeans, which were hard getting over my shoes that I had forgotten to take off first. I turned away from the bed to undress, and as I was pulling off my shoes, I looked up and saw her grinning in the dresser mirror, and I saw how silly I looked to her. And I looked down at the stuff on the dresser, combs and brushes and a plastic foam head for the wig and things, and there was a picture of a family there, all of them black, that looked like a mother and a father and three kids, two girls and a younger boy. The old man, he had his sleeves rolled up like he just came from working somewhere, and the woman had on an apron. The girls both had pigtails and those kind of dresses that hang down straight from the bones. The boy had kind of a devilish smirk on his face, but both the girls were looking pretty mopey, their mouths hanging a little open, their heads down, and their eyes drilling straight at the camera like they hated it. I don't know what interested me so much about the picture, maybe just the surprise that it was there at all, but it just drew me into it. It was like I should know these people, but I know I didn't.

"I'm the one in the middle," I heard Delly say, and I looked up to her in the mirror and back down at the picture, and I could see the resemblance plain, except she was a lot younger in the picture. It gave me a funny feeling. I got to wondering if she had any notion when the picture was snapped how things were bound to work out for her.

"You gonna come over here, Sugar?" Delly said. "Or's this a long-distance call?"

I tripped over my clothes getting to the bed and she made room for me and I lay down beside her pretty clumsy. There seemed like there was no place to put my elbows.

"What happened to the flagpole?" Delly says.

"I don't know." I'm not sure what was wrong with me. Everything I looked at seemed so clear somehow, the wallpaper design, the little doily on the dresser, the coke bottle on the stand next to the bed, it was all clear and strange. I don't even know how to begin to explain it. It was like I had been picked up and plopped down in the middle of someone else's life, or like a real clear dream where everything fits perfectly except me.

"Happens sometimes," Delly said. "They's plenty of time to fix it. More'n enough." And she started in to playing me like a piano, but so far I couldn't hear the music.

Time went by. There was a slice of moonlight which I watched creep across the bedspread, crawling along over the threads. there was still nothing to run a flag up. It's like the damn thing was out to embarrass me completely, if not one way, then another. "What do you suppose is wrong?" I said finally. I was guessing I needed profession-al help.

"First thing you got to do, Sugar, is say hey to yourself."

"Say hey?"

"To yourself. Like, hey, man, what's happening?"

"That's what I'd like to know."

"Go on, Sugar. Say hey to your toes and work up."

"Hey, toes," I said.

"Say it like you mean it, Sugar."

"Hey, toes," I said, real sincere.

"Go on."

"Hey, feet. Hey, ankles. Hey, leg. Hey, knee. Hey, thigh. Hey, hips."

"Say, hey, flagpole."

"Hey, flagpole."

"Again."

"Hey, flagpole."

Delly shook her head.

"It don't answer."

"Maybe we just not calling it by the right name. Try some other."

"Hey, Peter. Hey, Harry. Hey, George. Hey Benedict. Hey, Curly. Hey, Larry. Hey, Moe. Hey, Eanie. Hey, Meanie. Hey, Mynie. Hey, Archibald."

"Hey what?" she said.

"I am running out of names," I explained.

She tried just about everything she could think of on it——flattery, insults, threats——and nothing seemed to work. I got me a dumb flagpole that forgot to set its alarm and was way late punching in. I understood a whole lot clearer now about how Quick must've felt with Meals on Wheels. "How much time left?" I said after a while.

"Ten is all," she said. She was looking pretty rattled herself. I suspect her professional pride was taking a beating from two flops right in a row. I don't know which I felt sorrier for, me or her.

"I think we better call in Aretha," she said.

Fine, I thought, that was all I need, two of them looking pitiful as nurses at my lowdown, two-timing, fruit-of-the-loom snake-in-the-grass. But this was not what she had in mind, so it seems. She first stood up beside the bed and took off her wig and took it over to the dresser and put it on the foam head. Her real hair underneath was short and in that kind of real tight curls. It looked to me like a kind of improvement, in fact. Then she went back to the stereo and put on this big set of earphones and punched buttons on the stereo set. Then she started in to dance. You got to understand her back was to me at first, so the view was special spectacular. I saw in movies the ocean rolling up on shore, and that was the closest thing I can think of to describe it. It started in her hips, shifting one side to the other, and the rest of her rear end picked up the motion. Then her spine started to sway the top part of her body. If you have ever seen a cottonwood bending under the wind of a prairie storm, you have got some idea. She was holding out her elbows and turning around real slow as she put her weight on one foot and then the other. Here's the thing—I still didn't hear the music she was dancing to, but I saw it. It was there in her body, not just the beat, but all the little inside beats and the peaks and valleys of the song. It seemed like to me that someone bright could invent a way of turning all her movements back into sound again. It's got to be one of the loveliest things I ever have seen.

She was holding another set of earphones to me. So I scootched over to the side of the bed and I clamped them on and the music was there like that, a band pounding somewhere right behind you, it seemed like, and this girl moaning in your ear. Delly held out her arms for me to get up and dance with her and I did. I am not much for that kind of dancing, never having done it too much, but it doesn't take a lot of learning. If you listened close, it seemed like you could hear those Indian drums in it, and even night-hawk cries, too. And all you have to do is let her body swarm in and take yours over and the dancing was as easy as falling.

In a while I felt her push away from my shoulders a little and I opened my eyes up and she was making words with her mouth I couldn't make out. I reached up and pulled one earphone out to listen.

She was grinning. "Hey, Flagpole," she was saying, like someone shouting over a wind.

And at the same time I heard someone hammering at the door. I looked over at it, not wanting to stop dancing.

"What's the matter?" Delly said. She reached up and lifted one of her earphones too. The door was hammered again. Delly pushed away from me, looking a little scared. "Who that?" she said. She was taking off her earphones altogether.

"Quick," a voice said through the door which I'd know anywhere and anyway could've guessed at. Who else would have such perfect bad timing? "I got to talk to Rodney," he said.

Delly looked over to me and I nodded and said, "Goodbye, flag-pole."

She let him in, kind of hunching herself behind the door and holding a little towel or something over the front of her.

The old fart came right on over to me. I was setting on the edge of the bed now, feeling kind of wilted. "Rodney, you better get dressed."

"What for?" I said. My voice was sounding pretty unfriendly, I noticed.

"You got to check out this car," he said, and he handed me a title slip. I took a fast look at it. It was for a Jeep wagon.

"Where'd you get this?"

"The Big Shot. He's down to his socks. It's got me worried. I think he's getting more suspicious than usual."

"I told you that C. T. Colton business wouldn't work." I don't know if I ever actually did or not, but I'd thought it pretty strong.

"Not just that," Quick said. He made his voice a shade quieter. "I been cheating a little."

What could you do about such an impossible individual? He was just like a flood or a blizzard or some other natural disaster. There was nothing to do but save your ass and try to pick up the pieces after-wards. "What do you want me to do?"

"Check out the car. He says its out in back in the alley. He's putting it up for one last showdown. Says its worth six thousand. That sounds high to me."

"Why don't you just bail out?"

"He'd kill me on the spot. He's figuring to get some of his money back."

"You took it all?"

"The others got a good deal of it, but it's me he hates."

It's not too hard for me to see how that could be. I started scrambling around getting my clothes on.

"I skimmed about five hundred," he said. "If I get in a jam I figure I can leave him what's left on the table and walk. But I'd rather ride. A Jeep would be perfect for a fishing car."

Do you see the way his head worked? The walls were shaking around him and he was thinking about fishing.

"I got to get back," he said. "Check out the car and get back to me in the card room." And he went on out. I don't think he even noticed Delly still behind the door.

I was dressed now except for my shoes. I sat down on the edge of the bed to pull them on. Delly came over and watched me. "You still got five minutes coming, Sugar."

"Save it for me," I said. I got up and gave her a little squeeze and started out.

I went back through the big room, which had thinned out a lot, and down the back hallway and out the door by the card room. There was a rickety wooden fire escape which I headed down. I found the Jeep pretty easy. I gave it a quick lookover. It was two years old but it was in good shape. Six thousand might be stretching it a little, but these four-wheelers get good trade-in. I started back to the stairs, and this flashing red light caught the corner of my eye as I walked by a side alley. I stopped and took a look and got sick real fast. What I saw was a cop car pulled up behind the orange VW where I had parked it, and two cops were looking over the car real careful. And with them was that slick-looking gentleman I saw with the Doll before, the curly one.

I high-tailed it back to the wooden steps and going up I met somebody wrapped up in a long coat coming down which it took me a little while to figure out was the Doll. She gave me a little poison-dart look and skipped on past me. It didn't take me long to figure we were in real trouble. When I got to the top of the steps I was panting as much from nerves as the climb. I busted into the card room and everybody looked up at me like I was some kind of a ghost that popped in. I jerked my head to Quick to come out in the hall and stepped back and waited for him.

"What's she worth?" he asked me when he got out there.

"Not shit," I said. "The cops are onto us." And I told him what I saw.

He took the title from me, which I had been carrying all this time and kneading into a rag. He didn't appear all that worried. Here was where Quick would fool you. I didn't know if he was exceptional brave or exceptional stupid, but he would not get too stirred up where the average person might yank on the flusher.

"What are we going to do?" I said, being a more excitable type myself.

"I'm going to play out the hand," he said, and turned and marched back into the card room. Me now, I just looked after him with the kind of drop-jaw feeling you might get watching a twister coming at you or a rattler about to strike. Then I stumbled in after him.

He was putting the title in the center of the table and pushing all his chips and bills in after it. "As advertised," he said to the Big Shot. "Call."

The Big Shot ran his cards over grinning like a coyote. "Four kings," he said, "and an ace for insurance."

Quick was shaking his head. It was hard to tell what it meant. The Big Shot started to pull in the pile, but Quick put his hand on the Big Shot's arm, still wagging his head. The Big Shot's eyes got their usual scared look back in them.

"For Christ sake," the Big Shot said, "you drew three cards."

"Straight flush in hearts," Quick said, flipping his cards, "jack high."

The scared look in the Big Shot's eyes turned into something uglier now. "What in hell were you drawing to?"

Quick just shrugged. "Guess I'm a natural optimist."

"And damn handy with the deal," said the Big Shot. "I thought I saw something funny."

"I didn't hear you laughing," said Quick. He tossed the title back to the Big Shot. "I think this needs to be signed."

The Big Shot just looked at the title, working his jaw like he was chewing on something tiny and tough. You could see his feelings working on him, those that told him he was being taken and those that kept him from doing anything about it. He might've kept on wrassling himself for an hour if Reggie hadn't stepped in just then. "Gentlemen," she said, "I just got a call from a friend at the sheriff's office. They are about to pay an unscheduled visit. You might want to break up this party."

"Shoot," said the oil-drilling cowboy, "just when it was getting interesting." He reached for his hat.

The dentist picked up his coat pretty calm too. "I think I know the way out," he said.

The Big Shot stood up, just about knocking over the chair he's been setting in. He looked like a cornered rat that you can't tell which way he will jump.

"Sign the title first," Quick said, pushing it at him.

So the Big Shot got out a pen and signed and tossed the title at Quick and scrambled to the door.

"Hold on," Quick said. "No hard feelings. There's an orange VW out front you can use." And he nodded to me and I dug out the keys and threw them over to the Big Shot, who looked at them like it was some kind of trick. "And I suppose we better have the keys to the Jeep," Quick said.

And the Big Shot got out some keys and put them on the table. Then he gave Quick one of his ugly looks and took off.

"You still a notary public, Reggie?" Quick asked.

She grinned and nodded. "I got my stamp behind the bar." And out she went.

I had had about all the calmness I could stand. "For shit sake," I said. "It's us they're after."

"I don't trust that character," Quick said. "I think he's some kind of lawyer. I want to make this perfectly legal."

I just about choked on that one. Here was an individual who had robbed and cheated and committed mayhem, and he was worried about getting a legal title to a car that wouldn't do us a spit-wad worth of good if we waited another minute.

"Go get the bag and the rod case, Rodney," he said. And there was nothing else to do, it seemed like.

Coming back with the stuff I met Reggie carrying a big nut cracker. We both went back into the card room. Quick had started himself a game of solitaire. "Ray is holding them off in front," she said. "They're just setting out back now." She signed the title and stamped it with the nut cracker.

Quick played a card. "Looks like there's no place to go but up," he said. He looked over his spread and shook his head. It's plain he was beat. He tossed down the cards and picked up a bunch of bills and handed them to her. "For your trouble," he said. "That's honest money. They just want us."

"There's an old stairway down to the restaurant," Reggie said.

Quick folded the title and stuffed it in his shirt pocket, then he grabbed the rod case out of my hand. "Lead the way."

We went down the hall a ways and she pointed to a door. "I think it's boarded from the other side. They use it for storage."

Quick waved her away and gathered himself up and pounded his shoulder into the door. He just bounced off. "Shit, I think I broke something."

"Not the door anyway," Reggie said.

"Rodney, you try," Quick said. But I couldn't budge it either. Then the Angel came down the hall. "They're coming in," he said, sort of matter-of-fact. "Wouldn't listen to reason."

"Ray," Reggie said, and pointed to the door.

The Angel sized up the door, then he leaned back against the wall of the hallway and put a foot against the door and pressed. You could hear the agony of wood and nails give way and the door flung open.

"I'm obliged," Quick said, and handed the Angel a bunch of bills. To Reggie he said, "There's always a next time."

And she said, "Look me up in California." And the last we heard of her was that big booming laugh as we headed through the door and down into the dark. There was a turn at a landing. Quick was ahead of me and went around it and stepped off. There was a racket like a ponderosa pine going down.

"Mr. Quick?" I said, feeling my way careful. "You all right?"

I heard a moan somewhere down below and that let me know he was at least alive. There were all kinds of things setting on the steps that I had to make my way around except for the path that Quick had cleared.

"Who was it?" I heard Quick say.

"It was you," I told him. "You must've tripped on something." I felt around and found a doorknob and turned it and the door went open and enough light came in to see that Quick was sitting at the bottom of the stairs on a busted-open sack of something white and was all-over white himself, and was holding on to his rod case like it was an egg he just saved from getting broke. He licked his lips. "Cornstarch," he said. "The cornstarch saved me."

I got him up and brushed him off a little and looked around to figure out where we were and I saw a Chinese gentleman standing in the doorway gawking. "What the hell?" the Chinese gentleman said.

"It's all right," I said. "He isn't hurt."

"Lot you know," Quick said. "I'm killed."

I looked at him and he did look like a ghost at that. I tried to get some more of the cornstarch off him.

"What the hell?" the Chinese gentleman said again. In his excitement he was repeating himself.

I pulled Quick past the Chinese guy. Now we were in a kitchen. I propped Quick by a counter and went to check the back door. I saw a cop car out there waiting. When I got back to him, Quick was chewing on an egg roll.

"We better try the front," I said.

"We better get a dozen of these to go," Quick said, and licked his fingers.

"What the hell?" It was the Chinese individual again. It sounded like he was completely stuck now.

Quick pulled out some bills and put them on the counter. "For your trouble," he said, "and a pint of chow mein."

I jerked him up and through a swinging door that went into the front. All the customers seemed to be up around the front door, checking the commotion in the street.

"Let me through," I said. "I've got a sick man here."

They cleared a way for me. "I think it was the shrimp," I said. And Quick's pale complexion and uncertain step looked pretty convincing.

"The shrimp," someone said. And I think I heard someone start to gag.

We had broke through to the street by then, and like I figured, the cops were paying no particular attention to the restaurant, so I just led Quick out and took a fast turn and down the street as natural as possible under the circumstances. One thing that helped was that there was quite a crowd around the VW, and peeking through I saw the cops there talking to the Big Shot, who had reached some kind of record in looking uncomfortable and was talking fast enough to sell a popsicle to a penguin. We took another corner and got to the Jeep. I unlocked it and pushed Quick in and tossed the flight bag in back and got in the other side and took off. The Jeep had considerable more power than the VW and I laid down a little rubber and threw our weight into the cushions getting started. Through the whole thing Quick had somehow managed to hang on to his rod case. Now as we pulled out it was like he came awake all of a sudden and waved the rod case around so I had to hold up my arm to keep him from hitting me. "I told you," he said. "I told you it would be a hell of a fishing car."

14.

"It's pretty clear," Quick said after I gave him the details of what I saw. "It was the Doll tipped the cops to us. Her sweepstake's come in." He was a good deal more clear-headed now. "Hang a right."

"I wonder if Delly's still waiting for me to come back," I said. I gave him a little sideways look after I made the turn, wondering if he felt at all sorry for busting in on us.

He shook his head, looking a little disgusted. "Man that can't get laid in a whorehouse," he said, and let it trail off. And there's my answer. I don't think it's in him to feel sorry for a thing he ever did.

"The Big Shot did, though," he said.

"Did what?"

"Get screwed." And he gave one of his evil cackles.

The moonlight was pretty bright, which made it easier to crank around those mountain roads. Nobody followed us, but I was naturally a little worried. "Where we heading now?" I said. It's pretty obvious we were going generally west. "How about San Francisco?"

"Place I know," Quick said. "Not far from here. Hold on. Look there."

I pulled over and stopped. Quick pointed through the trees to a mountain that stood out in the moonlight. It had been sheared of trees in strips up its sides and was strung with cables and towers like a banjo. "Ski lift," he said. "What do you think of that?"

Later on, of course, it would look a whole lot uglier to me for what happened there, but right then it was more of a puzzlement. "Why do they want to do such a thing for?" I said.

"Pleasure, I guess. Maybe just to get the best of something. There's a certain kind of person looks at a mountain and asks himself what he can make out of it, and isn't satisfied until he's cut it down to his size. Only revenge the mountain's got is to outlast him, like some kind of disease that will run its course. Wait till he's stringing Z's with the dinosaurs. Go ahead on."

I kept following his directions. We got into this kind of junky looking place he said was an old mining camp, then back along a railroad grade a ways, then further still to a place where there was a spring in a pasture and an old skeleton of a house leaning, about ready to fall over. We stopped there and took a kind of inventory. There was some camping stuff in the Jeep, and Quick was happy to find a fishing net in the back. Where money is concerned, we didn't have a whole lot more than we started with, Quick gave away so much to everyone for their trouble.

"This is not too bad a place to camp, anyway," I said.

But Quick said no. We had to pick up some groceries for one thing, and for another, this was where he was raised, right in this house.

"My daddy worked for the Annie Creek mine," he said. "My mama and me took care of the place. I can't stop here long. All I can see is ghosts."

So we drove on, back to a paved road finally, past a little crossroad store where Quick said we could get groceries next day, and up another little gravel road until he told me to pull over and stop. The moon was down behind the mountains now, so I couldn't see too good where we were, but we pulled out the sleeping bags and put them in the rear end of the Jeep with the hatch down and sacked out with our heads sticking out the rear end where we could see the stars glowing steady as a stare up above.

Quick was sawing away pretty fast, but it took me a while, I guess because of all the excitement in Deadwood. But now I had pretty much bought the idea that I was in for trouble long as I stuck with the old fart, but what else was there? Sometimes you get that kind of sick and hopeless feeling in your belly, like all this is what you're in for, no matter how hard you try to get out of it, so why try? I don't remember going to sleep, but I woke up with the sun in my eyes. Quick was still snoring, so I sat up and looked around, and I felt pretty good. That sleep had been just like some kind of a pill for me, and the view I got from the back of the Jeep was another dose of good medicine.

Where we were camped was just about the loveliest valley I had ever seen, with a string of beaver dams stepping along down from above and the ponds they made sorted out along the creek the way beads were strung on a necklace, small to large. One side of the valley, where the road runs along, was mostly ponderosa pine and spruce, but the other side, where the hills sloped down to the ponds, was striped with those pale aspen trunks, their little fluttery leaves kind of floating amongst them and above them like some kind of pale green smoke. The beavers must just relish those aspen, so many of them had been chomped down and their stumps left sticking up along the fringe of the trees like a pole fence with sharpened points.

The ground was so boggy and rich that the grass pushed up thick and with a dark cast that was hard to believe when you are used to seeing mostly scrawny brown stuff. If you looked close in the grass you could see purple and pink and yellow and white and blue and almost every color flower you could name, like a rainbow maybe broke up into a million pieces and floated down like colored snowflakes and got caught there. I wished I knew half of the names of them.

The ponds picked up the sky color when you saw them from a distance, but closer up you could see that the water was almost as clear as the air. And when you knew what to look for, you could see the trout down there as plain as anything, waiting still as stones or letting the water waver them like a tail of moss or lazing along feeding or darting and zigging if they caught sight of a person or if they spot a shadow moving against the flow.

Mr. Quick spent most of his day fishing, starting out at the big pond and working his way up to the smallest one. He was peculiar about that. A person would think he would work down to the biggest pool, but I never saw him ever do that. I figure it was a habit he couldn't break, making his way upstream like that. And he was hooking fish pretty regular after a while. Once he got enough for eating for the day, he would just keep on fishing and put them back careful and a darn sight wiser.

He let me fish with his rod sometimes and that little stick was so light and springy that I got the knack of whipping the line pretty easy. Catching trout was another thing, though. I figured they had to be about the finickiest creatures in the world, the way they would nose around a fly that you drop in front of them. They kind of sniff and back off, sniff and back off. And what got me was when Quick showed them the very same fly they would gobble it down like that. What was I doing different I would like to know. Even Quick couldn't tell me. Or wouldn't. I suspected he would just as soon I didn't know, to tell the truth.

I lost count of the days we spent in that place. I may be wrong, but it looked to me like that could maybe be the way a person was meant to live, as you get up in the morning with the day stretching out in front of you and nothing particular to do. I know there's some that would say they were bored with such a situation, but it just seemed awful free and easy to me.

There's a whole lot a person can do around a camp in the way of keeping it picked up and handy, and wood to chop from the bug trees up on the slopes and meals to get and all like that, but there's nothing says you have to do anything you don't want to, or no clocks to punch into like at the home, or no one to say you're doing it wrong. Quick and me, we just split up the chores without hardly saying a word and it all run pretty smooth.

But two or three times a day, along would come a car of some kind and I would dive for the nearest thing to hide me. The funny thing was, you never saw a car coming down the road. You wondered a little bit where all those cars were going. We got to noticing the plates on the cars after a while and they were from all over, but mostly California. Pretty soon Quick could hardly stand it. When a car went by, he would stop fishing and said, "Dammit, we ought to follow that one and find out what the big attraction is." But he never did. I don't think there was hardly a thing that could get him away from fishing very long when the fever had him.

One day he yelled at me to come. He was at the topmost pool, kind of dancing along the edge and pointing into the water with his rod. So I left the fire I was building and went to see what was the fuss. "Look at this," he was yelling. "I don't believe this. It is a wonder of nature."

"What?" I said. I was a little out of breath from running up to the pool so fast. I was thinking he had lost something in the water.

"That fish," he yelled. "Look at the size of him."

To be honest, I was just a tiny bit disappointed. Another fish, I was thinking. But then I saw him. It was a little shocking because I saw him first head-on and he looked to be about as big around as a woman's thigh. Then as he let the flow of the water swing him around, I got some idea of his length and from the side he looked skinnier, but long as a person's arm. His head was a lot bigger than it should be for the size of his body.

"He's a monster," Quick yells. "Where the hell has he been hiding all this time?"

It was easy to guess he might've been there all the time, actually. Because it catches the first strong rush of water down from the creek, this pool was really deeper than any of the others, and the flow had cast up a ridge of silt that had curled over the way a snowdrift will in a high wind, making a pocket where the fish could hide easy.

Quick cast over the fish a few times, but it didn't pay any particular attention.

"I don't think he's hungry," I said.

"He's probably used to something else. Something bigger."

And as we watched, the fish just settled down with his own weight and sunk into the deep shadows of the pool so you might not even believe you had seen what you did, like it was some kind of ghost. In fact, that was already what was shaping up in my brain as a name for it. Ghost Fish.

After that Quick changed his style some, still starting out every morning at the low pool and working up, but moving a whole lot faster than before so he was at the little top pool a good while before the sun was high, and he spent most of his effort there trying to roust out that big ghost fish. Some days he would not even see it. And then again it would rise up just like it wanted to keep the old fart on the hook, just to show itself, and drifted down again what seemed so slow, but you just blinked and you couldn't make him out no longer.

"He knows I'm after him," Quick said once after the fish had disappeared again.

Quick was of course of the belief that fish are a whole lot smarter than any person outside of a fisherman was willing to give them credit for. But what I saw of this spooky trout, it did seem to be more calculating than the average. The way I saw it, there's got be some reason he got to be that old and big. Things are so rough in this life, a person has to respect anything that made it that far.

"He's past his prime," Quick said. He was looking down into that deep hole in the pool the way a man looks into a fire sometimes, like what he's seeing is the shapes of his own ideas. "He's way past his prime. He probably fought his way up here at flood to spawn one last time, got stranded when the water went down. He is just — "
But about there he got stuck entirely in his ideas.

"Just what?" I asked him.

"Waiting," he said.

Then I heard somebody coming up the road and I ducked down in the weeds that grew up beside the pond. Quick heard it too and stood up again and started tossing out his line into the water. "If it's another one of those California cars, I'm going to get into that Jeep — "

Hearing him stop like that, I got curious. "What's the matter?"

"Get down there," he said. "I think they're stopping." And he went on fishing without missing a stroke.

So I snuggled down deeper in the grass and I heard now that it was not a car at all, but I was pretty sure two or three motorcycles. "It's that bunch we saw back in Deadwood," Quick said. "Shit." And I heard a splash and a roar of the cycle engines. "They forded the stream," Quick said. "I think they're planning to stake a claim. Might as well get up. I doubt they give too much of a crap who we are."

So I stood up as accidental as possible like it was the most normal thing in the world to be laying low in the grass like that. I took a look over to the other side of the creek. They had shut off their bikes by then, so you could hear yourself think again, and they were sure enough the same ones we saw going into the saloon, the two men and the skull-girl. They didn't pay too much attention to us, but just went about their business, setting up a camp. About the first thing they broke out was a portable radio, which they turned on as loud as possible with that kind of buzzing music thumping and squalling away. I don't know too much about it, but it wasn't like that that Delly played, though there was some of it in there. It was more like something you would use to drown out a noise you didn't want to hear.

"There's your electricity," Quick said, disgusted. But he was still going through the motions of fishing.

The motorcycle individuals set up a tent out of a pack on the back of one of the bikes. They had a time setting it up, the one without a bandanna, who was the stocky one, yelling what to do to the other one and making a pretty clumsy job of it, it seemed like. The skinny girl, she was unpacking other stuff. It was hard to believe the two bikes could hold as much stuff as they had.

"Maybe we should just leave," I said.

But Quick's eyes got to looking even more steely blue than usual and he set his jaw like somebody reining in a horse. "Maybe they could just leave," he said. "It's our camp."

"Looks like they are planning to stay a while," I said.

"We'll see," Quick said. I had heard that gravel in his voice before, and so far it had meant nothing but more trouble for us. I figured there was nothing to do but hold on for the ride.

15.

Quick kept fishing, but he wasn't catching much. He was keeping his eye on the bunch over on the other side of the pond. For their part, the motorcycle individuals put on quite a show. I never had nothing against motorcycle riders before, but there was something in the way this bunch acted that made me a little sick. The noise was one thing. They were yelling all the time at each other, except the girl who was pretty quiet, even when there was no cause to yell, and they had that radio going all the time full steam. It crossed my mind once or twice, maybe riding like that without helmets, the wind sloshing past their ears, might have hurt their hearing, but that is just my theory.

And then they got to acting like we were the ones busted in on them. They saw us watching sometimes and gave us a stare that made my eyes water all the way across the pond, but of course it didn't faze Quick much. One time I saw the bandanna one give Quick the finger in no unmistakable way, leaning back and shoving it up in the air like maybe he was driving a knife into somebody's chest. But Quick went on fishing like it wasn't more than a gnat buzzing around him. And pretty soon the bandanna one got to throwing rocks in the water. He was pretty cool about it at first, like it was for recreation, then he edged closer to where Quick was fishing and before long there was no doubt what he was up to. Quick just hauled in his line and moved upstream a ways.

Watching them carry on like that, I was a little bit reminded of when I was a kid and a bunch of individuals gathered on the brush land just outside the trailer park one summer and just set up camp like they had the right to be there. They lived in tipis, was what was funny to Lymon and me, though they were white. About the only tipis we'd seen up to then had been that flimsy kind you see at tourist places. It hadn't come to us anyone might want to actual live in them. Then these individuals were all the time going around giving that two-finger peace sign, so that us kids got to doing the same when we saw them just to see if they would do it back, and if they did, we would get a big kick out of it. They decorated their tipis with that sign for peace, too, the one in a circle that always reminded me of a rocketship about to take off, and upside-down flags and flowers. But the thing that really got us was the women liked to go around with next to nothing on, especially where their bosoms were concerned. Lymon and me would sneak down to their camp all hours just to get a glimpse of them which were the first bare ones I ever seen, I believe. I don't know but what the sight of them brought on some of my first bad attacks of horniness. And I can see them pretty clear even yet.

Come the first signs of cool weather, the tipis were gone, along with the painted up school buses and peace signs and bare bosoms. I remember Lymon and me poking around the camp after the tipi bunch left, trying to find something useful in all the garbage they left behind, but not finding too much. Lymon said something about them being like the snow geese that pass the reservation, sometimes even light for a while, but didn't want to spend the winter there.

That's what was in my head then, thinking we could outlast this motorcycle crew. I guess that could be the big flaw in my thinking from the start.

Before long the two men got on their bikes and went farting off through the aspen, getting a big kick out of scrambling up the slopes and posting over bumps and all that. I guess it was their idea of sport, though to me it brought to mind what Quick said about the ski-lift and some kind of people who just have to get the better of things. Anyway, they disappeared among the aspens, though they could still be heard, and I relaxed a little. It came to me that I had been watching them like some kind of a play, or one of those movies in high school where you have a quiz on it afterwards. The girl had gone into the tent and the stage, so to speak, was empty. I didn't see Quick anywhere either, but I figured he must be trying the stream above the pools, which he does sometimes for variety.

So I figured it was a good time to clean the fish Quick had caught for supper. It's one thing I'd just as soon do myself as watch Quick's attempts at it, even if he showed me how in the first place. The way he slashed around so careless I was half afraid he might cut off his own finger sometime. I got the bag of trout and the cleaning knife, the one with the heavy weight on the end for zapping them dead, which Quick calls a priest, and I went down to the stream and kneeled down and started in to cleaning them. Trout aren't nearly as hard to clean as catfish or even bluegills, and you end up with a whole lot more to eat. There is even something kind of relaxing and satisfying in it, the moves all so pat as they are. I took off their heads first, then slit their bellies and cleaned out their guts good and held them in the clear water to rinse them off good and laid them on the grass in a row. Most often we'd throw the remains across the stream to where the weasels or ferrets could clean them up, but I guess now we'd have to just bury them. In a way I like the idea of them going to the animals myself because of nothing really going to waste then. So I was cleaning the trout and wrapped up in it pretty much, when I heard this real close: "Really? I thought you were praying." And I looked up and there was the skull-girl knee-deep in the water in front of me, which I didn't even hear her wade in or catch any movement out of a corner of my eyes beforehand, and I felt like my skin was crawling right off of me.

"Or panning gold," she said.

I made some kind of sound, maybe like "Huh," and leaned back on my heels with the knife in one hand and a dead fish in the other, its guts dripping out.

"You do the dirty work," the girl said, and grinned. I wish I could explain what that grin was like, in combination with the sunk-in cheeks and eyes so set back in the shadows they seemed to be staring out of caves. It was like she was showing me how foolish I looked. But at the same time she was seeing the way I was looking at her, and she was making fun of that, too, the mixture of feeling sorry for her and feeling afraid at the same time. "He catches them, you cut them, right?"

"I caught a few too," I said. See, right away she had me defending myself, like there was something wrong with cleaning fish.

She had just waded into the water with her jeans on and was standing there, leaning a little against the flow. I didn't see how she could stand it myself, the water was so cold, probably just melted from the snow upstream. She didn't seem to pay any attention to that, though. It's me she had her eyes on. "He your grandfather or something?"

"No," I said. I tried to go back to cleaning the fish, but I had lost the rhythm of it now and kind of fumbled around.

"Just a friend, huh?" she said.

"Right."

"I get it," she said, and I looked at her and she was grinning again, so I couldn't keep my eyes on her face. I let them slide down to more my eye-level, kneeling there like I was. There was a gap between her gray-blue blouse and her jean top was showing a kind of whitish gray skin, her belly all sucked in.

"You want some of these?" I said, waving the knife at the fish. "We got more than enough."

"I'm on a diet," she said. And at first I thought she was making fun again, but when I looked I saw her face was earnest for once. It came to me for the first time she might be a little bit crazy. She hooked her thumbs into the waistband of her jeans and they rode down a little on her bony hips. They were just as tight as when I had first seen them in Deadwood, with the fold cutting so into her crotch there wasn't too much left to imagination. I guess she saw me looking there, because she said, "Want to fuck?"

I never quite had it put to me that way before, and it took me back some. It sounded to me like one of those trick questions in exams in high school or on driver's license tests. The first thing you got to do is figure out what it really means. "I don't know," I said in order to buy some time to think.

Maybe she saw how it threw me, because now she put it to me a little softer. "It's the same position, praying or screwing. We can go over in the tent." But it still came to the same question. Did I want to or didn't I?

There was no use consulting the flagpole on this one. I had already felt it twitching, which I took for affirmative on its part. But it was well-proven by this time that it didn't have the sense of a pup. This was one I was going to have to settle on my own.

She gave her jeans another tug, like a horse rider giving a little flip on the reins. "Or topsy-turvy," she said, "if you'd rather."

She was like the salesmen in stores that started in giving you choices between two brands of something before you've made up your mind to buy anything. If I didn't watch out, she'd start lining out the entire menu. I saw I had to come to a decision fast, and about that time I saw that the answer to the basic question was not a yes or no proposition. It was both. Yes in general and no in particular. So I took a breath and said, "I don't think so."

She gave me that deadly grin another time, "I get it," she said. "The old guy, huh?"

It took me a while to see what she was getting at, but then I kind of choked up because I didn't know how to tell her I was not queer but I would just as soon not have sex with a half-dead person, either, thanks a lot anyway.

Meantime she had come to her own conclusion. "That's cool too," she said. "Come over anyway. Junior will dig it. We can all get it on." And she started in to wading over to me slow.

"Hold on," I said, and without realizing it completely I stuck the knife out in front of me. I didn't mean it the way it must've looked, but she stopped anyway and took in the knife and my face and her grin got a little weak. "Unless you've got strong feelings about it," she said.

"I just don't want to," I said. "That's all." Meaning that's all I was willing to own up to. I didn't see why I had to explain everything I was thinking, even if I could.

But she started at me again, making her grin some kind of shield. "It's cold in here," she said. "I've got to get out." And she aimed her belly right at my knife so I had to pull it away before she gutted herself on it.

"There's plenty of room on the other side." Quick's voice came from behind me. I half-turned and saw him shouldering out from behind a clump of willows. "Kid says he don't want to play today. That should be a good enough answer for you."

The girl pulled herself up and let the grin melt away. "You his lord and master?"

"You better ask him that," he said.

She looked at me.

"We're partners," I said. For the time being I forgot about all that side-kick business he'd been handing me.

She got her grin back, like she was hearing an entirely different answer. Then she turned and waded back across the water to the other side.

"Sweetheart you got there," Quick said after she went into the tent.

I caught myself shivering like I was the one been wading in the ice water. "How much did you hear of that?" I said.

"Enough to get the general drift," Quick said.

"You could've stepped in earlier," I said.

He shrugged. "For all I know you might want to take her up on it, being so deprived as you have been."

"I don't think I'll ever get that deprived," I said.

"Lucky thing you didn't anyway," Quick said. "Here come her boyfriends back."

And I looked over and saw them come roaring out of the aspens and got to wondering what would've happened if they had found me in the tent with the skull-girl. Killing me would probably been easiest on me. I couldn't help trying to guess which one was Junior. I bet on the bandanna one. I started in shivering again, and I realized it's only partly that the sun was down and the cool night wind was flowing down the valley with the creek.

"You done with those, I'll cook them," Quick said.

I put the fish in the bag and handed them to him.

Across the creek they had got the radio blaring full throttle again.

"Looks like we're in for a night," Quick said.

16.

While we ate supper, we watched the goings-on over on the other side. It must've come to them all of a sudden that a fire would be needed, because the two men went clomping off up the hill and came back pretty soon dragging almost the whole trunk of one of those ponderosas the bugs have got at, pulling at it and cussing it as it caught in the brush or got hung up in the weeds.

"I think they are planning to roast a whole cow with that," Quick said. He was a great one for little fires, anyway. "Bigger the fire, bigger the fool," he liked to say. He made tiny tidy ones for cooking, letting them burn down to the coals before setting a pan on them.

The motorcycle guys didn't have a saw or axe or anything either, which didn't help them too much. They tried setting fire to the bark first, but of course it just went out. Then one got out a can of that charcoal starter, which Mr. Quick said is nothing more nor less than kerosene, and soaked an end of the log with it, and it flamed up pretty good for a while and went out. Finally they got the idea of using kindling, banking the small sticks up against the side of the log, and they got something to going at last.

"It's like watching cavemen," Quick said. "They got to work everything out from scratch."

Once they got the fire going, they were like a couple of kids that just learned to whistle, puffing up and yelling at each other again and looking over at us pretty smug, which they didn't dare to do when they were having such trouble, and altogether acting like they had just discovered fire. They set the skull-girl to cooking supper, which looked like it came out of a can, whatever it was, and out of the stream they pulled an onion bag full of canned beer and commenced drinking it up. It was completely dark by this time, and Quick and me had had enough of watching this silliness, so we got into the sleeping bags in back of the Jeep and tried to get some sleep.

"They are something," I said, listening to them yelling and watching the reflection of their fire glitter in the trees.

"Clowns," Quick said.

"Why do you think they act like that?" I said.

"I think they are trying to prove something."

"What are they proving?"

"They don't know, probably. I've seen punks like that before, though, a great many in my time, and they are the ones you have to watch out for. Those that know what they're after, them you can count on to behave a certain way. This kind, though, you never know what they will do."

One of them, I don't know if it was Junior or the other one, had this laugh that sounded like he had worked on a while to tune it so low and evil-sounding, and he cranked it out just then. It gave me another fit of chills. I pulled the bag up around me and zipped it high as it would go.

"Wild Bill," Quick was saying, "he had his hands full with that kind all his life, from the McCanles gang on up. And it was one of them did it for him at last, that Jack McCall, what now they call a crazy mixed-up kid. That and a little bit of carelessness." He gave a big yawn.

I got thinking maybe it's not such a good idea to close our eyes on this bunch. "Mr. Quick," I said.

He didn't answer.

"Mr. Quick?"

"What?" he said, yawning another time.

"You got your gun handy, don't you?"

"Thought you didn't like guns."

"I don't," I said. "I just want to know where it's at."

He yawned again. "In the flight bag."

I got up on an elbow and spotted the bag down at our feet. "Is it loaded?" I said.

He didn't answer.

"Mr. Quick?"

But all I got for an answer this time was his snore, and I knew it was no good trying to rouse him once he got his chain-saw going. I laid back down and tried to remember what I did with the fish-cleaning knife, wishing I had it there in the sleeping bag with me. I didn't know whether it was the flickering orange reflections of the fire on the pine needles or the sound of the clucking laugh that got me worse. The radio was sill churning out that terrible twining music, too, of course, which didn't help. And when I tried to close my eyes, I heard the water in the stream and I got to thinking it was the skull-girl or Junior wading across, and my lids flew open again. For a while it sounded like the men were arguing about something, but I couldn't make out what they were saying. Once or twice I heard the girl's little voice chiming in, but the men seemed to be doing most of the talking. Somewhere along there I must've slept, because I dreamed I was running and the skull-girl was on my back, riding me like a horse, and there was a big mob of people after us, C.T. Colton and the Big Shot and the red-faced guy from the liquor store, on and on. And I came awake fast like you do with an alarm clock sometimes, not knowing what woke me up, and I saw the firelight on the trees lower now, and hardly a sound but the chuckling of the water, and then the low wicked laugh again, and then just the water sounding like a crowd of voices. Next thing I knew the sun was bright on me and the birds were cheeping away like crazy and Quick was gone. I got out of the bag and looked across the pool and the motorcycles and the tent were nowhere to be seen, nor anything else to show they were there except beer cans scattered around, a wisp of blue-white smoke twining up from what was left of the pine log.

"They were gone when I got up." It was Quick, crouched down beside the morning cook fire boiling his coffee. "Must've took off before the sun rose."

So me, for one, I was pretty relieved, thinking we got off easy after all, so little did I know. Quick went back to his fishing, I went back to the little chores and lazing around the camp. In the afternoon after a sandwich for lunch, I took a nap and slept good, with no dreams. And after that I spent a good deal of time watching a water ouzel feeding, dipping along under water just like it was on dry land. Then the time of day came when I got to thinking about supper, and I knew I've got to get firewood, and I thought it wouldn't hurt to use what was left of that pine log the motorcycle bunch left. So I went downstream a ways where I knew a place to step over the rocks to the other side, and went over to poke around their camp, and that was when I found her.

She was lying not too far from the log, in the grass tall enough to hide her from the other side. Her clothes were off and she had been struck many times, with a knife, it looked like, although there was no knife around that I could see. Not that I looked too close. Once I saw what it was, I got feeling sick fast, and I tried to get away from there, but stumbled down to my knees, and the first thing I knew I was throwing up. Then I felt a little better and went back to look again, and started to gag, but held on better this time. I'd seen dead people at the Hillview Home before, and had to move them and sneak them out before the other ones caught on, but then you always half expected it, they were so old and on their last legs, not young like this and not killed this way.

But the peculiar thing about her was she was looking almost satisfied, her face relaxed out of that awful grin and looking fuller than before, her cheeks and eyes not so sunk in, though her lids were open a crack and she was looking out like someone half-asleep trying to stare down the sun.

I went to find Quick then and caught up with him at the little pool at the top of the valley.

"I saw him again," he said when I came up, meaning the Ghost Fish. "Can't interest him though. You want to try for a while?" Then he looked at me better and must of seen something wrong about me. "What's happened?" he said. "You cut yourself?"

So I told him what I had found.

He sat down on a rock and let his rod trail in the water. "I knew it was too lucky to be true," he said.

"What do we do now?" It was the question that had been on my tongue ever since I found the girl.

"One thing we can't do is call the sheriff," Quick said. "We're in deep enough there now. And I guess we can't stay here, either. They drove us off after all." He looked at me again and must've noticed me shivering, because he held out the handle of the rod to me. "Cast a while," he said. "It'll calm you down."

So I took it and gave it a few whips and it did seem to settle me a little. "It feels different," I said.

"It's a weighted streamer," Quick said. "Just give it more time on the backcast."

I concentrated on that for a while to get the feel of it, the rhythm. It seemed to help me, doing something halfway familiar.

"We better hide her better," Quick said. "Give us time to get in some distance before someone finds her. Some camouflage wouldn't hurt for us, neither."

"You mean like bow-hunters' outfits?" I said.

"Like that brook trout," Quick said. He was pointing into the water. "There's one over by that snag, see it?"

I cast over to the fish he pointed at, which looked pretty good sized.

"Even with the water as clear as it is, it's hard to spot them sometimes, they fit in so well. The two of us, we're pretty noticeable. No protective coloring."

"Maybe we should after all split up." I kept busy looking down at the line where I was sneaking it in.

"A deal's a deal," Quick said, like he always did. But I had a long time ago forgotten which one of us that made obliged to the other. "What we really need is some place we fit in better," he said. But I think he was just as puzzled as me where that might be.

I was pulling the streamer past the trout that Quick pointed out and the fish started to follow.

"You've got him interested," Quick said. "Give it a little more speed. If he thinks it's going to get away, he may grab it."

So I speeded up pulling in the line, and for a second the trout darted toward it and looked like he was going to take it, but then all of a sudden he ran away, just shooting off.

"Something spooked him," Quick said.

"What did I do?"

"It could be anything, shadow of the leader or the streamer didn't look quite right."

On top of it, the line had stopped coming in. It felt like it was stuck on something at the bottom. "I think I got a snag," I said. I'd had them often enough before.

"Just give it a couple jerks," Quick said.

So I jerked the rod, but the line seemed like it was stuck tight.

"Go ahead and break it," Quick said. "I've got lots more streamers."

So I gave it a good hard pull, and something seemed to give a little, like maybe I'd hooked into a heavy log or something.

"Oh no," Quick said.

And then the rod seemed to quiver in my hand like it was caught by one of those stiff breezes you got up here, except there wasn't a wind. It had me puzzled.

"Oh no," Quick said again.

And then the line started pulling out against my pull and I could feel there was something live on it.

"It's him," Quick said. "Give him some slack."

And so I let the line slip out a ways and in the meantime it came to me that I had hooked a fish.

"It's him," Quick said again. "You've got him solid."

And for a space there I was so shocked I could hardly move. I felt like my whole body had been shot with one of those shots a dentist gives you. It was one thing to hook a fish, but hooking this Ghost Fish was a different proposition entirely. To be honest, I was scared to death.

"Keep it taut," Quick yelled. "He wants to get a run at it so he can snap it off."

So I tightened up the line and the rod buzzed again as he tried to shake off what'd got him. "Maybe you better take over," I said.

"It's your fish," Quick said.

"Where'd he come from?" It had me so upset that I didn't see him coming.

"He must have been laying there in the shadow. That's what scared the other one away. And maybe that's why he went for the streamer. He thought the other one was going to get it first. Watch it."

The trout had made a fast dash off to the right, slicing the line through the water.

"Keep your rod high," Quick yelled. "Let it do the work. Keep him away from those snags."

You could see the wicked branches underwater where they were stuck by the beaver a long time ago and now all coated with fuzzy brown moss. I tipped the rod away and the pressure kept the fish from getting into the sticks.

"Don't let him jump."

And just after he said that was the first time the fish jumped. It seemed to me like he was coming up to see what kind of fool he had on the other end of the line.

"Oh no," Quick said again when he saw the Ghost Fish out of the water.

If you could frame one thing in the world you've ever seen and hang it on the wall to stare at the rest of your days, that jump would be the thing I'd choose. It could be the most lovely thing in creation the way he came driving up, the water rolling off of him like diamonds, like he wanted to keep right on going into the sky. His colors were just beautiful, silver blue fading into pink and then white on the belly. And then he shook his body and it was like a willow bending in the wind as he hung there, twisting his big head like he was trying to see everything. And then crashed down with the sound a beaver makes when it's mad.

"Keep the tension," Quick yelled. "Don't let him fall on the leader."

He jumped three more times and each time higher and more powerful than before.

Then the fish went down.

"He's tired of the fancy stuff," Quick said. "He's gonna try to overpower you."

The line was stretching down at a steep pitch now and the tip of the rod was bending almost into a loop as the fish pulled with a steady rhythm—pull, let up, pull, let up, pull. I was loosing quite a bit of line to him.

"Turn him around," Quick told me. "He's the one with the hook in his mouth. Make him feel it when he lets up."

So next time he pulled I waited until the surge was almost done and I started leaning back with the rod. And that must've broke him. The line cut a half circle in the water and the steady rhythm of pulls stopped.

Quick said, "You've got him backing away now, and that's harder on him. Now you've just got to be careful you don't pull the hook out."

So I brought the line in real slow and careful and there were a lot more little runs off to the side but I was gaining line steady.

"He's worn down," Quick said. "He's saving everything he's got left. If he's got anything left."

And before long the fish was close enough to see real clear. I suppose it was wrong to think that fish and things like that got feelings like a person, but it did seem to me that that particular trout might be thinking that he made a dumb fool mistake and now he had to pay the consequence.

"How am I going to get him?" I asked. Every other fish I have caught was so little I could just heft him up on the bank with the leader.

"Use the net," Quick said. He had the net fastened on his vest and was fumbling with it.

"You net him," I said.

"He's your fish," Quick said, and he had the net unsnapped and was handing it to me.

So I took it and now I had the rod and the net both to deal with and I was feeling fairly unhandy about it.

"Get your net down in the water," Quick told me, "and just float him over it."

So I waded out a step or two to where the water got deep and I kind of crouched down and dipped the net in the water and with the other hand I pulled the line. The fish still wanted to skip off to one side or the other, especially when he saw me, then he just came sliding in over the net and the rod whipped straight and I stood up and by god I had got him.

He was so long about a quarter of him was sticking up above the frame of the net. It was a real effort to hold him up to get a close look at him. "God," I said. "He's beautiful."

I couldn't explain too clear what I was feeling right there. All the time I was getting that fish in, it was like I wasn't really there at all, like I was kind of outside myself altogether. I had been thinking so hard about the fish that it drove everything else out. It was like my heart jumped right out of my body, and then after I had him, it just came crashing back into me. I felt like I just came back from a long ways off and just plopped down there still out of breath.

I looked over at Mr. Quick and he was fiddling around with something on his shoulder and was looking awful serious.

"What's the matter?" I said.

"The streamer," he said. And he showed me where it was hooked into his vest there. I was kind of shocked.

"You pulled it out right at the end. It snapped back and snagged me." He finally twisted the hook out of the cloth. "You coulda lost him."

"I didn't though. Look here."

"I see him." Quick didn't look too much more cheerful than what he had before.

I looked at the fish again. He had his mouth open and was kind of panting. And every once in a while he would give a shake. "What are we going to do with him?"

"It's your fish."

"Maybe we should put him back." It came to me that there was something wrong with getting him.

Quick said, "He'll just waste away. He's way past his prime."

I looked up at him and it began to come to me what I let myself in for. I forgot I had to kill the fish if I caught it.

Quick got out his knife and held it out to me. I leaned the rod down on the edge of the water and took the knife. "Make it fast," Quick said. So I grabbed the fish through the net and held him the way Quick had shown me and gave him a good hard hit with the priest, so called, behind the eyes, and the fish shivered and went still. I looked up at Quick and he gave me a nod as if to say I did it right.

We didn't say too much to each other the rest of the day, but just went about doing what had to be done, pretty well weighted down with the way our good time there had come to an end all of a sudden. I felt a little like I was walking under water, like that ouzel, against the flow.

It came to both of us about the same time that we better bury the girl, just to keep the animals away from her, if nothing else. There was an old army blanket in the car and we wrapped her in that and carried her up toward the aspens a ways and I dug a trench with a camp shovel not too awful deep because it was so hard. I kept running into rocks, and the little shovel was hard to handle and gave me blisters. And once as I was digging we heard a car coming up the road and had to duck down in the grass again, and I found myself stretched in the trench I had been digging like I was the one getting buried, and I got up again a little faster than I should, but it was just one of those California cars going up to wherever they go.

"Damn," Quick said for about the millionth time, "I'm going to follow them one of these times."

But then we both saw that there couldn't be many of these times left, and the quiet settled on us again like a cloud. I dug some and stopped. "Maybe we should go up there tomorrow," I said.

Quick shook his head. "Whatever they're up to, I doubt we'd fit in real well." And I went back to digging again.

After we put her in and covered her up, we just stood there for a time. I knew we both felt odd about it, like there was something we should say or do, but I guess neither one of us could think of anything. So we piled on some more grass and brush and tried to make it look natural and went on back to camp.

I had to cut the fish into four pieces to get him into the pan. It was more than enough for both of us.

"I took down the measurements," Quick said. "We get out of this, I'll vouch for it. It's got to be some kind of record for the Hills. Wish we had a snapshot."

He was setting on the remains of the pine log we pulled over from the other side. I was crouching down by the fire, getting the last of the fish out of the pan onto his plate. "I'm sorry," I said. It was something that's been on my mind to say since I got the fish.

"About which?" he said. "No snapshot?"

"Getting your fish. It was nothing but an accident."

Quick shook his head. "You played him about as good as he could be played."

"I almost lost him at the end."

"You did fine."

"I wish I had lost him."

Quick looked down at the plate and got a load of fish on his fork. "That's only for books, that about the big one getting away. Sob stuff." He took a bite and chewed and swallowed. "Besides, he is getting away, isn't he? They all do. You can catch them, but you can't own them."

I got my plate full and sat down beside him on the log. We ate for a long time without saying anything. There was still a glow in the sky above the aspens where the sun went down. A tall spruce close to us was outlined against the light, and you could see the long strands of moss draped over its low branches, what they call old man's beard.

"I hate to leave here," I said.

"We have to," he said.

"I know."

"How do you feel now about the fish?"

"Strange. Happy and sad. Both."

"Good," Quick said. For about the thousandth time I thought to myself what a weird old guy he was. But things went so smooth here before, when there was just the two of us, I didn't want to think what was going to happen when we got back amongst people.

There with the fire crackling in front of us and the smoke floating up and the moss on the spruce and past that the ponds and the gabbing of the creek and the aspens and the sky glowing, it seemed like it would be a pretty decent world if it wasn't for people.

17.

Next morning we packed up the Jeep and set off back down to the crossroads. When we got there, I said, "Which way?"

Quick shook his head. "You choose." It was the first time I ever heard him turn down an opportunity to give directions. I guess he must've been feeling pretty low at that.

I took the south fork and we rode quite a while. We started getting into touristy country again, which was clear from the signs we started seeing. I pointed some of them out to Quick as we went by, like "Trout Ranch—Rope 'em, Brand 'em, No License Needed," or "Infinity Point—Defies Gravity, Mystery of the Universe," and so on. Quick just shook his head, looking sad and disgusted. "They just can't leave it alone, can they?"

Then we started seeing others: "Golden West—History Comes Alive." "Golden West—Pancake House and Museum, Coffee Still Five Cents." "Golden West—Pageant Nightly except Mon." "Golden West—Campground and Motel." "Golden West—Fill 'er Up, Lowest Gas Prices." "Golden West—Pan for Gold." They were coming at us about every half mile. "Golden West—Five minutes Ahead," the last one said.

"We could use some gas," I said.

"Not that bad," Quick said.

"Golden West—Free Cider!" the next one said. "Golden West—Cowboys! Indians!" "Golden West—Rock Candy Mountain!" "Golden West—C'mon Pop, Let's Stop!" And finally, "Golden West—-Here It Is!"

What it looked like was another one of them phony old-time towns you saw so much around here, but maybe a little gaudier.

"Keep on going," Quick said, "before I start to gag."

And as soon as he said that, just like an answer almost, the decision was taken out of our hands. The Jeep started in to pulling over to the right.

"What the hell are you doing?" Quick said.

"The tire," I said, trying to hold the wheel steady as we went over a curb. "I think we got a flat."

Quick just moaned.

I got the car stopped, and it turned out we were right at a gas station, in front of a big sign that said, "Lowest Gas Prices!"

A guy came out of the station wiping his hands on a rag. He was wearing a baseball cap with a big "G-W" in yellow on it against the red, and a face that would come in handy playing poker, one of them that looked like it was permanently frozen by boredom. He leaned over and looked in the window on Quick's side. Quick rolled it down. "Do something for you?" the bored guy said.

I pointed to the right front corner of the Jeep. "Flat," I said.

He leaned back and looked at it, then bent forward again. "Sure is. You want it fixed?"

I gave Quick a look to see what he thought. But he screwed up his face like he smelled something dead in the glove compartment.

"How much?" I said.

"Special this week," the guy in the cap said. "Ten bucks even."

I looked at Quick again for some sign, but he didn't say a thing. "Go ahead," I told the guy, and started to get out of the car.

"You can get come cider in the cafe while you wait," the guy said.

"How long will it be?"

"Half-hour," he said, squinting. "Three-quarters."

Quick got out, bringing the flight bag with him, and with that grumpy expression, and we headed toward the cafe across the street.

"Just as well do it ourselves," Quick grunted.

"It's only a ten," I said. "And the cider is free."

"Half hour," Quick said. "He'll probably stick us here all morning."

"You could've said something," I said.

But he just grunted. I figured it was giving up fishing that was making him sour.

It turned out that the free cider comes in a cup a little smaller than the pill cups they used at the Home. And a sign by the counter said, "Refills ten Cents."

"And the five-cent coffee is probably a quarter," Quick growled.

But anyway we went to the booth and ordered some. "And what else?" the waitress said.

"Just coffee," I said. "The five-cent kind."

"With meals," The waitress pointed to a sign behind the counter. Sure enough it said you've got to order a meal to get the nickel coffee.

"How much otherwise?" I said.

"Fifty cents."

Quick's eyebrows did a little dance for me.

"What is the smallest meal you've got?" I said.

"Egg salad sand," she said. "With potato chips and pickles."

"How about toast?" I said. "Is that a meal?"

"French toast is," she said. She pointed to a chalk board behind the counter with all the meals listed on it.

"French toast and coffee," I said. I looked over to Quick.

"Nothing," he said.

"Go ahead," I said. "We got a half-hour here."

"Water then," he said. "A glass of water. That's free, I hope."

"With meals," the waitress said, and pointed to another sign.

"Christ," Quick spit out. "How do I get the sign-making contract here?"

"You want anything then?" The waitress was flicking at the pages of her order book.

"Bottle of catsup," Quick said, "and a straw."

The waitress gave him a pitiful weak smile and took off. "Christ," Quick said again.

"You can have part of my toast," I said.

"I don't want your toast," he said. "Or your coffee either, or your water. I just want to get out of here with my gold crowns still in my mouth."

I tried to shush him a little bit, but he just grunted and got on his sour look again. The cafe was about half full. "They can't all be stuck here with a flat tire," I said.

"Don't bet on it," he said. Then, "What's the matter?"

Quick saw me shrinking up a little bit when I saw this big guy coming toward the booth. He had on a purple western shirt and fancy knit slacks and was carrying a coffee cup and was staring right at me and smiling in a determined kind of way. He had one of those square-shaped faces and was wearing glasses. My first thought was that he was some kind of lawman who had recognized me as the accessory after all kinds of facts. He came right up beside the booth and planted himself.

"Howdy," he said.

I was looking down at my hands on the table now, sure we had been caught.

"What?" I heard Quick croak out.

"Howdy," the guy said again. "You passing through?"

"Trying to," Quick said. "They don't make it easy."

"That's the idea," the guy said. "The way I planned it."

I looked back up at the square-faced individual. He was smiling yet and stirring his coffee with a spoon.

"Monte Long," he said. "I run this place. You tried the five-cent coffee?"

"I would," Quick said, "but I haven't but ten dollars on me."

Monte Long grinned that one down. "Just as well," he said. "It's on the strong side." And he pulled out the spoon and there was a big hole in the bottom of it, like it had been eaten through with acid. I could hardly keep from smiling at that, and I saw Quick's surprised look.

"You mind if I squat a while?" Long said.

It looked like Quick might mind, but Long had already squeezed in beside him. "I couldn't help noticing," Long said to me. "You're Indian, aren't you?"

"Not that I know," I said. I supposed it was all that time I'd been spending outside lately that had got me browned up. If I'd been thinking, I'd've kept covered better.

"From around here?" he asked.

"Not too close," I said.

"Got a job at the moment?"

I looked over at Quick.

"We're on vacation," Quick said.

"From what?"

"Everything," Quick said.

"You ever act before?" Monte Long asked me.

I thought about that for a while. "High school," I said. "Senior play, if that's what you mean."

"What did you play?" he said.

"It was just a little part," I said. "When the mob stormed the jail, I held up a piece of rope and said 'Give him what he deserves.'"

Monte Long nodded solemn at that like he'd just read a three-page resume. "How'd you like acting?"

"Fine," I said. "Especially the cast party."

Quick was getting impatient. "What you got in mind?"

"I need a Crazy Horse," Long said. "My Crazy Horse took off last week with my Calamity Jane and the proceeds from the sarsaparilla concession. General Custer's been doubling in the role, but it's not working out. He hasn't got enough time for the change."

"I'm not really an actor," I said.

"Neither was my last Crazy Horse," Long said. "He wasn't an Indian, either. He was an Armenian kid from New York. His nose was right for the part, but it got all the good lines, too." He pinched his nostrils together. "'As Long as duh grass grows and duh watah flows.' The part's not supposed to be that funny."

I looked over at Quick. To be honest, I was a little interested. This Monte Long was such a talky character you couldn't help but like him a little. Quick of course seemed to have taken an instant hatred to him. "We got better things to do," he said.

"Thirty-five dollars a week," Long said, "and a fifty-fifty split on the sarsaparilla."

"He don't need the money," Quick said.

"Free room. One meal a day," Long went on.

"No deal," Quick said. About then the waitress brought my French toast and coffee and I dug into it.

"Does he speak for you?" Long asked me.

I nodded, chewing on the toast, which was anyway a little on the tough side. I'd just as soon stay out of it.

Monte Long had shifted around in the booth and was looking at Quick like he was seeing him for the first time. "I could probably find a part for you, too."

Quick's eyebrows went up and his steely blues got narrower, "Like what?"

"You're perfect for the old prospector," Long said. "Same deal as your friend except for the sarsaparilla."

"Old prospector," Quick said. "That's a part?"

"No lines," Long said, "but a good mime bit."

"Mine?"

"Mime. Pantomime. Using gestures to tell the story. Take my word. Nobody knows casting better."

"I've acted," Quick said. "In the movies. In Hollywood."

"What in?" Long said.

"About a dozen things. Lines too. Westerns. Bronco Billy. William S. Hart."

"Did they have sound then?" Long asked.

Quick shrugs. "They had lines."

Long nodded. "What kind of role you have in mind, then?"

"I don't know," Quick said. "You got a Wild Bill Hickok? A Charlie Utter?"

"Our Wild Bill is filled," Long said, "and I never heard of—what did you say? Udder?"

Quick snapped his teeth together and glared over at me. "You about done?"

"Let your friend be the judge," Long said, nodding to me. "What do you see here, Wild Bill or the old prospector?"

I gave Quick a once-over as I finished my toast and washed it down with the coffee. He hadn't shaved, I don't think, since he had run away from the home, and his beard was grown out pretty full and white, and of course he had on the same tattered clothes that had got in only a couple more rinsings in the creek. I saw an old prospector sure enough, glaring at me like he might make me swallow my cup if I said a word. I shook my head and stood up.

"It's on me," Monte Long said, taking the check. "Why don't you stay over tonight, see the show, think it over. I'll give you a deal on a motel room."

Quick was following me, trying to herd me out faster. "You can pay the bill if you want to," he said, "but we got to be in Newcastle, Wyoming, by dark."

The three of us moved across the street to the gas station all in a bunch. The bored guy came out toward us wiping his hands on a rag.

"Tell you what," Long said, "I'll throw in the work on your car. A free fill of gas."

"Trunions," said the poker-faced individual.

"The motel bill, too," Long said. "The whole thing."

"Trunions," the poker-face said again.

"Is the flat fixed?" I asked.

"Long time ago," the guy in the cap said. "But it's not the tire. It's the trunions."

"The what?" I never even heard of them before.

"Trunions," said the guy, and gave me one of them looks that only professional mechanics or doctors can get on their face when you don't know what the hell they are talking about. "You can't steer without them. Yours is worn down to a nub."

Monte Long was standing there blinking behind his glasses, taking in the news pretty calm.

"Put a new set in then," Quick growled. He throws Long a dirty look. "We'll wait here."

"Can't," poker-face said. "Haven't got any here. Have to send to Rapid for them." He tugged on his cap and set his jaw and folded his arms together.

"Shit," Quick said, and groaned. "I knew it. We're never getting out of here."

I turned to Monte Long, who was smiling a little again. "I guess we'll take you up on that motel room," I said.

"Sure," he said. "Thirty per cent off."

"You said the whole thing," I said.

"You said Newcastle by dark," he said. "I guess we were both wrong." And he hands me back the cafe check.

"Shit," Quick said again. "We're here till doomsday."

18.

Now I think about it, along about then was when Quick started getting more and more strange. First it seemed like nothing could satisfy him, then he started going into sulky spells when you couldn't get a word out of him, then he would bust out in a long line of chatter that you figured he must have been saving up and working on for several years at least. I guess it was just a sign of what was to come.

There was just about nothing in this Golden West place he could find to like, and in a lot of ways he had a point. Like the big rock candy mountain turned out to be a three-foot pile of jelly-beans colored to look like pebbles, and the museum was a bunch of old furniture and clothes and stuff supposed to be used and worn by the pioneers but looked more like it had come from one of those Rapid City rummage sales. The town itself was nothing more than some false fronts stuck onto two long cement block buildings on either side of the road and divided up into shops selling all kinds of tourist trash. In some of them you could see people doing actual things, like a woman making candy or a guy that shaped little animals out of glass, but most of them just sold souvenirs and postcards and plaster ash trays and all like that.

Down at the end of the street, on the hillside, there was a gold mine, so-called, really just a tunnel dug into the hill about thirty feet, and outside it a pile of sand and a trough of water where you could wash for gold. They rented the pans out, and there was a sign that said, "Keep All the Gold You Find!" Which I'm guessing would add up in a day to about enough to dot an i. Across the way, on the valley side, there was a tipi set up and a sign that said, "Take Your Pictures with Chief Manyponies, One Dollar." The Chief was setting outside the tipi on a wooden kitchen chair. He had on a full warbonnet and deerskin suit like you see on movie Indians but which most real Indians never did wear. But he looked pretty Indian otherwise, with that real dark skin you see sometimes, and some good wrinkles coming on. Just as me and Quick crossed the street toward him, the Chief jumped up out of his chair and went running after this car that was starting to drive away. "Hey!" he was yelling. "Hey, you wait a minute there!" And he was waving his peace pipe at the car and got up beside it and put his hand on the hood like he was going to hold it back, and the brakes creaked and the car bounced to a stop. He went to a side window. "One dollar for the picture," he said and pointed to the kid in the back seat who was still holding onto the camera and had a scared look on his face like he was about to get scalped. I didn't hear what the other ones in the car said, if anything, but when the Chief came back to the tipi where me and Quick were standing, he was folding a bill and stuffing it into the pouch he had hanging at his waist.

"How about that?" he said to me. "What do you think of these cheapskates anyway? The dumb thing on their part is they could just as well get a nice pose, my arm on their shoulder or something. But they always try to get away with something. You want a picture?" He was looking around for our camera.

"No," I said. "We don't have any film or anything."

"I've got film. What kind do you use?"

"No camera either."

"Which we wouldn't use if we had," Quick growled.

The Chief looked at Quick and looked at me. Up closer he appeared to be maybe forty-something. I was trying to think if I have ever seen him before when he saved me the trouble. "I think I saw you at a dance at Weed not too long ago. I was working the p.a."

"Could be," I said. I flashed a look at Quick to see if he was upset I had been spotted so easy, but I think he was too mad being stuck in the Golden West to be concerned with much else.

"Clyde Manyponies," the Chief said and held out his hand to shake. "You're a friend of Lymon Twobows, aren't you?"

I nodded and gave my name.

"What you doing here? On your way to Rushmore?"

"Car trouble," I said. "It's getting fixed."

"Count on two days, minimum," Manyponies said.

"You live here?" I said.

"Summers. My fifth season." He saw me looking over the tipi. "Not in the tent. We got a trailer in the campground. I make a living. Gets us through the winter."

I was looking at the blanket he had spread out by the tipi. There were beaded mocassins and bags on it, all good designs and careful stitching. "Good beadwork." I said.

He nodded, looking at the blanket himself with a shake of his head. "My daughter does it. It doesn't move, though. I've got to charge too much for it. The tourists can walk down the street fifty yards and buy some cheap Taiwan or Korean crap that suits them just as well."

"Your daughter," I said. "I remember her from the wacipi, I think. She was queen, wasn't she?"

"That's her." He gave a grin.

Then he looked back at me. "If you're staying over the night, come on and have supper with us. We don't get that much company. Verine could stand somebody to talk to more her own age."

"I'm not Lakota, you know."

"I didn't think you were. But if you're a friend of Lymon's, that's good enough for me."

I looked over to Quick, who seemed to be in one of his sulks again.

"Bring your friend," Manyponies said.

"We're supposed to go to this show," I said. And I told him about the offer Monte Long had made me.

"He wanted me to take the part, too," Manyponies said. "Forty a week. For Crazy Horse. Even Major Reno gets fifty."

"I don't think I'll be taking it anyway," I said. "But he wants us to see the show."

"Stop in after, then," Manyponies said. "We'll save something for you. First trailer you see in the park." He was staring past me at something. And as me and Quick moved away, Manyponies took off after another car, waving his pipe: "Hold on a minute! Stop right there."

The place where the show was held was in a natural bowl on the valley side of town, past a big parking lot. The people who came to see it sat on benches that were built on the slope of the bowl, looking down to where the actors were. You came in when it was still light and you could see the Indian camp—-four tipis—-on one side of the bowl and the army fort with its flag and pickets on the other, and in between them a stage with a low fence behind it for a back wall, and past that the other rim of the bowl and then just the pines and cliffs. After it got dark enough you heard the Indian drums start to go, and then a voice out of the loudspeaker I recognized as Monte Long's started in to tell the story, and then the lights shined on the fort or the Indian camp or on the stage up front, which stood for all kinds of indoor places, depending on the furniture, or on the other rim of the bowl where most of the animals got in the act. See, besides the people there were a bunch of horses, a team of oxen and a burro. One time when Monte Long was going on about the buffalo that roamed the plains by the hundreds of thousands, the light came up on the far rim and for a while there was nothing, then there was a single buffalo cow peeking over the rim kind of timid and backed down out of sight again. That was one of the biggest laughs of the show, but there were others, like when somebody stepped on Sitting Bull's robe and pulled it off and underneath he had on a pink teeshirt with real white arms sticking out, or when General Custer was setting on board his horse Comanche and the narrator was talking about Yellowhair going to meet his fate at the Little Big Horn, and the horse lifted his tail and dropped quite a load before they got the light off him.

One thing that interested me was that Crazy Horse got to ride a white horse and talk pretty good grammar instead of that kind of baby-talk Indians in movies tend to get. Of course it still wasn't too real, to me, since it seemed to always go the long way around—do not instead of don't and will not instead of won't and so on. I guess the writer figured Indians didn't know about apostrophes. But anyway it wouldn't be too much of an embarrassment to do the part, I didn't think.

Quick, naturally, couldn't find anything at all good to say about the play. Myself, although it was a little chopped up, I thought Monte Long's voice held it together pretty good. But as we were picking our way through the cars in the parking lot afterwards, Quick sputtered and muttered about this and that thing wrong with it, but mainly the way it screwed with history.

"You'd think they would at least read a book or two before they wrote something," he said. "Like about Charlie Utter and the fact that Wild Bill had a wife. And they make out Custer like some kind of hero instead of a damn-fool egomaniac."

"The horse took care of that," I said.

"That's another thing," he said. "They set him on Comanche, which wasn't even his horse, and was a bay instead of a black, to boot, and promote him to General and leave on his golden curls—"

"I don't think it is supposed to be all that real," I said. "It just gets at the feel of it. Like a legend or a myth or something. Crazy Horse comes out looking pretty good."

"A whole lot like Custer," Quick said. "Sounding like him too. It's the first time I ever seen Custer wearing war paint. That's different, anyway."

By now we were almost back to the motel, and I figured it might be good to get to the point about staying on. "You got to admit we would fit in pretty good here," I said. It was a card I had been holding out to play at just the right time. "You couldn't find better what you call protective coloring."

Quick gave a snort. "So you can get out in the spotlight on top of that white stallion."

"I heard you say myself if you want to hide something, put it in plain sight where nobody would think of looking."

If there's anything Quick couldn't stand, it was having his own words thrown back in his face, so now he bunched up his mouth and went quiet.

We were at the motel then, and I unlocked the door and went in and Quick followed me. I went into the bathroom and washed up and when I came out Quick had flopped on the bed and was staring at the television.

"Aren't you going down to the Chief's trailer with me?" I said.

He didn't say anything.

"They're bound to have some good food," I said. But even that didn't get a rise. I looked at what was on the TV. It was a news program. "Anything on there about—" I didn't quite know how to finish, but he knew what I meant.

"Not yet," he said.

I finished wiping my hands and threw the towel on the back of a chair. "I'll go on by myself then," I said.

"I want to see the weather," he said. "How it will be for travelling tomorrow." Just so I could see my argument hadn't got anywhere with him. Then he threw in, "Maybe there will be a John Wayne picture later."

So I left him laying there and went on to the campground alone. I had pretty well given up on staying, much as the Crazy Horse part suited me. But I knew that there's no use wasting words on Quick when he got his mind set. Besides, who knew when somebody would start poking around in that camp and find that girl? Or how many people had seen the Jeep parked there? Quite a number from California, for sure. So at that point I thought, okay, maybe it's for the best anyway to get out of the area altogether.

At the campground the first trailer I saw had "Office" on a sign in front, which surprised me so much I went on to look for another one, but I couldn't see any other that looked right, so I went back and knocked on the door and Clyde Manyponies opened it. I almost didn't recognize him because his hair was cut so short, which I hadn't been able to see under the warbonnet, and he had on jeans and a tee-shirt that said "Red Power."

"Come on in. Where's your white-beard friend?"

"He's feeling a little down," I said, not wandering too far from the truth. "You run the office?"

Manyponies nodded. "But don't give me too much credit for that. Monte likes to split things up like that to save money. This way he gets a campground manager and a cigar-store Indian for the price of one." He motioned me to set down on a sofa and took a chair himself. There was somebody else in the kitchen past the partition. "Got room for some stew and fry bread?" Manyponies asked me.

I couldn't help but grin at that. My diet had been pretty limited lately, leaning heavy to fried trout and canned beans. I looked around the trailer, which was small but real homey, and my eyes got stuck on a picture beside the sofa so I had to lean over for a closer look. "That's Leonard Fourwinds," I said. "And you." I looked at him to check the resemblance. He was some younger in the picture and with a lot shorter hair, one of them crew cuts, and he and Fourwinds were standing with some others on top of a big rock with cliffs and hills fading off in the haze behind them.

"Nineteen seventy," Manyponies said. "That's us on top of Teddy Roosevelt's head at Rushmore."

"I remember that," I said. "I was just a kid. It was on TV and in the newspapers."

"There'll be another one there this year," he said. "Tenth anniversary protest."

I was looking at him in a whole new light now. People are full of surprises sometimes. I would never have figured him for a protester.

"COUP is staging this one, which may make a difference," Manyponies said. "I didn't see a whole lot of change out of the last one. Took the Wounded Knee and the FBI killings before anybody started paying attention." And he looked up and smiled at the girl who'd just come into the room carrying a bowl of stew.

"This is my daughter, Verine," Clyde Manyponies said, and he got a look on his face of someone showing off a secret treasure, a new hat, maybe, or a special piece of jewelry.

The girl kept her eyes down in that shy Indian way as she sat the bowl of stew down on the little table in front of me, but she was one of those beautiful girls that couldn't keep their loveliness hid even if they threw a cowhide over it. It gave me a sinking feeling of the type that comes over you when you see a new valley open up in front of you that you'll be going down into before long and a beautiful ridge of mountains across the way that you're headed toward. I think I must have decided right then to try again to turn Quick around and stay there after all.

19.

The weather next day helped some. I swear I smelled it coming when I stepped out of Clyde Manyponies' trailer after midnight, smelled that coolness and dampness in the wind and looked up and saw the stars blotted out by clouds. So I got a pretty righteous feeling in the morning when I woke up and heard the rain sputtering on the thin motel roof. It was no weather for travelling after all. Not that we could have anyway. The Jeep was still short trunions, which were supposed to be coming on the noon bus. But I knew that Quick's head was already halfway down the road under sunny skies, the Golden West fading like a bad dream back there somewhere. It was going to take some doing to snap him back to the here and now, and the rain was bound to do some good in that direction.

I guess I was on to his ways enough now to know you couldn't just step on the brakes and expect him to come to a dead stop. You had to gear him down like a loaded truck on a downgrade and be damn careful he doesn't get away from you in the process. Meaning you got to do it without him knowing. So I lay there a long time pretending to sleep, letting the rain do a job on him. He was bumping and thumping around, clearing his throat, cussing to himself, pulling back the curtain to look out, going to the bathroom, running water, making more and more noise until finally he just lost patience and yelled out, "You going to sleep all day?"

I pretended to wake up, then, and rubbed my eyes. "Morning already?"

"Damn near eleven."

"Is it raining?" I said, trying to sound surprised at hearing that loud pea-shot clattering on the roof.

He made a disgusted sound in his throat, meaning yes, it's raining and no, he wasn't going to let it stop him.

So I got up and started pulling on my clothes. "We better get something to eat," I said. "I'm hungry as a coyote."

Now, truth to tell, I'm not all that famished, having had at least four bowls of that stew last night just to have an excuse to hang around Verine Manyponies a while longer. But I did know that some kind of pangs have got to be getting to Quick, unless he'd been sneaking snacks without me seeing. Outside of a couple cupcakes he wolfed down for lunch yesterday, he hadn't had much to munch on. He seemed to be thinking if he took food here, he signed himself to something. I figured that's just another thing I got to work on him. "How does pancakes and eggs with sausage and hot coffee sound to you? I saw it on their menu yesterday."

He made that growling noise another time, meaning yes it sounded good, no he's not giving in that easy. "I just as soon check the garage first, see how the car's coming."

"They can't even start until they get the parts." I reminded him. "Sometime this afternoon, if the bus isn't held up too long."

Growl, snarl, he went again, but I thought he was weakening. With Quick, it was the major part of the struggle just to get him to recognize the plain facts. "We better be out of here by dark," he said. "I'm not staying another night."

"Wasn't your bed soft enough?" I tried to make it sound like an innocent question, but I knew what mine felt like to me after all that time in sleeping bags on the cold hard floor of the Jeep.

Of course he was not admitting to comfort outright. "It wasn't the bed so much. It was you and your snoring."

"My snoring?" I was too surprised to laugh in his face. When I'd come in the night before he was ripping away in his usual fashion. He hadn't even missed a stroke when I accidentally dropped a shoe on the floor between the beds. Or even when I threw down the other one on purpose.

"You snore," he said, and he curled his lip up like he was daring me to say he was wrong. The thing is, we both knew there was just no winning this kind of argument. There's no way to prove to anyone he snores. Even if I was to record him at full throttle, he would claim I got the sound from a passing diesel truck or something. For my part, I knew I slept quiet.

"You snore like an elephant farting," he said. "I damn near cut your throat myself."

"You never mentioned it before."

"I was trying to spare your feelings," he said.

That would be a first, I was thinking, but not saying. I finished dressing and stood up.

"I'm going to eat," I said, trying to double clutch into another gear.

And he snarled and snapped the air like a bobcat in a cage. But he followed me out, I noticed.

Not having a raincoat between us, we got pretty soaked on the way to the cafe. We shook ourselves off and went and sat in a booth and I ordered the pancake special and Quick held on to his stubbornness enough to take just a donut and coffee, which of course he's got to pay extra for.

Monte Long was making his usual morning round of the customers with his trick coffee spoon, and when he saw us he came over to our booth and sat down. "Morning, gentlemen," he said. "You catch the performance last night?"

I kept my eye on Quick as we both nodded. At least he kept from growling this time.

"What did you think of it?" Long asked.

I jumped in fast to keep Quick from voicing his well-known opinions. "I liked the Crazy Horse part."

Long said, "It's yours if you want it."

"Don't I have to try out or anything?"

"I'm a pretty good judge of talent," Long said. "You look good for the role, you've got a good voice. You'll do fine."

"He won't neither," Quick croaked out just then. "We're leaving as soon as the car's fixed."

Now Long looked at Quick the way you might look at a hair you just found in your custard pie, then he looked back at me. I shrugged to show it was not my idea. That got Long on my side. He looked at Quick again like he was trying to read him through his glasses. "You didn't like the pageant, sir?"

Quick smiled kind of thin and shook his head.

"May I ask why not?"

And Quick's smile got thicker, relishing this moment with all the meanness he could squeeze out of his mean old carcass. "You really want to know?"

"I wouldn't ask otherwise," Long said.

"Okay," Quick said. "It is the biggest pile of horse manure I've seen since I used to swamp out the livery at Deadwood City when I was a kid." And then he proceeded to go through what he said to me about it last night, but with all kinds of little elaborations and flourishes. In my opinion, Quick wasted his time in all those other jobs he has held through the years, or says he held. He ought to have been one of those critics. I don't believe any of them could have outdone him for gall and nastiness and venom. Toward the end of his tirade, I even began to feel a little sorry for Monte Long, his pride and joy was being so totally torn apart and picked over, like hungry relatives going over a fried chicken. But I guess I might've underestimated the man's resources. When it was clear Quick had run down on the awfulness of the play and I was expecting Long to put together some kind of defense, what he said instead was, "There's a lot in what you say, sir."

"Damn square," said Quick.

"The playwright is young, a neophyte. He has more taste for the colorful fictions of legend and his own imagination than the even more compelling confluences of actual history."

Quick looked a little set back by some of the grammar Long was coming up with, but he spurred along. "Pretty obvious."

"The basic script, though is sound, I think, don't you?" Long asked.

Quick shrugs. "It's got most of the right people in it, anyway."

"What it needs is a squaring up, wouldn't you say? A setting to rights."

Quick went for that like the fat pitch that it was. "That's ex-actly what it could use," he said.

Then came the curve. "You seem to know a lot about the history of the area. How'd you like to be our historical consultant?" Quick squinted at Long, his jaw set to the side.

"With pay, of course," Long said, casual, "and a credit in the program, and the part of the old prospector, too, if you still want it."

Quick shook his head slow, his mouth fell open, like a home-run slugger that's just been fanned by a rookie.

Monte Long got up out of his seat. "I'd better get back to my other guests," he said. "You two think about it, talk it over. I'll check back later."

The waitress had brought our breakfasts, and I buttered the pancakes and poured on syrup. "You don't get that kind of offer every day," I said.

Quick was back to his yes-no growl again. "I see what he's up to." He bit off half his donut and chewed it, his eyes a little glazed over. Then he tossed the other half in and licked his fingers and took a gulp of his fifty-cent coffee.

I dug into the pancakes. I figured it's better not to say anything, the way he could stiffen up to an argument. But I couldn't help smiling to myself the way he got suckered into that old high school club trick where the main complainer ends up chairman of the committee to do something about it.

Quick looked down at his plate like he just woke up after a short nap. "Where's my other donut?" he said.

"You only ordered one," I said. "You made a big point of it."

He gurgled a little in his throat and fixed his eyes on me eating. I was trying to be enthusiastic about it, even if I was still up to my tonsils in stew. "You eat loud enough," he said after a while.

"First I snore and then I eat loud," I said. "I can't do anything right today."

"You could close your mouth while you're eating anyway. It's disgusting."

I guess it probably was. It is something I've often noticed that eating is pretty gruesome to witness as long as you're not doing it yourself. If it's you doing the slurping and the crunching, that's all right. It all depends on where you're sitting, like a lot else I could name. I pushed my plate away. "I've had enough anyway," I said, stating a plain fact. "You want to finish it?"

He looked at the plate. "Why did you order so much if you couldn't eat it?"

"I thought I could. Go ahead. I haven't even touched that half."

But it'd gotten to be a principle with him. He shook his head. I shrugged and wiped my mouth with a napkin and left the plate setting in the middle of the table where he could watch it, which he was doing like it was the center ring of a circus.

"Manyponies is going to Rushmore on Monday," I said. "Asked us to come along if we were still stuck here."

"We won't be," Quick said, like he'd been put in a trance by the pancakes. "Rushmore?"

"The faces," I said. "Teddy Roosevelt and the rest. Monday is their day off here."

"Teddy Roosevelt," Quick said. "T.R. There's a man. They ought to put him in their show."

"Maybe you can talk them into it." I let it go there, not to be too obvious.

"He had a ranch out here," Quick said. "Over by Elkhorn. My mother took me to see him once. He shook my hand."

I nodded solemn and interested. It sounded a lot to me like another one of Quick's wishful lies, but I wanted to give him lots of line. He is one fish that won't stand being horsed.

"I wouldn't mind seeing him again," Quick said. "Might be worth it."

I looked out at the rain. It was pouring down just like I ordered it for breakfast. "I guess we couldn't see too much today," I said.

Quick tore his eyes away from the pancakes long enough to look out the window.

"Can't hardly see across the street," I pointed out. But just then all my careful setting up got a big jar. The bus pulled in alongside the cafe. I looked over to Quick again, who's smiling.

"That'll be our trunions," he said.

And sure enough, when Monte Long went out to greet the driver, he was handed a box that couldn't be nothing else, along with a bundle of newspapers.

"Your parts are here," Long said when he came back in. "I'll get on a coat and take them over to the garage right away." He set the bundle of papers on the counter by the cash register and peeled off the top one and brought it over to the table. "You talked it over yet?"

"Enough," Quick said.

"Don't rush it," Long said. "It'll take a while to get your car back together. You want to take a look at the news?" He handed Quick the paper and took off again with the box of parts.

Quick opened up the paper. "Where's the weather? It'll probably clear up before two." But then his own face got dark like a cloud just went over it.

"What's the matter?"

He just shook his head, reading. He had the paper held way out and his head pulled back because he'd left his glasses somewhere. When he's finished, he gave me a grim look and handed me the paper.

This is what I read, right on the front page:

Gunmen Suspected
In Death of Woman
Found in Hills

DEADWOOD—The Lawrence County Sheriff's office says it has a lead in the apparent murder of a woman whose body was found buried in a shallow grave near here yesterday.

Sheriff's Deputy Glenn Stone said officers are looking for two men connected with armed robberies in Rapid City and Sturgis. Notices have been sent out to neighboring states as well, Stone said.

The body of the woman, as yet unidentified, was discovered by campers in a valley about ten miles southwest of Deadwood.

The examining physician said the woman died only about 72 hours before being found.

No description of the two men was released. Stone said the sheriff's office didn't want to endanger the public by engaging it in the search. The suspects are armed, Stone said, and distinctive enough in appearance that lawmen would have little trouble tracing them.

The Sheriff's office said earlier that the victim may have been picked up by the suspects while hitchhiking.

I looked up at Quick feeling pretty shaky and sick, which just shows you how that kind of news will affect different people. He was chomping down the last of my pancakes.

"Long as we're staying," he said between bites, "No use in starving to death."

20.

It was easy enough to see what Quick's thinking was, especially since I planted most of it in him in the first place. The news about the girl being found was just the clincher. He was figuring we lay low here for as long as it takes, keep off the roads where the law would be looking hardest, then get a new start. Meantime he was going to set the record straight in the Golden West Pageant. What I didn't see was that he had something else in mind, too—something that was tearing him up inside. That I didn't figure out till a lot later.

For now, most of my thinking was taken up with what I have gotten into as the latest model Crazy Horse. I had lines to learn and practicing to do. Lucky for me, I had Verine Manyponies to help me with the words. Since it was raining, we worked in Clyde Manyponies' trailer, which was pretty cozy and nice with the main disadvantage that the Chief was there all the time, too. He was out of business when the rain came, of course, but I got a feeling he would have found some way to keep an eye on us otherwise, too. It was pretty obvious I was not going to get away with anything. Not that I wanted to. I do believe I turned some kind of corner in that respect. A short while earlier I might have been all over her like a blanket as soon as I got the chance. Now it seemed just about enough just being around her. I got warm from her like she was giving off a glow. It was a little like the feeling you get when the sunlight washes over you on a cool morning. And when she put her big eyes full on me or when she gave me a shy smile, it was like the fire jumped to me, and it kindled and kept me going all day.

Besides that, she really helped me with the lines, not just in learn-ing the words by heart, but getting at what they meant, and where to put on the pressure and where to leave it off. Like once when we were working on that long last speech I got, which was such a ballbreaker, she said to me. "How do you feel about what you say here?"

"I feel like I don't know what the next sentence is," I said.

"Don't think about the words," she said. "Think about how you feel. The white man's moved into your holy place, the Paha Sapa, he's put your people on the bad land of the reservations, he's broken his promises and made war, he's tried to wipe out the new Ghost Dance. How do you feel about that?"

"Not too good," I said. But I could see from her eyes she wanted more than that. "I feel mad," I said. "I feel mixed up. What does the white man want from us anyway? Sometimes it's like he's trying to be friends, then he's trying to rub us out entirely."

She gave me a little smile to show I'm on the right track. "How do you feel about getting rubbed out?"

"For me," I said, thinking hard, "for me, personally, I don't care too awful much. But it's not just me. It — It's not the people either. It's — the world. The world the way it was. It's like the end of the world." I looked at Verine Manyponies again, and she nodded, pretty solemn now. "That's about the saddest thing I could think of," I said.

"Now say the words," she said. And it was like some kind of mir-acle. I didn't have a bit of trouble remembering. That whole long speech just flowed out of me, beginning to end. It was like the feeling of it was the stream and the words were just the leaves and pebbles and twigs that were caught in it and showed the power behind it. When I was done, I looked up at her and the warmth was pouring out of her eyes and into mine. And I glanced over to where Clyde Manyponies was standing having a cup of coffee by the kitchen counter and his eyes were filled up with warmth too, and he nodded slow and deliberate, two nods, and that felt better to me than any of the clapping I ever got from it in the actual show.

The rehearsing was another thing, though. The rest of the actors had been doing the show over a month already, and knew it so they could do it in their sleep, which some of them claimed they did. They were mostly college kids who signed for the summer to be able to spend some time in the Hills. Two or three, like General Custer, were actual actors who couldn't get better work other places. They all had in common a dislike for Monte Long. I must have been told eighteen times the first day how Mickey Mouse the operation was and how chickenshit Long was. They every one of them swore he rooked them one way or another in terms of money or what their duties were or something. Which pretty much matched my ideas. I would say a hundred years ago he would've been one of them medicine show men, and probably would've made a pretty good living at it. But the point is, all of the actors looked at their time off as their real wages. And I came along and need rehearsing and they wanted to make short work of it so they could get back to their own plans.

Add to that, because of the rain we had to practice inside the recreation hall, as Long called it, of the dormitory, as he called it, which was a medium-sized room with a ping-pong table, a card table, a television and a bunch of chairs, part of the building that fenced off the arena from the parking lot. The actors had little rooms with bunks partitioned off from the rest of the building, and the rooms looked for all the world like jail cells, only without the bars or the comfort. In the recreation hall, so-called, Long tried to set up the arena in miniature, a table here being the Indian camp, a bunch of chairs there being the fort, the table being the ridge, more chairs for the front stage, and so on, okay, let's go. They skipped all the parts that didn't pertain to Crazy Horse and left out all the lines except just what came before mine and pushed me and pulled me where I was supposed to go and explained what's supposed to happen in the meantime. The whole thing took about an hour, and by the end of it I was more mixed up and scared than I was in the first place.

Monte Long, though, seemed pretty satisfied. "Your lines are good," he said. "You're a quick study. You might as well start tonight."

That didn't soothe me in the least. "I don't even know how I'm supposed to get to where I'm supposed to be for my first speech."

"The other boys will show you," Long said. "No problem."

"Maybe we better go over it a couple more times," I said.

But Long just shook his head and waved his hand out at the room. I looked and there's nobody left but him and me. Everybody else had gone to whatever they had planned. "It'll be fine," he said, pounding me on the shoulder. "Just say the lines good and loud."

Lucky for me that first night there was still a mist in the air and only about a dozen people showed up. I got led and pushed around that arena like a blind man and got through most of my lines good enough just because I didn't have time to think. But before the last speech there was a long wait while the play concentrated on what was happening to Wild Bill and General Custer. I got thinking about that speech I had coming up and going over it in my head, but it seemed like I couldn't get more than two or three sentences into it before I dried up and had to start over. Then before I knew it the lights were on me and Monte Long was telling about Crazy Horse talking to the tribal elders one last time, and I couldn't even think of the first lines I had been going over and over, but I just stood there with my mouth a little open and wallowing like a trout out of water.

"My brothers——" I said, but it was no use. I didn't think any amount of priming would get me going. It crossed my mind like lightning what Verine Manyponies told me about the feeling, but the only feeling I could come up with at that moment was scared shitless, and that didn't budge any words out of me at all. I thought about trying to make something up, but all I could think of didn't seem to come up to the situation. So there I stood, trying to lick some wetness back into my lips, trying to swallow, and finally just hanging down my head until the light went off me. The other actors just laughed it off and said it's all right, but I went back to the makeup room feeling like I just swallowed a grapefruit whole. When Monte Long came in afterwards, I couldn't look at him. I thought, there goes my theatrical career. But all he did was to clap me on the shoulder and say, "Look at it like this: It was an eloquent silence."

It never happened again. And pretty soon I was even getting some clapping, and I didn't think I did too bad at that.

Quick, of course, didn't need much rehearsal for the old prospector part, which was mostly just leading the burro in and then kneeling down with a pan and making out like he was washing for gold. But the business about consulting on the history he took pretty serious. When we'd been going about three or four days, Monte Long called another afternoon get-together in the recreation room, which naturally caused a good deal of pissing and moaning among the actors. Long had them all set down and told them there was going to be some changes in the script. More groans.

"There have been some complaints about the play not conforming to historical truth," Long said. "Mr. Darling has graciously offered to make some strategic alterations." What he didn't mention is that the complaints as well as the gracious offer both came from Mr. Darling, as Quick now called himself. (Holden Darling, no less. Don't ask me where he came up with it.) "To start with," Long went on, "General Custer will be Colonel Custer from now on."

I tossed a look at General Custer, who first opened his mouth and then closed it with a snap and gave his golden curls a shake. His hair was his pride and joy and he used it to get a lot said. He had eloquent hair, Long might say.

"And since Comanche was a bay and we haven't got a bay, we'll have to do without the horse for a while," Long said.

"Ahem," General Custer went, and was holding up his hand and rattling his curls. Long pointed to him and General Custer stood up and propped his hand on his hip. "Just what am I supposed to do then? Just stand there?"

"Just do what Comanche does, George," one of the other actors said, and followed it with a pretty dirty noise he made with his tongue. Custer sat down again fast, his face turning pink.

"And we're cutting the farewell speeches, Custer's and Crazy Horse's," Long said.

That came as quite a blow to me, seeing I just spent so much sweat learning the speech and I just now was getting it out right and getting applause for it. But Custer was a long ways more upset than me, and was on his feet again, shaking his hair and turning his face from pink to red. "I have just one question," he said. "Why?"

Now Quick jumped in with his usual bad timing. "They never said it, that's why. Custer's is stole from Lincoln, the second inaugural, mostly, with a couple of echoes of Gettysburg. And Crazy Horse's is lock stock and barrel from Chief Joseph, hole-in-the-nose tribe. They are outright thefts."

Now to me all this sounded pretty amusing coming from a man with Quick's record of honesty. But Custer wasn't taking it so humorous. "But they work," he said. "They are the only good thing that this pitiful pageant has. They are the pivot, the center of the whole play." And every time he hit a word extra hard he gave his curls a jiggle.

Quick said, "To me that's no excuse for messing with the facts. We're going to be sending young kids away from here thinking Custer was a saint and Crazy Horse was another William Jennings Bryan. But maybe you don't care how you corrupt the young people."

For some reason, General Custer took particular exception to the last remark. "Well," he huffed. "I've never——" And he flounced out, his hair speaking volumes to make up for what his mouth couldn't.

Long broke up the meeting then, and there was a lot I don't know about how the thing was settled, but I do know that General Custer stayed a General, Comanche stayed a black, and the farewell speeches stayed in the play. It turned out to be a pretty sad day for truth and honesty. I suspect that was exactly what Monte Long thought would happen, and is another example of the special way that swindler had of getting his way.

Whether it was that or something else, Quick's disposition seemed to take a big nosedive about then. Considering what it had been, you can see it must've got pretty bad. All I saw at the time was he's wrassling hard with the business of true and false. My own notion is that a person can have two ideas almost exactly the opposite clunking around his head all his life and not have any trouble with them. Then something will happen where the ideas knock into each other at last and the person sees that one of them has got to go. Either that or he's got to weld them together somehow to make a whole different one. Quick had a respect for the truth, for sure, and a downright disgust for the kind of sham that went into an enterprise like the Golden West. But there was part of him I think was a little in love with the lie part, too, and he certainly had a knack for embroidering his own personal history with all kinds of fancy scrollwork. What I saw, it's something like he'd turned a corner and run smack into himself going the other way, and one or the other had to give.

But the strange part I couldn't entirely figure was why he took it out on me. The new quarters might have contributed. The cell we had to share in the "dormitory" was quite a comedown from the motel room, and I would rate it a good deal lower than that camp we had in the valley. He naturally grabbed the lower bunk, and about twice a night I would get waked up with a jump, getting a sharp prod from below with his fly rod case he kept leaning by the bunk for the purpose. "What the hell," was my usual response. "You're snoring," he wheezed. "Go to sleep," I threw back. "I'd like to," he'd say, and so on. Then a couple hours later my eyes would fling open again and I had the rod case sticking into my backbone through the thin mattress: "What the hell," and the whole thing all over again.

Then he got a cold from the damp weather and he was sniffing all over the place. As I say this, I know it sounds like a puny thing, but I swear he knew the sniffing got on my nerves and would sniff all the harder just to rub it in. I was in the bunk reading and he started in. Sniff. Silence. Sniff. Silence. SNIFF. Eloquent silence. SNIFF! "Jesus," I yelled. "Blow your damn nose!"

"I'll blow yours," he said, giving another mean sniff, "with black powder and a fuse."

I even took to tossing him my bandanna when it started to get to me, but he just threw it back and sniffed with a vengeance. It's my guess there's many divorces got started with a sniff, partnerships broken up by a snore. I wouldn't be surprised if there wasn't governments fell somewhere because of the way somebody crunched on an apple or sucked up soup.

If I could've seen where it was leading, I might've done different, but I doubt I would've put up with his tricks at Rushmore, no matter what. We couldn't have come to a parting of the ways faster or more permanent if he'd planned the whole thing.

21.

All the ruckus I'd been through with Quick had changed me some, I guess. Tippy-toeing on the edge of a canyon, scary as it was, at least lets you know you are alive. In a lot of ways I felt more alive than ever, and stronger somehow, like I'd found muscles I never knew I had. And the feeling I got about Verine Manyponies was part of it. Being with her it was like looking into a kind of mirror where you see things about yourself you never noticed before. At first I couldn't even believe that she'd want to spend time with me, but the mere fact that she did got me to thinking maybe I'm not such an entirely worthless individual as I sometimes felt like. It got me to thinking maybe there's things I can do I never dreamed of. Like being in the play, and all that, but even better.

We packed off to Rushmore that next Monday. I tried to talk Quick out of going along, thinking that they might just recognize us together whereas I would blend in pretty good alone. But you know by now how easy it was to talk Quick into or out of anything. He'd got past that short numb stage where he didn't seem to care where he was led. Now he's all for going to see T.R., as he called him, and it got pretty obvious he would not be put off.

"We can't take the Jeep," I told him. "They'll spot it sure."

"I'll ride with the Chief," Quick said. "In his pickup."

"There's only room for three in the cab," I told him.

"You can ride in the box," he said.

"In the rain?" It had been raining off and on all week, usually in the days, clearing up at night enough to put on the show. Besides, I was thinking that would cut me out of riding beside Verine Manyponies. "You can ride in back if you want to."

"I haven't got a raincoat," he said.

"Neither have I."

"I've got a cold already," he said, and gave me one of his sniffs to prove it.

But I was in no mood to give in. "That don't mean I have to get one. That would be fine, Crazy Horse with the sniffles."

"I forgot you had lines," he said. "Old prospectors that don't have lines can just as well die of pneumonia."

That got to me as much as anything, the hint that I was being superior to him. "All right," I said, "I'll ride in back. I'll get a sheet of plastic to cover me."

"Never mind," he said. "I guess I can ride in back if you want me to."

You see what he was doing. Anything to get to me. "Dammit, ride there, then," I said.

"You'd enjoy that, wouldn't you?"

"You want to come, ride in back. If not, then don't." Maybe I was hard in doing that, but he'd been chipping away at me too long. I had as much as I could stand.

He rode in back with a plastic ground cloth of Clyde Manyponies' pulled around him. It was raining pretty good, too. I tried not to think about it, tried to make talk with Clyde and Verine, but it was no use. I kept twisting around to look at him. He was huddled up there in the corner of the box on the left side, his back to the cab, with the plastic folded over his head like an Indian blanket.

"He'll be all right," Clyde Manyponies said to me when he saw me look for maybe the fifth time.

"Sure," I said. But it seemed like there was no way to win with Quick. Now he had me feeling guilty as sin.

"He's quite an old character," Clyde said.

"You don't know the half," I said.

"I don't suppose it's any business of mine," he said. "It does seem a little odd, you two travelling together."

"He's just an old guy I got mixed up with," I said, which I think is what one of my teachers in high school used to call a vast oversimplification.

"What's he got on you?" Clyde said, kind of smiling to hide the fact that he really wanted to know.

I looked at Verine setting between us, but she's got her eyes looking down like she knows there's serious talk going on. "Nothing," I said. "He's got nothing on me." And I got to thinking it's true. There's nothing he can do to get me in any more trouble than I already got. That about telling the cops I planned the holdup, that didn't hold too much, what with the other scrapes he'd got us into. And I'd got us out of. I really don't owe him a thing. So went my thinking.

"I'm glad to hear that," Clyde Manyponies said. But he didn't sound too sure.

"He's getting to be more trouble than he's worth," I said, watching the wipers slashing across the windshield.

"Never mind," Clyde said. "I've been mixed up with people myself. I know how it goes."

"Who did you get mixed up with?"

"The movement, for one thing. We were gonna change the world. It's not that easy." He drove a while longer. "Verine's mother. We were out to change the world, too."

"What happened?"

"We didn't change the world, that's for sure. We met at college. It was an optimistic time. J.F.K. years. Before it all started to go bad. It seemed liked it might be possible for somebody like me and somebody like her to have some kind of life. White girl and an Indian, so what? We're all human beings. That's what we thought. That's how dumb we were."

Nobody said anything for a long time. The wipers worked. The tires squished on the wet pavement. I was waiting for Clyde to finish the story, but I guess he thought it was finished.

By this time we were at Rushmore and pulled into the parking lot and I kind of forgot about this little discussion.My problem right then was to keep Quick from drawing too much attention to us. About the first thing I saw was all the ranger uniforms around, and they were close enough to cops to make me pretty nervous. I got out of the cab and walked around back. Quick was trying to get out from under the plastic.

"Christ," he said. "I'm all cramped up. I don't think I'll ever get straight again."

I helped him out of the box. "Just don't try to stand out too much." But even when I said it, I saw it was almost a lost cause. For one thing, he had taken a shine to the costume he wore as the old prospector, that fringed leather shirt and the beat-up old hat, and that was what he was wearing now. There was about as much chance of his not sticking out as a basketball player at a pygmies' ball. Besides that was not his personal inclination. I think he might feel something was wrong if he didn't have people staring at him like the main attraction at the freak show. As soon as he got out of the truck, he headed up toward the visitor center.

I took Verine's arm. "We better keep an eye on him." I said. "But lag behind. Pretend you don't know him."

"You go on," Clyde said. "I'll see if I can scare up any of the COUP bunch."

So me and Verine set off on Quick's trail, up the walk that has all the state flags hanging on each side. There's a big concrete and stone porch on one side of the visitor center where you can look at the faces, and that's right where Quick headed. We hung back from him and take in the stone heads up above. I'd never seen them before in real life, and to tell the truth I was a little disappointed. Maybe it was the situation and the weather. There was clouds skittering over and around, sometimes hiding them altogether, and the rain had made big wet splotches on them. One, I think maybe it's Jefferson, the one that looked kind of soft and womanish, he had a dark stain coming down his forehead like he'd got wounded there and was bleeding.

And Lincoln looked for all the world like he'd been bawling. But the main thing was, it seemed like a waste of a good mountain, besides being a terrible vain thing. Like Quick said about the ski-lift (here's another place it seemed like he was of two minds), you wonder why anybody would want to do such a thing. Then, big as you know they are, they don't look all that large in comparison to the surroundings. And you know a good earthquake could wipe them out, or a couple hundred years of just getting rained on, or a million years, which like one of my high school teachers says is no more than a tick where the world is concerned. It seemed to me it had just the opposite effect of what was intended. It showed us up for the stubborn, conceited, foolish creatures we are. I don't see much difference between that and carving your initials in a tree or painting your name on a rock or chipping the outline of your hand into the sandstone. Every park I been in, they got rules about not doing those things, but I guess if a government does it, or a big company, that's all right. My thoughts were running along about like that when I felt Verine yank on my arm and I looked where she was nodding and there was Quick, who'd climbed up on the stone ledge of the porch, which was maybe four feet high, like he had to get a better view than anyone else.

"Shit," I said, and sneaked some looks around to see if there were any rangers in sight. By some kind of miracle, there was nothing but tourists, some of them starting to look as interested in Quick as the stone faces. I walked fast over to the ledge and Verine went with me.

"Get down off there," I said, not too loud to call attention to us. "You're making a damn fool of yourself." For about the thousandth time, I could just as well have added.

Quick tipped his face down to me, and he's got a look on it of the kind you see a lot in religious pamphlets, that kind of saintly look of a guy who's just said a prayer or let a fart. "There he is," he said to me. And looked back up at the heads.

"Come down here," I said. "People are starting to notice."

"Don't he look like he could chew bullets and spit sinkers?"

"Which one?" I said, trying out a new idea. "Come down and show me."

"Right there, dammit." He waved his hand up and he wobbled a little on his perch, almost thrown off balance. "There's no mistaking that face."

I reached up to grab his hand, but he danced on down the ledge a little, out of reach. "A genuine war hero, too," he said. "Not just an officer or a president who happened to get into a war, but a hero. San Juan Ridge."

I was getting pretty desperate now. I whispered to Verine to go stand over by the steps and yell if she saw a ranger coming. Then I tried to edge closer to Quick, being as casual as I could force myself to be. "I never heard of it," I said. "Tell me about it." See, I was trying to get his mind on something else so I could get close enough to catch hold and haul him down. Now I look back, I see it was a big mistake.

"Never heard of it?" Quick said. "What do they teach in history classes anymore? Colonel Roosevelt and his Rough Riders with those Mauser bullets ringing around their heads, but up they go, T.R. himself leading them all, on board of his horse Texas."

Looking around I see quite a few tourists watching Quick like they were halfway suspicious he was part of the show the U.S. government had provided, sparing no expense to the taxpayer. I saw I may already have missed my best chance. Quick was doing it to me again.

"Look at me here," Quick yelled then, and me and about fifty tourists who up to then had been ignoring him, now took a good look. "Look at me up here on top of Texas." That's what he said. "Me on a horse and you on foot, and who do you think them Spiks is going to choose first for a target? So don't get any ideas of diving for cover. Long as you see me, you know we stand a chance."

Quick was waving his arms and getting into the spirit of it pretty good. I noticed a lot of tourists with cameras starting to take pictures of him.

"Miles of wire with catclaw barbs," Quick was saying, "a steep slope of open ground to run up, a sleet storm of Mauser fire that could cut a man down like a stalk of corn, and Spaniards dug in as snug as June bugs. Not even to mention the artillery fire. Ninety of them are bound to die, but up they go, and Colonel Roosevelt himself ahead of and above them all."

He had his hat off now, flapping it and pointing it up the mountain, and there were mumblings and rumblings coming from the tourists like they were getting ready to follow him to the top, just like he was T.R. himself. I felt a tug at my elbow and Verine was saying to me that there was a ranger coming up the walk. But Quick was going full throttle now. "Men are falling all around him, but up he goes, until Texas gets caught in the wire. Then he jumps off and goes it by foot, his polkadot scarf flapping in the wind. The Spanish see he can't be stopped, and half of them turn tail and the other half is plugged and before you can say bully, there he is at the top. Colonel Teddy Roosevelt, walking soft, carrying a big stick and saying, Look at me here. And he's still up there, same fire in his eye, same grit in his teeth, same—"

But just then I saw my chance and reached up and grabbed a handful of fringe on his leather shirt and jerked and he teetered a second and came flailing down like some big bird that's been shot, landing in a heap at my feet.

The tourists, half of them figured it's part of the show, gave him a pretty good hand of applause, but some I heard saying he doesn't look much like Roosevelt, and others saying it would be better with music and sound effects. I was bending over him just to see if he was still alive, shaking him and tugging at his shirt. First thing I knew there was a ranger in a hat beside me bending over him too. "What's wrong with him?" the ranger said.

"It's the altitude," was all I could think of to say. "I think the thin air got to him."

"A stroke," the ranger said. "Keep him here. I'll get some oxygen." And he ran off.

As for keeping him there, looked like there wasn't much choice. The old fart was out cold, but he was still breathing. "Help me," I said to Verine, and we got him up between us like a drunk, and drug him off the porch and around the corner of the visitor center and onto a stone bench where we sat him down. He was starting to come around then. "Who was it?"

Something just went bust inside me then. "It was me, you silly shit," I yelled. "You got our tails in the soup again. You and your damn T.R. and Zane Grey and John Wayne and Wild Bill crap."

He just narrowed his eyes and made them into two blue steel bullets and said, like a line out of a book or a movie, "You hit me one too many times, you little bastard."

And it was that that finally did it. I got up and stormed off down the walk, mad and disgusted as hell. I even forgot about Verine, I was so hacked off. Right then I didn't care ever to see his ugly face again.

I was just outside the gate, marching toward the pickup when I heard someone calling to me. "Hey, stuck up. Hey, where you going, stuck up?"

When I looked around to see who it was, I saw Lymon Twobows with Leonard Fourwinds and Clyde Manyponies and another one who looked a little familiar, tall and with old-fashioned braids. They looked like they were doing an imitation of Mt. Rushmore.

22.

Lymon was looking good, with that face more and more like it was chiseled out of stone. He was the one who called "stuck up" to me, and he gave me a grin when I recognized him. The others were looking solemn.

"You know Leonard," Lymon said. "This here is Purcell Wolf," he said, motioning to the tall one.

It hit me then why he looked familiar. He was the one who founded COUP. I'd seen him often enough on the TV, and in person he looked just the same, only a little less real. I mean, when you finally meet someone you've only seen on television, it is a little like a dream. You don't know how to act. I didn't know whether to shake hands or switch channels. Lymon had a good laugh on me, the way I was mumbling and fumbling around.

There were all kinds of currents flowing around Lymon and me, questions we both had, and things we had to say, but we were holding back because of the others being there.

"What're you doing here?" is about all I could think to say.

"Making plans," Lymon said. "Working out the details for the anniversary demonstration."

"What about your job at Hillview?"

"I quit. It's a long story. We're at Thunder Mountain camp. You need a place to stay?"

"We got a place at Golden West. It's another long story."

Verine came up about then and said she'd got Quick back in the pickup. She said after I took off an old lady came up to him who saw him on the ledge and figured he's a worker for the monument and asked Quick where she could mail a postcard. Where he told her to stick the card would take a whole new zip code. And the old lady ran off to find a ranger. So I said we'd better all get going before the old lady gets together with the ranger who went for the oxygen and they send out a search party for me and this old fart that is supposed to be half-dead with a stroke. So Verine and Lymon and Leonard and Purcell and me all piled into Purcell's station wagon. Clyde Manyponies took Quick in the pickup, so the old man could stretch out on the seat a little.

On the way back to Golden West I told Lymon what all had happened since I'd seen him last, once in a while shooting a look over to Verine to see how she was taking it. I spared them a few gory details, but it felt pretty good to get it off my chest. I didn't realize until then how tough it'd been keeping it all to myself with no one but Quick to talk about it to.

When I was done, Lymon shook his head, "Colton's bull would be bad enough. With you it is one thing after another."

"How did it go with Colton?" I asked him.

"About what you'd expect. He had his goons coming to Celia's place asking questions, giving everybody a hard time. I went to Leonard, and he went to Purcell, and COUP raised a big stink about it, saying Colton was harassing Celia. That's how I met Purcell and everybody and decided to join up with them. I am kind of their poster child, I guess."

"Lymon is being modest," Purcell Wolf said, who was driving. "He got a lot of publicity for us. You've got to keep people thinking about things like that, or else it's like killing a turtle. You've got to keep killing him or else he will put his head back on and crawl away."

Everybody else got a chuckle out of that. I looked at Verine and she was looking at Lymon and I got to feeling that something was happening all over again. "What happened to the German girls?" I said. I hadn't planned on saying anything about that, but something mean inside me made me.

Lymon gave me a flat kind of stare. "They left." There was more to the story, his eyes said, but he wasn't gonna let it out there. I let it go.

"Maybe you want to come down to the camp tonight," Lymon said as we pulled into Golden West. "You and Clyde and Verine," he added on, but it was Verine he was looking at.

"White guy wanted by the law," Leonard Fourwinds said. "Just what we need." He looked at Purcell Wolf.

Purcell pulled up to park in front of the motel. "We've had our share of people the law was looking for. I doubt they'd look for him there, anyway. Let him come, if he wants to."

Verine and Clyde and me, we got Quick out of his damp clothes and into his bunk. We got some hot soup from the restaurant into him. He was quiet, but he didn't seem right to me. He'd been taking his pills all right, far as I knew, but I was worried that something had gone wrong the way it had before, when his daughter had put him into the Hillview Home in the first place. I was still pretty mad at him for calling me a little bastard, too. It wasn't so much what was said, but the way he'd said it, with so much venom, like he'd wanted to hurt me. I didn't see how I'd deserved that.

Verine was spooning soup into him when he looked up at me and swallowed and said, "What happened?"

"You know what happened. You made a fool of yourself."

He blinked at me, his eyes all runny, and shook his head. "Checkers?" he said.

"You don't remember?"

"Someone was cheating. I gave them a hit."

"That was a long time ago. Eat your soup."

I went outside with Clyde and we talked a while. It was pretty obvious there was something wrong. I didn't know if we should try to get the old fart to a doctor. He'd been like that before, and he'd pulled out. Clyde thought he'd be all right. "He just needs some rest, probably."

I was thinking how I'd like to go to Thunder Mountain camp and talk to Lymon, but I should stay there in case Quick had another spell. And finally Clyde said, "You and Verine take the pickup and go. I'll stick around and keep an eye on him."

I still wasn't sure. Quick had me feeling guilty again. But when we went back in, he was asleep already and looking pretty peaceful, and after we'd had some supper, he was still sleeping, so I took Clyde up on his offer.

Thunder Mountain was a camp that COUP had set up over by Pactola, right in the middle of national forest land, in order to show they had the right to be there. They claimed that the land had been stolen from them in the first place, so it was legally theirs. Naturally, the government was at sixes and sevens about what to do about it. So it was a kind of a standoff. The government let them be, which turned out to be a rare smart thing, because unless the government made some fuss about it, the camp didn't make the evening news, and everybody forgot about it.

You got to the camp by way of an old logging road and then a foot trail through the spruce. Then you came to a clearing where there were a lot of tipis set up in a circle and inside the circle a space for people to gather and talk. Really, it was a pretty nice place, even if it was a little like something someone would think up if they only knew a little bit about Indians. Tipis in amongst the pine trees struck me funny right away. I kept thinking, why didn't they make some log houses? But who was I to say anything? I figured they must know what they were doing.

That night they'd built up a fire and we sat around on rocks and logs and just talked a lot at first. I got a lot of cold stares from people who didn't like my looks or something, but just as many people came up and said hello. There were other people there didn't look any more Indian than I did, and some a lot less so.

Lymon and me had a good talk, when there were just the two of us. He finally told me about Ingrid flinging herself at him and about him flinging himself back. "I knew you'd been giving her the eye," he told me, "but you didn't seem to want to do anything about it. Besides, you were gone by that time." After all that flinging, they took some time to talk, and that's when things changed. "You start thinking what it would be like, married to a white woman. And at first you think, hey, pretty good, like maybe getting a credit card and no limit. But then you think about guys like Clyde Manyponies who did that, and how it screwed them up. There've got to be resentments, both sides."

"Verine turned out pretty good," I put in.

"She was too young to remember her mother very much. Clyde just raised her to think Lakota. You try to have it both ways, that's when the pinch comes."

"So you and Ingrid came to that conclusion?"

"Sort of. Anyway, it came time for her to leave, and she did leave. She said she will write." He didn't sound too sad about it, but it still seemed sad to me, somehow. I wondered how Ingrid felt about it, whether she was happy to have done her bit for the plight of the Indian or felt like she had come up short. And I thought about Lorrie, too, who had grown on me as time went on. It's funny how people will stick with you like that.

"This about pretending to be Crazy Horse," Lymon said. "What's that all about?"

"It's just a kind of play," I said. And I told him about the camouflage idea and everything. Besides being one of the first things I ever felt I could be proud of.

"Like 'I'm not a doctor, but I play one on TV'?" Lymon said.

"Something like that."

"I worry about you sometimes. You're not Lakota, you know."

"I know that."

"Sometimes you act like you think you were."

"I've got more sense than that."

"Sometimes I wonder."

Lymon shook his head at that and held out his hand to shake, and I took it. "It doesn't make any difference," he said. "Only you got yourself in one hell of a fix, if you ask me."

I couldn't very well argue that.

"I'm going after the vision," Lymon said. And he gave me a steady look, waiting for me to say something.

"When?"

"As soon as they get done making the sweat lodge. Leonard will help me get ready for it. Then I will go to the mountain."

"What made up your mind?"

"I'm not certain. After that business with Colton, and all that publicity, I felt different about it. Like maybe I'm cut out for something special after all."

"I always thought so."

"It scares me some, though. What if I go through all that and nothing happens?"

"Don't you get another try?"

"You can try as much as you want, I suppose. Some have been known to."

"Well, then," I said. All I knew about going after the vision was that it's not a thing to take too casual. For the old-time Lakota, the vision was something you looked for to tell you who you really were. For some, the vision came without asking, and some had more than one, but for others it was pretty hard work to get to the point where your eyes opened to it. There were fasts and the sweat lodge and climbing to high places to wait it out, and I don't know what all. Flesh offerings. Sacrifices. And what you got out of it is just knowing where you stand in the world. Not just your name, though that may be part of it, nor some silly white man thing like a title, professor or president or general, but what I guess you could call your center, your center of gravity, maybe, where you balance. And what you've got to decide ahead of time is what it's worth to you to know.

"And what if I catch a thunder vision?" Lymon said. "What if I turn out to be a thunder-dreamer?" And he gave me a wide-eyed look like he really expected me to answer that one.

Lymon had told me before about Heyokas, thunder-dreamers, which seemed to me about the strangest and most awful thing a person could turn out to be. They dreamed about flying, and in their visions they learned to sing thunder songs, and they had great and secret powers to bring benefits to their people, but, come right down to it, they were like clowns, kind of holy fools, and they were always poor, dirty, in rags, and alone. In the old days, anyway. "Is there such a thing in this day and age?" I asked Lymon.

"Leonard says there is. They don't all own up to it. Some of the drinkers are like that, he thinks. People laugh at them and pity them, and feel superior to them, but they can do these wonderful things, these miracles, but only for other people."

I wondered if I knew anybody like that. Maybe some of my Uncle Blanks, who always kept everybody laughing until they hit the floor and passed out. Some of them you liked so much, and they seemed to have nothing but good feelings for people, not like those that were punching all the time. They made you laugh and they did magic tricks, and somehow you felt good just to've known them. But they couldn't rise in the world. And pretty soon, like all the others, they wandered off.

"Anyway," Lymon said, "I'm going to do it. I guess I'll find out, one way or another."

Purcell Wolf came out about then and sat down and started talking a little. He had a stick, and he poked at the fire with it. People asked him questions, and he carried on a conversation. It wasn't anything so special, I suppose, but people listened to him careful. There was something about him made you want to listen. He gave the impression of knowing things you hadn't even thought about. I can't even remember much of what he said, but just have a picture of him there, looking so Indian with those braids and the way he was dressed, squinting into the fire, and talking slow and low. "Nobody's going away," I remember he said once. "It's no use anyone hoping for that. We're here and the Europeans are here, and nobody's going anywhere. So it's just a matter of what's fair. It comes down to that. And the only way we will get what's due is to keep reminding people we're still here." It was all pretty calm and plain, it seemed to me, and with none of that angry, gravelly talk that you hear him saying on the TV so much. And nothing like the fancy speeches in the play, either. He seemed to make pretty good sense.

I went looking for Verine after a while. I saw her with some other women, sitting and talking, and I started over to them, when a guy got in front of me and cut me off. He was shorter than me, and older, and wore glasses, and had a kind of sour look on his face. I figured he was just another one of them who didn't care for my looks. "You think any good will come of this?" he asked me.

I wasn't sure what he meant, so I just tried to shrug him off, but he stuck with me. "You think you're doing something special here?"

"I'm just visiting a friend of mine," I said.

"You're not even Indian," he said.

"My friend is."

"You think this is the way to go about getting back the Hills?"

"About as good as any other." I was getting a little irritated by now. "Who wants to know?"

He dug a card out of his shirt pocket and held it out. I held it up so that it caught the firelight. It said his name was Antone Reese and that he was a reporter for a newspaper. All I needed. "I don't have anything to say," I told him, handing him back the card.

"What's your name?" he said.

"None of your business."

"You think this is what the Lakota people want? You think Purcell Wolf is some kind of savior, some kind of super chief?"

"I don't think anything," I said. "Go ask someone with an opinion."

"He's got so many people fooled. He sets himself up as some kind of spokesman. TV people come from out east, he's the one they talk to. Like he's got all the answers. You know how many are in COUP? About three percent of registered tribal members. From other tribes, many of them. And the rest groupies like you."

"You seem to know a lot about this. I don't know what you are asking me anything for."

He grinned at me, then. Now he'd shown how ignorant I was he seemed halfway satisfied. "You want to add anything?"

"Sure, Mr. Reese. I like your peanie-butter cups." And I finally managed to get past him.

"You want to start back?" I asked Verine.

"Maybe so," she said. And she pulled her jacket around her and zipped it up and said goodbye to the women she'd been talking to.

"I saw you talking to Reese," she said.

"He acted like he had a cob up his butt," I said. "Why do they even let him in here?"

"They never turn down a reporter, from what I can tell. Especially if he's an Indian."

I waved goodbye to Lymon and started on down the trail to the car. It had cleared off pretty good by then, and the moon was full, so there was no trouble seeing. When we got to the pickup, Verine leaned back against it and looked up at the sky.

"It's a pretty night. Let's not go yet."

Fine with me. It was one of the first times we'd ever been completely alone. "Your father keeps a pretty close watch on you," I told her.

"It's been worse this week because of the rain," she said. "But he's always pretty protective. I think he's afraid I'll get away from him like my mother did. He trusts you, though."

That seemed to me like a terrible thing to say. Now I had to live up to being trusted, just when I had entirely different ideas.

"My mother left when I was three," Verine said. "I hardly remember her. I always thought she'd died, for a long time. Then I found out that she ran off with someone."

That got me thinking again of how people are made to act a certain way. "What I told about in the car," I said. "I'm sorry I couldn't tell you about it before. I did other things, too. Things I can't even tell you about." I was thinking about all that chasing after women I'd been doing.

"I can't believe you'd do anything very bad," she said.

"It's not so much what I did," I told her. "It's what I had in mind to do. I'd really feel bad now if I'd gone through with it."

Where the pickup was parked, along with the other cars, there were rocks slanting up out of a cushion of pine needles, and past them a cliff that fell off into a valley. You could see a stream away down below like a silver thread that's been dropped in big open loops. We leaned against the pickup and looked at it all. The moon was so clear you could see the gray patterns on it, the craters and mountains and the cold, dry seas. And Verine said, "The old Lakota said the moon is a woman. She runs after the sun until the sun catches up with her."

I thought how pretty that was, and true in a way. The moon lags behind more and more every night until you can see it in broad daylight at the same time as the sun. But right then I saw another light moving in the sky, and I pointed to it.

"What is it? A plane?"

But it was moving too steady and fast and quiet for that. "I think it's one of those satellites," I said. "A spy in the sky, maybe."

"Not as pretty as the moon."

"The moon is just a ball made out of rock," I said. "It's just what it looks like. Men have walked on it, driven around." I remember that because of seeing it on TV when I was a kid.

"It's still pretty. Like wrinkles on an old person. It doesn't have to spoil anything."

"Only you can't go back to not knowing something. No matter how bad you want to. Once you've learned it, you just have to put up with it."

We talked a long time like that. She was easy to talk to. I guess I thought I was in love again. Not the way it was with hers truly Karen Stephenson, maybe, nor with Ingrid nor Lorrie nor Delly, but in a way I'd never felt before, whole and warm and satisfied.

When we got back to Golden West, the sun was coming up. Clyde came out of the dormitory when we pulled up. "Quick is gone," he said. "He was sleeping sound, and I went out in the rec room and settled into chair and slept some myself, and when I went to check, he was gone. He took the Jeep, it looks like."

Quick had been about the last thing on my mind. Now that old tight feeling came back in my throat. I thought I should go after him, but then I realized that this time I had no idea where he might be headed. He did mention Wyoming before, but who knows where his crazy head might be leading him?

"I'm sorry," Clyde said. "I should've been keeping closer watch."

What could I say? It wasn't the first person who got away from him. I figured he must be feeling pretty bad.

When I went back to the room in the dormitory, I found Quick's rod case laying on my bunk, along with the medicine wheel Aunt Celia gave me. And was a little relieved, thinking he'd be back, that he'd never leave for long without his fly rod. It never occurred to me at first that he meant it as a gift.

23.

I had a hard time getting to sleep. For one thing, it was broad daylight, and for another, I couldn't help thinking about everything. I lay
in my bunk wondering about all that had happened and how strange
a fix I was in. I kept going back over everything from the beginning,
with the stuff at Hillview, the res, Colton's bull, Deadwood, the
Ghost Fish, the Golden West and Mt. Rushmore, and now, just when
I was feeling halfway good about things again, Quick gets his mon-
key-wrench in the gears as usual. About half the time I would be mad
about Quick getting me into all these scrapes, and the other half I
would be worried about him and what he was up to. My mind kept
going back and forth like a tire swing until I got a headache, which I
hardly ever get. And then when I did get to sleep, I caught a nightmare worse than I've ever had.

I was on a swing, getting pushed higher and higher, and I was
scared, the way I usually was, and then something broke and I went
sailing off hanging onto the tire, and the next thing I knew I was on a
motorcycle whizzing along one of those curvy two-lanes in the Hills.
You know how nightmares are. They seem to make sense even when
they don't. It didn't strike me as strange I was straddling this hog,
roaring along hunched over with the cool wind blowing past my ears
making the sound you hear in seashells, in spite of the fact that I'd
never been on a motorcycle before and didn't even like the damn
things. There was another person on a Harley in front of me, and we
were winding along on one of the roads where the cliffs jut up on one
side and the other side is a dropoff. There was a kind of easy rhythm

to it, hardly any effort at all, leaning into the curves. But then the guy ahead of me slowed down and so did I. There was a car dogging along in front of us. I saw right away it was a Jeep wagon, but I didn't think anything about it at first. As soon as the other motorcycle guy found a place to pass, he pulled around the Jeep, and I started after him. I have no idea where we were headed, but we seemed in a big hurry to get there. As I came alongside the Jeep, it started to look more and more familiar, and even from the rear I could see the driver's steel-gray hair and grizzled beard, and by the time I'd pulled even with the driver's seat, there wasn't any doubt it was Quick. He looked over at me and there was a pale blue fire in his eyes that was terrible to see. He looked like one of those pictures you see sometimes in history textbooks of John Brown, where his righteousness seems to be just burning him up. And before I could rev up and get past, he cranked over, nudging the bike closer to the dropoff. I didn't have time to think what to do, and the next thing I knew the motorcycle bumped onto the shoulder, swerved a little, and then went charging off into nowhere. The machine dropped away under me and I was flying, aimed right toward the trunk of a big ponderosa pine.

If I'd've had any sense, I would have woke up right then, but instead everything just went black, and then before I knew it I was sitting in a waiting room, blinking like I'd just come to after nodding off, and I had to think for a second where I was. It was pretty obvious it was a waiting room, because there were a lot of people sitting around looking like they'd just as soon be anywhere else, some of them reading dogeared old magazines, some of them staring at a television in one corner of the room, and some of them sneaking glances at the others like they didn't want to be caught looking or just looking off with that kind of stunned look people get when they are actually looking into their own heads.

Nobody said anything to anybody else, and they all looked like they'd just as soon not be talked to, like they might just kill somebody if they got asked about the weather, even. The room was all wood of various kinds and colors, oak paneling for the walls, with walnut trim, and maple furniture. The pictures on the walls were the kind you see in waiting rooms, the kind that looked like they were painted in Mexico by somebody who was getting paid for how many he could turn out in an hour. There were windows, but it was dark outside, so all you could see in the glass was the reflection of the room. At one end of the room there was one of those glass windows to a little room where a receptionist sat. She was dressed all in white, and she looked about a thousand years old. Beside that window there was a paneled wooden door, ash, I think, although how I knew all these different kinds of wood just by looking at them, I don't really know. From the other side of the door came sounds of someone half-gagged, squealing with pain, and the sound of a dentist's drill whirring and grinding up and down a scale from a high whine to a low growl when there was so much friction that something was probably starting to smoke. There was not much question what kind of a waiting room it was. Once in a while, when the muffled screams got really bad, almost everybody in the room would look at the door. But some just licked their dry lips and let their eyes roll back in their heads and tried not to think about it.

The television was showing some kind of educational program, it looked like, about famous people who'd got shot. It was a black and white set, and there were still photographs of Abraham Lincoln. To get some movement into the picture, they kept sliding around, one side to the other, or top and bottom, until it almost made you dizzy watching. Or there would be etchings showing Lincoln watching the play, and John Wilkes Booth coming up behind him with a gun. And they would fade from one etching to another like it was some kind of slow motion. The sound was turned too low to hear, but you could about imagine what it was saying, and there was thin, tinny music, too, kind of putting in exclamation points and telling you how you should feel. Then came Wild Bill Hickok and Jack McCall, and then Crazy Horse and Sitting Bull, and then President McKinley, and then JFK and Bobby Kennedy and Martin Luther King, Jr., the later ones with all that tape and film everyone has seen about a million times,

John Kennedy and the one about asking not and King saying he had a dream.

When I lost interest in the television, I kind of peeked at some of the other people. Some of them looked pretty familiar, and some I recognized with no problem at all. Jake McManus, for one, who ran the cafe where my mother worked. He was sitting there in the apron he always wore. And beside him sat the guy with the Lysol breath I'd seen in Weed, with a half-smile on his face, showing the gaps in his teeth, day-dreaming. There were two or three Uncle Blanks there, too, looking like they were about ready to give somebody a sock. Right across from me was a skinny woman with her face buried in a glamour magazine. Then she let the magazine down and looked up at me and grinned, pulling her thin lips back over her front teeth, and it was the skull girl.

I couldn't stand the look she gave me, so I went back to the television and there was Zack Twobows, who must've been talking Lakota, because there were English words printed at the bottom of the screen: "Ho. Little Brother, there are many things that are strange in the world which we cannot grasp with our own poor eyes. We have to see with other eyes, the eagle eyes and the coyote eyes that are inside us. Then we will see who we are and where we are. Do not be afraid to see who you are. Let the dream come."

And just then the door opened up and out stumbled a person holding his hand over his mouth and moaning. He fell into a chair and sat there rocking, holding his mouth. And the receptionist was standing in the door. And she smiled this terrible smile and nodded at me.

I woke up shaking so bad I had to pull a blanket around me. It seemed like a cold blade had been laid along my spine. It took me over an hour to get my warmth back and stop shivering. I tried to forget the nightmare, but it was too real. It stuck with me like one of those movies you can't stop thinking about, the kind that seem to mean one thing when you first see them and something entirely different after you think about them for a while. I was spooked for sure.

One thing was, I recognized the road where the motorcycle skidded off. It was along the way from Rochford to Cheyenne Crossing. Quick and me, we'd just been along it, going the other way, a couple weeks ago. In the dream, Quick was headed north, but who knew how much stock to put in that?

When I finally crawled out of the bunk, it was after noon. I should've been hungry, but I wasn't. I went into the rec room, where there was a phone, and I tried calling my mother's number collect, but there was nobody home. I let it ring about a dozen times, and then told the operator to forget it.

I picked up a magazine, but I couldn't seem to concentrate on the words, so I tossed it back on the sofa and went outside. It was pretty warm, and the pine smell was strong in the air. I started down to the trailer court, thinking I'd talk to Clyde and Verine a little. Purcell Wolf's car was sitting outside Clyde's trailer, and I thought, good, I can talk to him, too, and see what he made of the words I'd seen in the nightmare. But the door of the station wagon opened up and Verine slid out, and after her Lymon. I pulled up short when I saw them. I don't know why, just something about the way they moved, like they were doing some kind of slow dance, took me by surprise and made me think there was something strange happening. He closed the door and they stood there by the car talking. I couldn't hear them, of course, but it seemed to me they were telling secrets to each other, the way she seemed to look everywhere but at him, the way he couldn't seem to look anywhere but at her. And then he put his hand on her waist and pulled her close and kissed her. She pulled away right away and turned and scurried on into the trailer. He stood and watched for a few seconds after her, then he opened up the car door again and got inside and started it up and backed it up and swung it around and started up the road toward me. I pulled back into the shadows of the pines, and he rolled on past without seeing me. It was a simple thing, I suppose, and could be explained any number of ways, but I took it just one way. I was getting to wonder if I could ever win. I didn't grudge Lymon, really, nor Verine, either. Nothing strange about it at all, except the way I felt, which is pretty much like odd man out.

I can't remember a lot about the next few days. I went ahead with the pageant and the sarsaparilla concession and everything. I kept trying to get my mother on the phone, but nobody ever answered. I was getting worried about that, too, but by that time, pretty much nothing would surprise me, especially if it was bad news. There was no word from Quick, naturally. I kept watching the paper, though, and finally there was a little story in the Journal about a biker going off the road north of Rochford, and getting killed. The story was on like page five, it was such a common thing, but it said the name of the biker was Garrett Bonner, 31, from Snoquomish, Washington. They didn't say his name was Junior, but they didn't need to. I got the chills all over again.

That night, just before the pageant started, I tried my mother again, and she answered.

"Honey," she said, "where are you now?"

"I'd better not tell you. I'm all right. You sound tired."

"Do I? Maybe I am. I've been on double shifts. When are you coming home?"

"I don't know. Have the police talked to you any more?"

"About every week, it seems like. They had you up at Deadwood, one time. You must get around."

"Sure," I said. "I'm everywhere. Listen, Jake McManus—"

"You heard about Jake?"

"Not really. I was just wondering."

"He keeled over in the kitchen last Saturday. Massive heart attack. We called the ambulance, but he was dead when they got there."

I couldn't say anything. I felt that cold blade pressed against my back again.

"Rodney, you there?"

"That's why you're working double shifts?"

"Kind of. His daughter is trying to run the place. She's a hairdresser, but she thinks she knows how to run an eatery. Marge quit right away. I've been thinking about it myself. Jake could be a real ass-hole sometimes, but his daughter is worse."

"What about the liquor-store guy?"

"He's out of the hospital, only crippled up, I guess. One side of the body useless."

"What are they saying? We're to blame?"

"He'd had other strokes before. It was just a matter of time. You can't be to blame for everything."

I didn't know what to say. I felt guilty enough.

"You're not a bad boy, honey. Too good, if anything. You don't have the kind of meanness it takes to get along in this world."

"Do you think so?"

"The world is ruled by tight-asses with not a kind drop of blood in them. You're lucky you're not like them."

Something about the way she was going on struck me odd. "Are you all right?"

"I'm fine. Maybe a little tired, like you said."

"What about Red? How is the professor doing?"

There was about a half a tick before she answered. "Red's gone."

"Did he get a job offer from a university or something?"

"He got an offer, all right. Not from a university, though. I'm not too sure she graduated kindergarten."

"Another Uncle Blank."

"Don't say that. You know I don't like that. Just put him out of your head. He's not worth remembering."

"I've forgot him already."

"Forgot who?"

"I don't remember," I told her. "What were we talking about?"

"Rodney, I'm scared."

"Don't be scared. I'm fine."

"Not just about you. Me too. I got nothing to fall back on. I got nothing put away. What am I gonna do, waitress until I drop? I've got varicose veins. I'm losing my looks."

"The son-bitch got into the cookie jar, too, didn't he?"

She didn't say anything.

"How much did he take?"

"Two-hundred some. My fault for leaving it where he could get at it."

I could've cried, it was so typical of her. The asshole leaves her and takes her money, and somehow it's her fault.

"Rodney, come back. You didn't do a thing that wrong. Just tell the truth and they will see."

Hit her with all the clear evidence otherwise, and she still thinks things can work out. Just tell the truth.

"Mama, I've got to go."

I waited, but she didn't say anything more.

"Goodbye, Mama."

"Okay."

And I hung up. Now to go out and bring a little entertainment to the folks.

Half hour later, I was by the corral and somebody was patting me with a damp sponge and Molly, the wrangler, was talking to me. "Buddy's been skittish today," she said. "Don't know why. He's off his feed."

"Me too," I said. I hadn't eaten much since the nightmare, but I didn't really feel hungry. A little sick to my stomach, if anything. How can you eat when things are coming apart like that?

"Don't push him too hard, is all," Molly said. "Let him set his own pace." Molly Long is Monte's daughter, who I've never seen in anything but Levis and cowboy boots and a plaid shirt and beat-up straw hat, with a body that looks like it's built out of tipi poles, all straight and narrow.

"I never have pushed him," I said. "I didn't know you could." Buddy was this big old white quarter-horse that they decked out with feathers and put a blanket over a roping saddle and called Crazy Horse's mount. He was pretty old and tame from having taught about two generations of girls how to ride. He was slow, but not stubborn, and was the only reason I even dared to get up on him in the first place, because I had never ridden much before. Buddy felt solid under you, like a platform, it always seemed like.

"Stand still," the guy with the sponge said, who was a hanger-on, a kid about 16, maybe, who did whatever odd jobs he was asked to do.

"What is this stuff anyway?" I tried to hook my chin over my shoulder to see what he was dabbing me with.

"Body makeup. Number 11. Sunburn. You're getting paled out," Monte said. Maybe all the clouds we've had lately. Your tan is all faded."

Just another thing to cheer me up, I was thinking. Then there was this fast drum music that was supposed to be my cue, and I climbed on Buddy. He seemed just the same as always. I heeled him a couple times in the flanks, and he walked on, just doing what he was told. I found my mark, which was chalked out on the ground, and reined up. Then there was a gourd rattle over the p.a., and the spotlight came up on me, and I was ready to start my speech, and then another rattle which I thought was just the sound guy having trouble for about the hundredth time, and all of a sudden Buddy went dancing around, snorting, and I tried to hold him, and then he started in to rearing, and he bucked and boom, I was flying again, shot off like a rocket.

And kept going. It didn't even hit me as strange that I was spiralling on up. I just looked at everything, real interested, the way you do when something is going on you've never been through before. It's not like you know how to act, but you take things as they come. And they were coming like a freight train. I was already high above, looking down on the Hills, amazed at how beautiful they look from that distance, like one of those relief maps, only sharper, with the streams and lakes gleaming in the light from the moon, which was just now coming up round and full. From that distance, the Hills looked like a giant Indian camp, a neat circle around, and the peaks like tipis. And out of one of the lakes this spout shot up, like some kind of silver tornado with pale colored streaks, right up past me and into the sky. It looked like it was made out of water, only lit from inside. And it

234

spread out above like the boughs of a tree, and I went circling around it, climbing, reaching out to what looked like pearls dangling from the branches of the tree, and then again more like bubbles, with that glint of rainbow colors in them. And when I touched them, they popped and disappeared. Only some of the bubbles had people inside, or what looked like people. One of the first I saw was my mother. It looked just like her, only more shimmery. She was crouched inside the bubble, holding onto her knees and staring off like she was thinking of something far away, and just kind of bobbed and bounced there, and then floated off. And then there was hers truly Miss Karen Stephenson. She was in her nurse uniform and had the fingers of one hand over her lips and her head cocked funny like she was listening to music and almost dozing off. I looked close at her eyes and they were blue. Then there were Ingrid and Lorrie, both wearing tee-shirts, and their arms on each other's shoulders, like they were posing for a picture. All women, it seemed like by then: Delly dancing to music which she was the only one to hear, and Verine, of course, but also Miss Frank, Aunt Celia, Regina Ball and the China Doll, teachers I'd had in grade and high school, on and on, almost every woman I'd every seen in my life, all in these bubbles. And the bubbles swirled around and floated off. And then the glittering trunk of the tree started to look like the northern lights, like a curtain of colors wavering in a breeze, and then the whole tree seemed to turn into stars, and there I was, so high by now I saw the curve of the horizon. It was like I was some kind of satellite, looking down and watching as the big ball turned, so far away that you couldn't see anything like people or anything that people made. And I got to wondering, where are those lines you see so plain on maps that show countries and states and all the roads and things? Was the world really this strange and simple, all in one? And if it was, what then? If there were these balls of rock and water and air and fire and stars and great whirlpools of stars, and whirlpools of whirlpools, on and on, the way they said, what happened to all these little bubbles we lived in till they popped? There was nothing to do but to make out people as pretty pitiful who couldn't see what terrible little their tiny lives counted for, and how temporary they all were in comparison to the rest. And when I looked around me I saw these other bubbles with people in them, and now they were all men, going about their business like they had all the time in the world. Ef-ef- Freddie, for one, pumping iron weights, and C.T. Colton oiling a revolver, and Harold Joli reading a paper, one after the other, and one of them was a person in a uniform, and he was reaching up under an airplane wing, doing something with a wrench, and I realized that it was Lonnie Deuce. And the strangest thing, the only feeling I had was, I felt sorry for them. Who am I to feel sorry for anybody? And who is a bully like Ef-ef-Freddy to feel sorry for, anyway? Or a creep like Colton? But I couldn't help it. It was like they were all in the dark about what they were doing, that they were making it up as they went, thinking they had some big plan, when the truth was they were getting blown around like snowflakes in a winter wind. And if the wind had a plan, it wasn't saying. Then there was this guy all dressed in a black suit and vest and black hair and he was staring down at something. He was looking into a pond, and in the pond you could see fish swimming. And there was one white fish in among them you could pick out easy, not silver like a rainbow, but actually white, and pretty good sized, at that. And the guy was following the fish with his steely blue eyes as it swimmed, making figure-eights in the water. And damned if it wasn't Daniel O. Quick, the guy, I mean. He had me fooled with the suit and the black hair, but it was him, all right, looking like he did once before that I remember, like things had gotten out of hand, like he didn't hold the cards any more. And I reached out to tap him on the shoulder, and piff, the bubble broke, and I was thinking, now what have I done? And I started falling. I was miles up, now, and falling and picking up speed, and all the time thinking, I'm gonna die, I'm gonna die for sure.

Then my head was aching, and I opened my eyes, and I was on my back looking up at the stars, and there were all kinds of people around me, looking down.

"Don't move," Molly Long said. "Your neck may be broke."

"His neck's not broke, Molly," Monte Long said. "If it was, he'd be dead."

"I'm not dead?" I said.

"What did he say?" Monte Long said.

"He says he's not dead," Molly said. Everybody laughed. I was laying there flat on my ass, getting a big laugh.

Monte kicked me in the knee and I said, "Ow. What are you kicking me for?"

"You felt that?" Monte said. "His neck's not broke."

"We're not moving him anyway," Molly said. "We'll wait till the ambulance gets here."

"Should be here by now," Monte said. He kicked me in the other knee with the heel of his boot.

"Stop kicking me," I told him.

"He's got feeling both legs," Monte said. "His neck is no more broke than mine." He kicked me in the ankle.

"If you kick me one more time, I will break your damned neck like a stick," I said.

"He's fine," Monte said. "Can you move your arms?"

I held up my right hand where I could see it and opened and closed my fist.

"See there," Monte said.

"Don't move," Molly told me. "Put your hand back where it was. Daddy, get these people out of here and get the hell out yourself. He's gonna stay right where he is until somebody who knows something says it's all right to move him."

"Jesus," Monte said. "All right, everybody."

And the people started shuffling away, but they didn't want to, you could tell. I guess they thought they might miss a good laugh.

So finally it was down to me and Molly. She was kneeling down alongside me.

"How you feeling?" Molly said.

"Head hurts. What happened?"

"Buddy sent you flying. You landed hard." She dug a finger into her plaid shirt pocket and pulled out something that looked like a short string of beads.

"What is it?"

She gave the thing a shake and there was a dry rattle and I finally figured it out. Just in case I didn't, Molly made it clear. "Diamondback. They show up, time to time, not often at night, unless it's warm. My guess is he rode in on the load of hay we got today. Buddy made loose meat out of him."

"How long was I out?"

"Twenty-some minutes, is all."

I laid there looking up at the stars, trying to remember. I heard the ambulance sirens blowing way off.

"You want a souvenir? " Molly said. She tucked the rattle into my fist.

"Tell me something," I said. "Who am I?"

She got a shocked look on her face. "You don't remember?"

"I just want you to tell me."

"What are you talking about? You got amnesia or something?"

"Just say who I am."

"Jesus Christ, Rodney, you're Rodney."

"Who's Rodney?"

"You are. Now stop it. You're making me scared."

"I know I'm Rodney, I just don't know what that means."

"You're just Rodney. The guy that plays Crazy Horse."

"I just play him?"

"You act him. What else? You're not him, for chrissake. You're not even Indian."

"You don't think so?"

"I know an Indian when I see one. I don't know what you are, but you're not Lakota or anything like that."

"I know what I'm not. But what am I? I'd like to know."

"You're a sweet kid named Rodney."

"I'm a poor bastard named Rodney."

"I didn't say any such thing. The ambulance is coming. Just lay still. I'll go show them the way."

And she left me there, stretched out in the sawdust and dirt and horseshit, looking up in the stars and holding the snake rattle in my fist. And out of the clear moonlight sky there was a low rumble, like a rockslide or something in a far valley. Not even a wisp of a cloud anywhere, but that was thunder if I ever heard it.

I rolled over and got my arms and legs under me and boosted myself up till I was standing. My head was hammering now like it would bust open, but I managed to walk pretty well, once I got the beat of it again. Nobody paid any attention to me. It was like I was invisible. And I just sauntered off into the pines.

24.

Sunup next day I was leaning against a woven-wire fence, my fingers poking through the gaps, watching a white fish make circles and figure-eights in a pond on the other side. It was the old fish hatchery at Spearfish. Soon as I'd seen old Quick looking down at the fish in my dream, or whatever it was, I remembered seeing it in one of those field trips in high school, biology, I think. I'd borrowed Clyde's truck and I'd driven most of the night to get here. I'd gone back to the dorm and got into my own clothes and then went to Clyde and told him what'd happened, and he let me borrow the truck. Like me, Clyde figured the dream meant something. So there I was.

"You're early," someone said. I looked and it was a lanky guy in coveralls on the other side of the fence. He was carrying a pail and had a cigarette clipped into the hinge of his lips. He was looking at me with one side of his face all squinted shut around the cigarette. "Gate opens at eight," he told me.

"All right," I said. "I was just looking for somebody, anyway."

The guy clinched his face tighter around his smoke. "Who did you think would be here?"

"An old gentleman I know. He's got a thing about fish."

The guy in coveralls nodded. "Well, look, as long as you're going to wait, I'll let you in. You can give me a hand, if you want to." When he walked over to the gate, I noticed he had a limp. He set down his pail and dug a big chain of keys out of his pocket and found the one he wanted and opened the padlock. I walked around and he swung open the gate and I went on in.

"Give you a hand doing what?" I asked him.

"Feeding the fish." He picked up the pail and dug his hand into the brown pellets inside.

"What is it?"

"Fish food. Ground up stuff, animal and vegetable. I feed it to my cat, too. Gives her a slick coat." He scooped out a handful of the stuff and flung it out onto the pond. The fish saw it raining food and came up to snatch it, some of them poking half out of the water. The guy in coveralls giggled. "They're hungry. They get a lot from the tourists during the day, but by now they've worked up an appetite. Here, have some."

I got a fistful and tossed it out. The brown trout scrambled for it.

"Spread it out more," the guy said. "Don't just put it in one spot." He showed me how, swinging his arm wide. "Just like sowing seed."

I tried again, doing it better that time. "That white one," I said. "I never seen anything like that before."

"Albino. Just a freak, is all. Happens ever once in a while. Never see them in the wild, though. Too easy a target, I suppose."

We kept on feeding the fish.

"This friend of yours," the guy said. "Does he come here often?"

"Well," I said, "he might. He's a strange one. Maybe you've seen him. An old guy?"

"There was a strange one here yesterday. I don't know how old he was. Dressed all in black, like a preacher or undertaker or something. We don't see many people in suits out here."

I stopped and looked at him. "Three-piece suit? Dark hair?"

"The hair looked dyed, to me. Or maybe a wig. He was here all afternoon, just looking at the fish."

"Did you see when he left which way he went?"

"I wasn't looking that close. He had a car, I think." He squinted at me and dragged at his cigarette and blew the smoke away. "You interested in fish, too?"

"Some."

"You want to know something? Fish from this hatchery went all over the West. First brown trout in Yellowstone were from here. Lot of people think brown trout were native, but not so. Cutthroat, yes. Browns come from Germany. Rainbows are American, but most of them out here are planted. Brookies, they're another matter." He shrugged. "Guess it don't make too much difference now."

"Thanks," I told him. "I've gotta go, now. Maybe I can help feed the fish some other time."

"Sure," he said, but he looked a little disappointed. I don't suppose he got too many people he could talk to about fish.

I went back to the truck and got in and started her up and sat there thinking. If I was a crazy old fart like Quick, where would I go from here? He'd come to look at the fish. Okay, score one for my dream. But why would he do that? And why the funny suit and everything? It didn't seem like Quick. You wouldn't think you could get him into a suit like that unless he was dead and laying in a coffin. And that's when it hit me and knocked the wind right out of me. He was fixing to die. And where would he be heading to do that? I couldn't come up with any answer but one: upstream.

My head was throbbing again. I dug into the glove compartment and pulled out a bottle of aspirin and took a couple in my hand and tossed them down my gullet. Then I jerked the truck in gear and backed out and headed for the exit, and then on up Spearfish Canyon. I clicked on the car radio thinking I would get some music, but there was nothing but the early morning news, stock prices, farm reports, weather. I kind of went into a trance, I guess, winding up into the Hills again, watching the sunlight orange on the canyon cliffs. I came to in the middle of a news story, thinking I'd heard someone call my name: " . . . near Terry Peak. Acting on a tip, the sheriff's office has blocked off roads in the area. The two men are wanted for robbery in Rapid City and are suspects in the death of a woman whose body was found in the Black Hills last week . . ." And so on. Quick was born near Terry Peak, he'd told me. So I at least knew about where he was headed.

At Cheyenne Crossing I turned left and headed up Icebox Canyon toward Terry. At the turnoff to the ski lift, there were about four cop cars, so I went right on by. I pulled into the driveway of a lodge a ways further on. I got out Quick's rod case and I set out hiking, following the curve of the mountain up until I got to a string of cabins along the skilift road. I tried to hang back in the trees and bushes as much as I could. I was sore from the pounding I'd taken the night before, but the effort helped work out the aches. It took longer than I thought it would to get up to the ski lift. One thing, there wasn't a lot of traffic. I kept listening for engines, all ready to jump behind a tree if I needed to, but there were just a couple cars came by, and neither one of them even saw me. The sun was up pretty high by the time I got to the ski lift parking lot. There weren't that many cars there. The Jeep wasn't there either.

The lift was running, but there weren't all that many people around. They got a couple once in a while to go on it, and they hustled them in and got them planted in the right place and the chair came up behind them and they sat down and went swinging off up the slope. There were towers strung along up and then over the bend of the hill so you couldn't see the top.

I was beginning to think maybe the cops were mistaken and I put my balls in the noose for no good reason. I went on into the cafe. I took a look around. No Quick. "Shit," I said to myself.

Then I spotted him. No wonder I didn't see him before. He's shaved clean and he's got his hair colored black. It was blacker than any black you ever seen on hair. And he'd got a suit and vest somewhere, just like my dream, and was wearing sunglasses. Even an outfit like that will work for camouflage if you are looking for something entirely different. He was huddled in one of the booths. He was bent over a plastic foam cup of coffee, just stirring it with a plastic spoon, stirring it and never even taking a sip.

I sat down in the booth across from him. "Mr. Quick, what are you doing here?"

"Waiting," he said. He lifted up his head and he must've been looking at me behind those glasses. "Hello, Rodney."

"Hello, Mr. Quick," I said. "What are you waiting for? It's kind of dangerous here, if you want to know."

He kept on stirring the coffee. "Just waiting," he said.

"Maybe we better call it off," I said. "Go fishing. I got your rod right here." I showed it to him and propped it up in a corner of the booth.

"How old do you think I am?" he said.

"Old as the century," I said.

"Right," he said. "If you want to know, just look at the calendar."

I said, "That makes you eighty years old."

"No," he said. His voice had that kind of sound that didn't allow a bit of doubt. He shook his head.

"You're not eighty?"

"You must be looking at the wrong calendar. Forty-five my last birthday. The body and mind of a man of twenty-five."

"Well anyway, that's nice black hair you got," I said. "Looks like you got it in a bottle of boot polish."

"Rodney," he said, "I did it. I followed one of those California cars. Guess what they're doing up there?"

I shook my head.

"Waiting," Quick said.

"What for?"

"The end of the world," he said. "The faithful shall be borne away."

I was set back a little. I never heard Quick talk religious grammar before. I mean, he used some of the words, maybe, but he wasn't praying or anything. Far as I knew he didn't belong to any faith except maybe the Church of the Inside Straight or the One That Got Away. "Is that where you got that outfit?"

"Three-piece suit," he said. "By their apparel they shall be known. There was a girl there——" His voice trailed off. "Have you seen my wife?" he asked me.

"You showed me her picture once," I said.

"I've got it right here." He got his wallet out of his pocket and opened it up and spread it out on the table in front of me. "That's her. Heart as big as a tub."

I looked at the picture. It was the same one he showed me before. "She's a kind looking woman."

"Have you seen her?"

"Mr. Quick, can I ask you something?"

"She promised to meet me."

And that did take me back so I didn't get out what I was going to. "You're waiting for your wife?" I said.

"She promised she'd come. Lula Bea. Isn't she a grand looker?"

He took off the glasses and rubbed his eyes. They were beginning to leak a little, like they been staring too hard toward the sun. "She said she'd meet me. Maybe I better wait outside." He started to get up, all business all of a sudden, picking up his billfold.

"Hold it," I said. "I'll make a deal with you. You come with me, and I'll take you to your wife."

Even if I live to be as old as him, I'll never forget that look he got on his face then. It started out to be suspicious, then it just started to fall apart and come together in this look of gratefulness. He put back on his dark glasses.

"The cops will believe us," I told him. "See, it's the running makes us look a whole lot guiltier than we are. If we give ourselves up, that's got to stand in our favor."

But as usual, he was not listening too close. "She always takes me back," he said. "She doesn't have to, but she does."

"We could give back the money even," I said. Most of it's got to be in the bag yet." Speaking of which, I got to looking for it, but it was not there. "Where's the bag, Mr. Quick? Where's the money?"

He just smiled. It wasn't one of his evil ones, but it didn't tell me anything.

"It's got to be in the Jeep," I said. "Where did you park it?"

I didn't get a thing but that weird smile for an answer. I figured he was pretty much around the corner by then. "Come on," I said. "We'll just walk down to the turnoff."

"There's more than one way," he said. "There's more than one way up there."

I got him on his feet. He was pretty shaky it seemed like. "Old logging roads, Indian trails, deer paths," he was saying. "Up to where the first grass was parted by the rain."

"Come on," I said. I've got ahold of his arm and was helping him along toward the door.

"There's always a back way in or a back way out," he said.

I got him out the door.

"She's up there," he said. He was looking up the mountain to where the lines of the ski-lift bent over the slope.

And I finally started to see what he was talking about. "The Jeep," I said. "You got the Jeep up there by a back road, didn't you? And rode down the lift." You had to admire the old fart sometimes for his slyness. It seemed like sometimes he'd got more wriggles than a snake.

He turned to me then and there was a look of alarm about his face. "My rod," he said. "We forgot my rod."

I sat him down on the bench that was there outside the door. "I'll go back and get it," I said. "You wait here."

So I went back in and found the booth and got the rod and came back out again and he was gone. I started cussing myself out for how dumb I could be. I looked down the steps and saw two cops coming up them. And I looked over to the boarding place, and there was Quick getting scooped up by one of those chairs. I figured he must've seen the cops coming and it spooked him. So I went after him.

"Stop the chairs," I said to the girl there. "You got to stop them."

She just looked at me. She was one of those college girls who worked there summers. "You have a ticket, Sir?"

"That old guy," I said. "He's sick. He can't go up that high."

She was looking confused now. "He had a ticket," she said. "Return ticket to the top." All she's got on her brain is tickets.

"How much is a ticket?" I said.

"Round trip or one way?"

"Shit," I said. I got out my wallet and took out my last five dollars and handed it to her.

"One way," she said.

I shuffled out on the platform and got myself set to get in a chair.

"Wait," she said. "You've got change coming."

"Keep it," I said. And the chair swooped up behind me, caught me behind the knees, and I sat down and the chair swung me up.

"Pull down the bar," I heard the girl saying behind me. So I pulled the safety bar down in front of me. I looked back over my shoulder and I saw the two cops come up and talk to the girl on the platform. And I thought, well, that's it, any second now they will throw this thing into reverse and haul our asses right in. But we kept right on going, and I looked around and saw what I let myself in for. Quick was three chairs up ahead of me, and we were going upwards at a pretty steep pitch. I have to say I have never been overly fond of places where my feet are not firmly planted. Having all that space under my heels gave me a kind of wheezy feeling in my stomach. The towers themselves must've been fifty or sixty feet high alone, and where the cable stretched out over dips it was almost twice that to the ground. Add to that we were climbing and off to either side the hills were sinking and the sky was taking over. It was like my dream of flying, only moreso, because this was real. You started to see miles, one mountain after another stretching out, and it was like a Ferris wheel where you were afraid of the wind because it sets the chair to swinging. And you had to remember to breathe.

We went over one bulge. And I thought, what is keeping the cops? If they are going to haul us down, why don't they go ahead and do it? I would not much mind now. I looked back again, but I couldn't see the bottom now, because we were over that hump. What I could see is the Homestake Mine buildings at Lead and a little bit of Deadwood. I turned back again. Some way it seemed easier on my stomach to watch the mountain unrolling in front of me.

I saw Quick up ahead setting pretty calm and holding onto the bar of the chair and his feet hanging down with Uncle Zachary's shoes still on them looking too big for those scrawny shanks of his.

But while I was watching I saw his head start in to shaking from side to side and his hands came up and slapped down again on the bar, and his feet started in to pumping and swinging like he was some kind of puppet that just got all his strings pulled at one time. Then I was pulled on up over another hump of the mountain and I saw what he must've, away up there at the top. It was a red light wheeling around. And you could see the cop car and Jeep there beside it plain as anything, and the uniforms of the cops, too, up there waiting. I saw why now the cops down below didn't stop the contraption. These others tracked the Jeep up here and found it and waited until he came back for it. And now they were just reeling him in.

Then I saw Quick lift up the safety bar, and I thought, oh no, the old fart is going to try something rash as per usual. Then I saw him pull his feet up and kind of hunch around and grab the back of the chair and stand up in it. Oh no, I'm thinking, but there was nothing I could do. He got ahold of the pipe that hangs down and stands right up in the chair. And now I said "Oh no" right out loud because I could see what he was aiming to try. There was just one more tower between him and the top, and he was going to try to jump off onto it as he went by and climb down and get away.

I cupped my free hand over my mouth and yelled, "Mr. Quick."

But as usual he was not listening to me. Who knows what he was listening to then? There was something telling him to jump, maybe, and he did.

It was an amazing jump for a man of his years. It was like all his feebleness before was just a matter of saving up for this jump. He went out and up and got his hands hooked over the cross bar of the tower and hung there, dancing with his feet, trying to swing them over to reach the tower. But he couldn't. And his hands gave way and he fell, still reaching with his hands and legs, like he was climbing a ladder made of air.

I couldn't look any more. I had to look at the sky. I didn't hear him yell or anything. And that was the last I saw of him falling and climbing at the same time. I don't know when I breathed again, but before I hardly knew it I was at the top and the cops were yelling at me to drop it and were braced and holding out their guns at me with both hands. "Drop it. Get your hands up," they yelled. And it was like I was hit with something hard that numbed my brains. I couldn't figure it out. What was it they wanted me to drop? Then I looked down and saw that some way I had kept ahold of Quick's rod case all that time. And they must've thought it was a shotgun or rifle or something. So I let loose of it and it clattered down on the platform and I reached for the sky like they said, and the cops moved in and grabbed me.

25.

So now you know everything. If Mama is right, I've done all I've got to do, which is tell the truth. My lawyer says the same. Myself, I'm not so sure the truth has anything to do with what people think. Anyway, I gave it a try.

To me, it is all like a dream, in a way. If I hadn't lived through it, I wouldn't believe half of it. Even so, there are things I can't explain.

They wouldn't let me go to Mr. Quick's funeral, of course. They cremated him, the paper said. Cheaper for the daughter than buying a casket and everything, I guess. Loretta is suing the Hillview Home for negligence, they said, and I am being named in particular for letting things get out of hand. So he gets off the hook, as usual, and I am left to take the rap. I'll bet he would have a good laugh about that, too.

The lawyer was appointed for me, seeing that I couldn't afford one of my own. She is pretty good, near as I can tell. She has talked to my mother and to Miss Frank and to Harold Joli and to Lymon and she says they will all be good character witnesses, if I need them. What she means, I think, is when it comes down to how much time I will have to serve, they may help it go easier on me. It is the facts of the matter, naturally, that will decide what all they will try to hit me with. They have found the other motorcycle guy, and my lawyer is hoping they will get a confession out of him about the skull girl. That would still leave all the rest, but at least maybe not murder on top of it.

Here's a surprise. One day they said I had a visitor and who does it turn out to be but hers truly Karen Stephenson. I was so shocked, I stopped stock still in the doorway to the visitor's room and the guard had to give me a shove to get me going again.

"Hello, Rodney," she said. She was dressed in a nice blue suit.

I sat down to the table and looked at her. "What are you doing here?"

"The people at the Hillview Home all asked me to come," she told me. "Miss Frank and everybody else. They want you to know they are behind you."

"Even Ef-Ef-Freddy?"

"Him too. We took up a collection to help pay lawyer fees, or whatever."

I didn't know what to say to that. I got to wondering how much Ef-ef-Freddy threw into the pot. Maybe you don't know people as well as you think you do.

"Are you all right?" Karen Stephenson asked me. "Do you get enough to eat and everything?"

"More than enough. They treat me fine. Ask a lot of questions, is all."

"What're you looking at?" She brushed her cheek with her hand. "Do I have something on my face or something?"

"Just checking out your eyes. Seeing if I remembered right."

"About my eyes?"

"Never mind. Just something Quick said once."

"What a bird," Karen Stephenson said. "You had your hands full with him, I'll bet."

"He wasn't so bad. I got to like him, some ways."

"After all the trouble he got you into?"

"It wasn't all his fault. He just did what he wanted to do." I got to looking at her again. Her eyes were blue, all right. "How come they picked you to come see me?"

"I don't know. Because I was your friend, I guess."

That just about floored me. "Really?"

"Sure. We are friends, aren't we?"

"I guess so."

"Well, then," she said. And she gave me a big smile which was almost worth everything I'd been through.

I got a note from Antone Reese saying he wanted to talk to me. He was doing a story about white guys who pretended to be Indians, he said. I wrote back that he should take a walk. It wasn't the first or last time the subject came up, though. My own lawyer kept hitting that, one way or another. Not to mention the police. Like it was somehow my fault I'd grown up with Lymon or that people took me for an Indian sometimes. I suppose it just gave me an odd angle, or something. I didn't see the profit of getting into all that. Nothing will change the way people see things. Everybody thinks he knows.

Lymon came to see me, too. The COUP people didn't want him to. They didn't want to get involved any more than they were already. He came anyway, he said, because he couldn't do any different. He said he figured I would do the same if it was him that was in trouble.

I told Lymon about getting bucked off Buddy and the dream I'd had when I was out cold. He didn't know any more what to make of it than I did. He'd been up to the mountain after the vision, but it didn't come to him. He said he would have to try again.

"Maybe the dream missed you and hit me," I said. "I heard thunder, plain as anything, and not a cloud in sight."

"Nothing new about that. Everybody hears thunder in the Hills. It goes way back."

"Did you hear thunder?"

"Only because there was a hell of a storm. And next morning a double rainbow. Twobows, get it? If it was a vision it was a funny one. A real joker."

"I was going to ask Quick about it, but I never got to."

"You think he'd know anything about such things?"

"He knew a lot of things. And there were the things I dreamed that turned out true, mostly about him. Maybe the dream was trying to tell me something."

"Or maybe you just got kicked in the head by a horse and saw stars."

We both had to laugh at that.

I guess I'll never know if there was any meaning to the dream. Maybe it doesn't make any difference if I know or not. Maybe it is a big mistake even to ask. Like asking what the wind is trying to say. What the thunder is talking about. Or the birds singing. Only I never will forget it.

I think about the strangest things, these days. All that stuff they took off me or Quick for example, and call it evidence. The gun, of course, and the fishing rod, and the snake rattle, and the medicine wheel, and the knife I used to clean the fish. All just things, I suppose. You could call them souvenirs. But if I had a medicine bundle, that's what would be in it.

I wonder what Loretta will do with the ashes. Myself, I would take them up in an airplane and dump them out over the Hills. I think about them sometime, floating down like snow. I don't know why, but it makes me happy thinking about that.

And another thing, the days we had in the valley where the ponds were. I can nearly smell the wood-smoke now, and see the old-man's-beard draped in the spruce, and the pale aspen trunks rising into the green mist of leaves. And that tapered rod, the way it would curve and the line bend so lovely raring back or shooting out to let the line settle with hardly a ripple on the water. And the trout holding or skittering. And that monstrous big rainbow exploding up out of the diamond spray and hanging there.